Praise for Mel Bossa

"This amazing first novel was one of the best new romances of 2011."
—Lambda Literary on *Split*

"If you only read one romance this year, make sure this is the one. Its ambition is only exceeded by its flawless execution."
—Out in Print on *Split*

"Bossa makes it work beautifully, smoothly, flawlessly. *Split* was a perfect, haunting read."
—Boysinourbooks.com on *Split*

"We're crazy for young author Mel Bossa. She's got a distinctive voice and a terrific story-telling gift."
—TLA GAY.com on *Franky Gets Real*

"Bossa has created a masterpiece of romance writing."
—Lambda Literary on *Into the Flames*

"*In His Secret Life* is her best book to date and is one of those incredibly rare books that comes into your life and leaves you feeling changed somehow."
—Anthony Simpson, *The Gay UK* on *In His Secret Life*

Craving's Creek

Mel Bossa

SAMHAIN
PUBLISHING

Samhain Publishing, Ltd.
11821 Mason Montgomery Road, 4B
Cincinnati, OH 45249
www.samhainpublishing.com

Craving's Creek
Copyright © 2015 by Mel Bossa
Print ISBN: 978-1-61923-109-2
Digital ISBN: 978-1-61922-995-2

Editing by Latoya Smith
Cover by Lyn Taylor

First Samhain Publishing, Ltd. electronic publication: August 2015
First Samhain Publishing, Ltd. print publication: August 2015

Dedication

This book is dedicated to those of us who suffer or have suffered from mental illness. There can be light in our darkest hours, but that light can only burst through the dark when we find compassion for ourselves.

Spiritus

Chapter One

1994

I stir more butter into the orange mess of powdered cheese and then dump a ladle of the shiny noodles into two identical Cookie Monster bowls. I look over the kitchen counter, at the dining room. "Ready, girls?"

My sisters nod excitedly. They're *ready* all right. Each is seated in her high chair, looking like a famished wolf disguised in a summer dress and piggy-tails. "Here it comes," I say, walking over to the cluttered dining room table. "One for you." I set the bowl in front of Summer first. Yesterday, I served Winter first. I always try to make things right between them. "And one for you."

They're two years old. They notice these things and make me pay later.

"What do you say?" I give them a serious look. I know my dark-brown eyes intimidate them.

"Fank you," Winter says, speaking for both of them. Summer hasn't said her first real word yet. And that's all right by me. One babbling two-year-old girl is enough in this house.

I go back to the kitchen to grab my mother's lunch. If I don't bring her something to eat, she won't eat all day. She's been writing since seven o'clock in the morning. "Eat," I tell the girls. "And maybe I'll take you out in the yard and push you on the tire swing later." I head down the hall to my parents' bedroom. "And don't you choke," I threaten the girls over my shoulder. "One noodle at a time."

I knock on the bedroom door, but all the while, my mind is on *him* again. I'm always thinking of him.

My Alistair.

While I wait for my mother's invitation to come in, I stare out the hallway window, because through it, I can see our street, and at the end of our street is Alistair's house. It's a shabby, stucco, two-story house with dirty windows, rotting porch and neglected lawn. I wish he had a better house to live in. Thinking of his face, I watch the yellow curtains move in the attic's tiny round window. That's Alistair's room. His own private sanctuary. I know he's up there right now, cutting up old curtains or something. He wasn't at school yesterday or the day before that. I knew he wouldn't be. He doesn't really have any friends to say good-bye to, except for me.

"Come in," my mother finally calls out. "I'm done."

I step inside my mother's territory. "I brought you some fluorescent noodles." I look around my parents' bedroom. I'm always a little shocked at how bad my mom is at housekeeping. If it weren't for my dad, I'd never have a pair of clean socks to wear. "Here." I offer her the bowl of lumpy noodles. "It's a rare delicacy."

She looks up at me, but she's not quite present yet. She's still trapped in her story. I can tell by the vague expression she's giving me. I try not to think of what she was writing before I came in. My mother, Hilary Kent, used to be a school receptionist. But when she was pregnant with the twins, she started writing at night, and lo and behold, she's really good at it. She published her first erotica novel last year, under the name Lorna Moon.

"Did you give this to the girls? I don't want them eating additives or food coloring—"

"Shit, I grew up on that stuff." I sit on the edge of the bed and grin at her.

"I know, baby, but I didn't know any better back then." My parents had me when they were both very young, and decided to have another baby at forty. They got two instead. She scrapes her fork across the mac and cheese. "Anyway, you turned out all right." She leans in and pinches me. "Well, pretty much." Then she frowns, cocking an ear to the door. "Are the girls okay? Don't let them eat alone."

"They're not alone. They're together." But I get up anyway. I know I have to play nice all afternoon if I want to get my allowance and go to Sheryl's party tonight. My first real summer party this year.

"Oh, and tell your father I'll be out in fifteen minutes. I just have to put down the shower sex scene between the pilot and Mary Lou, and then I'm done." She turns back to her typewriter, putting the bowl on her lap. "Your dad is still in the garage, right?"

Where else would my father be?

"Yep." I stretch and catch my reflection in the vanity mirror above my mother's fancy commode full of perfumes and creams. I grew too fast this year. My arms are too long. I need a haircut. My Soundgarden T-shirt is worn thin. I can practically see through some parts. "I'm gonna play in the yard with the girls a little," I say carefully. "And while they're napping, I'll go over to Mrs. Bastone's house and mow her lawn and all, and then—"

"You'll change into your Superman outfit and rescue a cat caught in a tree." My mother says this while she types furiously. "What do you want, baby? Just ask me. It's easier that way."

I step up to the mirror and rake a hand through my brown hair. "You think I should dye my hair?" I ask, out of the blue. I haven't even really thought about it, but I'm bored with my plain look. Grunge is dead. Cobain shot himself last April. I need a new look. I should go retro. Try a Billy Idol haircut or something. "Maybe I could bleach my hair."

I catch her eye in the mirror. "Like Alistair's?"

Why is it every time I hear his name, everything in me stands at attention like my soul's been called for battle?

"His is naturally white blond like that," I mutter, turning away from the mirror to hide the color in my face. "Mine would turn out yellow."

"Or orange."

In the dining room, the girls are hollering and banging their plates. I bolt out of the room. "I got this," I scream out to my mother. "But can I go to Sheryl's pool party?"

When I reach the dining room, I stop and frown at the girls. I didn't know it was possible to make wigs out of noodles.

I hear my mother shout from her bedroom, "You can go to the party!" She laughs wholeheartedly. "But you're a sly one, Ryde!"

Yeah, she's right.

It's hot out here. I'm sweating and the sweat stings my eyes. Just need to run the mower over a patch of high grass near the shed, and then I'll collect my five dollars, drain a glass of Mrs. Bastone's sweet tea and that'll be that. She's a nice old lady and I'd mow her lawn for free, but she insists on paying me.

"Thank you so much," she says as I'm turning off the rusty mower. She stands on her porch and holds out a glass for me. She's still shy around me. Never really looks me in the eye. My mother says it's because she thinks I'm handsome.

"Thanks," I say before draining half of the glass. I wipe my forehead with the bottom of my T-shirt. "You look nice today." She's eighty-five years old. Wiry and flat chested with very smart eyes that look at you through thick glasses. She's all veins and brown spots. But I think she must have been beautiful a long time ago.

Beauty is like a scent. It clings to you even when it's gone.

If Alistair's beauty had a scent, it would probably be lemongrass.

"Here," Mrs. Bastone says. "Don't spend it all in one place."

I finish the sweet tea and hand her the glass back. "I'll see you next week."

"School is over for you kids now," she says, keeping me a moment longer. "Are you gonna have a job this summer, Rydell?"

"Gonna help my dad with his business and all."

She leans in a little, closing her dress at the neck with her thin, knotted hand. "Is your father having any luck with his water filters?"

My dad and Lady Luck parted ways a long time ago. But he tries so hard, and I can't help believing that maybe, just maybe, this business, the new water filtering business, will be the one that finally works out. For the time being, he still sells contraband cigarettes to make ends meet. I'm not ashamed of that.

But I don't like to talk about it. "I think it's about to take off," I say, a little dishearteningly. "Just a matter of getting people interested."

She goes back inside and comes out with a white plastic flask. I recognize it as ours. My dad uses them to collect water samples around the neighborhood. Then he tests the water sample and fills out a chart, which he later leaves on our neighbors' doorsteps to let them know just "how terrible their drinking water is" and "how badly they need" his product. It's not exactly a scam. The water isn't too good around here.

My dad says one day everybody's going to be *buying* water.

Mrs. Bastone is embarrassed. "I know your dad says I have lead in my water, but you see, I'm still here, and as healthy as an ox."

I take the flask and my dad's technical sheet from her. "Don't worry about it."

I hate the way people pity my dad.

As I'm walking back home, I hear someone calling me.

"Hey, Ryde."

I look over my shoulder and see Sheryl and her friend walking up to me. Sheryl is wearing her old plaid shirt and ripped jeans. Her black hair needs to be introduced to a hairbrush. Maybe I should tell her it's 1994 and time to lose the woodcutter look. "Where you going?" she asks, stopping real close to me. "You're all sweaty and shit."

"I'm not going anywhere."

Isn't that the truth.

"We're going to eat these in the park." She shows me her stained hand. In it, she holds ten or twelve sour jawbreakers. "Wanna come?"

There's nothing to do around here but draw obscene things on our jeans with Sharpie markers, or sit around the swings, stuffing sour candy into our mouths to see who'll last the longest without spitting it out. I'm not in the mood for either of those stimulating activities. "I gotta go home and babysit."

"Yeah?" Sheryl stares at me. She's beautiful in a vicious way. The kind of girl who might make it out of here. She's bored enough to try and motivated enough to actually succeed. "Ever since Thing One and Thing Two were born, you're always stuck at home."

"Not true." I play tough. With girls like Sheryl, you have to. "Anyway, I'll see you at the party tonight." I step back but nearly trip myself up on my big feet.

Sheryl smiles and looks over at her mute friend. I know the girl. She used to date a friend of mine. The girl doesn't say much and she's a total nutcase. My friend Luis told me so.

The two girls exchange a look I don't like and strike off for the park.

Why am I going to this party anyway?

I knock on Alistair's front door and wait.

My palms are wet and I rub them hard down my jeans. I'm always too nervous when I go over to his house. His mother is on to me big-time. She sees right through my little "we're just friends and I don't want to get into his pants" game. I look through the screen door and see her ambling down. She's very heavy and hasn't been seen in anything but that faded blue housedress since Alistair was born. She almost died when she gave birth to him. His parents had him when they were both forty-five years old.

They call him their sweet miracle boy.

"What is it?" Mrs. Genet asks, her large, unhappy face peering at me through the screen.

"Um, is Alistair home?"

She stands in the door, barely allowing me in, but I slither by her anyway and quickly climb the steps up to the second floor, every creak of wood bringing me closer to him. Upstairs, I slow down and take a second to steady my heart. "Hey, it's me," I say, speaking up into the attic's open trapdoor. "Can I come up?"

I wait and listen to the sounds of suburbia coming from the open windows. After a while, I begin to despair. Sometimes he doesn't want to see anyone. Even me.

But finally I see his white hand sliding the narrow ladder down to me. As soon as the bottom of the ladder touches the floor, his hand disappears. I wait a few seconds and climb up.

I poke my head in the open floor. It's beautiful up here. All shadows and light. Like a church. And it smells like him. Everything up here is his.

He's sitting on the scratched hardwood floor, bent over something. I see his hands working furiously. He's sewing.

When I've made it up there, I bend my head so as to avoid knocking it on the slanted ceiling, and watch him for a while. I like watching him work. He's been making his own clothes for years. I don't know how he does it.

After a few minutes, I can't wait anymore. I want to hear his voice. I need him to look at me. "Why didn't you come to school yesterday?" I ask him, kneeling down, careful not to disturb anything around him.

He won't look up at me. His white-blond hair shines like a light in the dusty air. "I had a migraine," he says, the needle threading faster now.

"Was it bad?"

Alistair has had migraines since he turned thirteen. They sometimes cause him to have hallucinations, which he calls visions. I worry about him. I worry about his head.

He finally looks up at me. "Yes, and the angel came again." His eyes are more mysterious to me than the end of the world. "He was standing right there." He shows me the spot. "But he had black wings this time."

I swallow hard. I hate it when he talks about that damn angel. He needs to get out more. He's always alone up here. "What are you making?" I ask, changing the subject. I catch the scent of his breath. He's been chewing on blueberry gum. The scent of his breath makes me horny.

"A shirt."

"Yeah? It looks pretty good."

"You really like it?" He holds the shirt up to me, close to my shoulders, my neck. "Hm, it could fit you," he says, frowning. He doesn't notice I'm blushing so hard I think I might be glowing. "I can make some adjustments." He assesses the shirt I don't especially like. "I'll finish it for you then."

He seems pleased and that's all I ever want. Just to please him. "Cool," I say, leaning back from him. I know our first kiss is coming. It's going to happen soon, but I won't rush it. It'll come. It'll just come.

Alistair stares down at the mess around him and, for a second, looks like he's about to weep. I don't know why he gets the way he gets. It's like watching a solar eclipse. You know the sun will eventually slide out from under the moon again, but for a moment, your whole world is black.

"I haven't gone outside in two days," he whispers sadly. Sometimes his migraines get so bad, he can't stand the sunlight. It's caused him a lot of grief in the last four years. And he's lonely.

I don't want him to be lonely. "Wanna go walk around the new houses and write on the walls?"

"Yes, let's do that," he says, standing. He's short enough to stand without his head touching the ceiling. If he hugged me, which he's never done, I'd feel his mouth on my collarbone like a moth landing on my skin.

Deftly, he climbs down the ladder and I follow suit. He shuts the trapdoor and locks it. He sticks the key inside his pocket and puts a finger to his lips. His lips are always a little red because he chews on them all the time. "Don't wake my father up," he says, and when he says that, the hair on my neck rises.

His father scares the crap out of me. He's all about muscles and Jesus loving. The Genets are into religion hard. Alistair attends church three times a week.

When we reach the front door, Alistair looks back at his mother dozing off in front of the television. In the other worn-out armchair, his father is slumbering too. The television is blaring out more bad news about Rwanda.

I open the door for us, but for a moment, Alistair only stands there and watches his parents with tenderness. "God bless them," he whispers to my dismay.

I shut the door.

Chapter Two

When my parents bought our house here on Chambery Street, our backyard was just a field. Alistair and I used to ride our bikes up and down gravel roads and hide out in the woods around here.

Now everything is a construction site, a new development. But all they ever *develop* is more houses that look the same.

The construction boys never lock anything up, so Alistair and I like to walk around those big, new houses. I like the smell of them, plywood and dust.

Alistair likes it because it makes him feel like he's Jonas inside the whale.

"We haven't done this one," I say, showing him a gigantic house with the roof not quite done. It's just the way we love them: big, insulting and a little out of sight. I nod my head to the towering thing.

Alistair agrees and we look around at house windows and parked cars. The street is deserted. Everyone's out playing golf or shopping wholesale. After we've made sure the coast is clear, we sneak up the dirt driveway and check the door. It's unlocked.

Seconds later, we're in.

In some places, the roof is just a wooden skeleton, and the light pours through like water, cascading down into the lobby, over a large, romantic-looking staircase like the ones they used to have in plantation homes. "Shit," I say, really impressed.

Alistair takes a step into the well of light and looks back at me. "I wanna go up there."

My heart is pounding again. I want to go up there too.

We file up the marble steps and I wish I were barefoot. I bet the marble would feel smooth and cool against my naked soles.

Upstairs, we gaze down at the broad entrance, careful not to lean too close to the edge; there isn't a railing yet. "They don't have a chandelier," Alistair says, almost to himself. "How strange."

"So, where do you wanna write?" I usually write my somewhat political messages in the bathroom or in the closets. Things like, *While this house was being built, there was a genocide in a country no one cares about. Enjoy your first night here.* Or maybe, *In twenty years, your house won't be worth enough to pay for your kids' education.* Alistair prefers to draw the face of Jesus, using existing patterns in the dust. Under the saintly face, he'll write something like, *If you see this, don't worry. You're saved.*

It's uncanny how good he is at drawing Jesus. Not that I know what Jesus looks like.

"Let's not write anything here," he finally says, still staring at the ledge.

"Don't stand so close." I pull him back. "It makes me nervous."

Alistair looks at me. There's something in his eyes now. I've seen it before: something huge and ravenous, like a black beast waiting to be unleashed. "Remember when we used to play hide-and-seek?" When he says this, his voice is very low. Sometimes I don't recognize him. He's not himself these days.

I remember how I never used to find him whenever we played. But I want to try again. "You wanna play here?" I ask, coolly enough. "Could be kinda fun, I guess. Lots of places to hide." I like the idea and I get excited. "I'll count to a hundred. Go."

He glances around and quickly strikes off for the hallway.

"Hey, be careful," I yell out to him. "Don't bolt through open doors when you don't know what's on the other side!" I don't want him to get hurt. Maybe this is a bad idea. He can be so reckless. I wring my hands. Well, it's too late. He's gone. I lean my forehead on the wall and close my eyes. I count.

When I get to eighty-nine, the house is quiet and all I hear is my own breathing. Where is he? I start with the first room at my right. I check the walk-in closet. There are some plastic sheets and piles of rubbish in the corner, but Alistair isn't under there. I take my time. I walk slowly, exploring the second floor, going from room to room, door to door, and the seconds swell into minutes, the heat making me sweat or maybe it's the anticipation. I creep down the hall, into more rooms, lifting things, pulling doors open, knowing he isn't up here anymore. I want to make it last.

But I'm ready to blow.

Finally, when I've covered the second floor, I make my way down the stairs, trying to keep my footsteps light. On the landing, I stop. Listen. The light isn't as bright down here anymore. I look up to catch a gray sky leaning heavily on the roof. I smell rain in the air.

And Alistair.

With my heart drumming, I lean back and peer into the dark and vast room at my left. The windows there are still boarded up, but light rips through the cracks like long fingers scratching into the room. I stand in the middle of the room and call out his name.

I know he's here, and I know he knows that I know.

I spot a door in the right corner of the room. A pantry maybe. I can't hold back a second longer, and in two long strides, I'm standing at that door, with my hand pressed hard against it. How long are we going to play this game? "Alistair," I whisper. "You're busted. Get out." I smile because I can feel him smiling behind the door. "I'm opening the door in three, two, one—"

But the handle turns and he whips past me before I can put my hands on him. "My turn!" he shouts, his voice already far off.

"Where you going?" I turn but he's gone. Upstairs, I hear him counting.

I look around for a place to hide.

As we're walking back home, I sense Alistair's mood darken with every step. I want to ask him what's on his mind, but I already know, and I don't want to talk about it.

So he wasn't invited to Sheryl's tonight? Big deal. Not my fault. I can't make people understand him. I'm not staying home another Friday night to make him feel better about himself. People think he's weird and they might have a point. But they don't know him the way I do. There's nothing strange about him. He's just so shy, and his parents keep him cloistered like he's made out of porcelain.

As we're coming up on my house, my mom rolls by in our Dodge minivan. Summer and Winter are sitting in the back and waving at me. "Dinner's on," my mom yells, slowing down but not stopping. "Turn the burner down to medium-low in half an hour." She smiles at Alistair. "We're having chicken curry," she tells him and drives away.

"She wants you to stay for supper," I say, daring a quick glance over at his sullen face. Alistair never stays for supper anywhere. His parents don't allow it. So my mom doesn't really ask him anymore, just tells him what we're having. "*Cheers* is on in ten minutes," I add, checking my watch. Out of the corner of my eye, I see him shaking his head. No, he's not staying for light comedy television and curry chicken.

We pass my house but don't even look at it, because whatever the weather or time, I've always walked him home. When we reach his house, I feel like someone is squeezing my windpipe. I want to say something to him about the idiotic party and how trivial it is to me, but instead, I stuff my hands down my pockets and step back into the street. "I'll see you tomorrow, I guess."

He nods and looks back at his house. I know he's going to sit at that table and say his prayers and ask to be forgiven for something we haven't even done yet. At the door, he gives me one last look.

I can't stand it. "What?" I snap at him.

He slams the door in my face.

At the dinner table, I sit looking out the patio doors, watching fat pellets of rain drop like rocks into our aboveground pool. I've already wolfed down my share of supper and my plate is licked clean. I've grown four inches this year and nothing seems to satisfy my hunger. I can almost see the top of my father's head when I stand next to him. My mom says she's thinking of putting a lock on the fridge.

"More salad, hon?" She shows me the big blue salad bowl full of greens no one at this table will touch while there is still a scrap of meat left. Or bread.

At my right, Summer is babbling something to Winter, and I notice Winter's hair is getting fuller and darker like my father's. While my father chews and daydreams about the money we'll be making once his ship comes in, I study his long, serious face, and then I look at my mother; she's all freckles and laughter. I realize my sisters are copies of my parents. Winter is my father's spitting image, dark haired and intense, while Summer is just like my mother with her orange hair and slanted blue eyes.

Who the hell do I look like then? Maybe I'm adopted.

"Too bad about the rain, huh?" My mother picks up Summer's fork off the floor for the tenth time. "Still gonna go to the party?"

What am I going to do with my summer? I don't have a job, unless you count hanging empty bottles on people's doors as employment, but I lack the motivation to try anything new. I bought a used guitar last month, but that didn't last long. I've tried playing my old Atari games, but video games put me to sleep. I used to read a book a week, but lately, I can't even finish an Archie comic book. And I haven't submitted a short story to any magazines since my last rejection, which was last April. My brain is soaking in heavy, spoiled cream. I feel slow, like God's stepped on the remote, and now everything in my life is caught in one screenshot—everything frozen still—just waiting for that click.

I don't want to do anything but wait for Alistair to let me kiss him on the mouth.

"I'm gonna go anyway," I say, grabbing the last piece of bread. "I don't feel like staying home all night."

"Is Alistair going?"

I shrug and chew my bread.

"His parents are gonna have to eventually let him out of that house," my mother says, wiping Summer's face. "His whole social life can't just revolve around church."

I know my mother doesn't expect an answer from me. "Can I be excused?"

"You all right?" Her eyes tell me she understands more about my recent mood swings than she lets on.

But my father is oblivious to our silent exchange and suddenly turns to me. "Hey, tomorrow morning, we're doing the B section. I need you to be up bright and early, okay?"

Our little suburban town is divided into sections in which the street names begin with the section's letter. We live in the C section. I've renamed us the Cesarians. "How early?" I ask, hoping eleven. Another morning of collecting water samples awaits me. But three hours is thirty bucks.

"Eight." My dad rubs Winter's hair and grins at her. "You girls wanna go for a bike ride?" My father likes to tie up the buggy to his bike and take my sisters on long rides. Sometimes they're gone for hours. Who knows where they go.

"I'll be ready for nine," I say and wink, praying he'll let it slide.

He does. "All right, fine."

I climb up the stairs to my bedroom. Inside, I stare at my open closet, dejected. I pull out some jeans and my black-and-white, long-sleeved Empire shirt. I dig through my first drawer for clean undies, smelling through them like a bloodhound.

Downstairs my mother is hollering at me. "Ryde, phone!"

For a second, I wonder about making Alistair pay for the slammed door, but change my mind. I meet my mother halfway down the stairs and grab our new high-tech cordless phone from her. "It's Alistair," she whispers.

"Yeah, okay, thanks." I quickly go back to my bedroom and shut myself in. I make sure I'm cool. "Hello?"

But there's only dead air on the line.

I check my window and see him standing in his. I wave at him, and slowly, the embers inside me turn cold. I'm not angry about the door anymore. "Look," I say, "I don't care if you slammed the door in my face."

"You didn't go to the party?" He sounds upset.

But it's not about the party. I know this. It's something else. "Yeah, I'm still going, but not right now." I move away from my window. "So, what are you doing?"

"Nothing."

"Sounds fun." I lie back on my bed. Downstairs, I hear the clinking of dishes and my mother singing along with the radio. "Something happened at your house?"

I hear him sniffle on the line. "They're making me go to the camp again," he says.

Those words hit me hard and I sit up. "What? But I thought last summer was your last. Didn't they say you only had to go until you were seventeen and you're seventeen—"

"No, Ryde, I'll be seventeen next week. They say, technically, I'm still sixteen."

I jump off my bed and shoot for the window. How can they do this to him? To us? This was going to be our first summer together. He's been going to that Catholic summer creep camp all his life. Every damn summer. How am I supposed to kiss him if he isn't here? "They can't make you," I say, my voice sounding like a growl. "It's not fair—"

"Father Bilodeau says I'm gonna be like a counselor and that it'll be fun, because I'm good with leading others. He says—"

"*Fun?*" I lean my head on the glass, talking low. "But I thought you didn't wanna go away."

He's quiet for a while. "I don't," he finally says. "You know that."

I know what he's saying. What he means. Does he feel the same about me? Does he think of me as much as I think of him? I spend my time planning our lives together.

I watch his small attic window. See him standing there, half-hidden by the curtains. "What am I supposed to do all summer?" I ask desperately. What I really want to ask is, *How am I gonna live without you for two months?*

"Ryde," he says, "they don't want me to spend too much time with you. If you'd come to church, like I asked you to, they wouldn't be so scared of you and—"

"Fuck church, okay?" As soon as the words come out, I want to put them right back in my mouth.

"Oh, that is a nasty thing to say, mister, and I'm asking God to forgive you right now." He sounds so serious. He starts praying and I wait for him to finish. "And you're lucky too," he says after he's done. "'Cause God likes you."

I shut my eyes, bite my tongue. "All right, thank you very much for taking care of my soul."

"You're welcome."

I can't help smiling. I press my hand to the window. The glass is cool from the rain. "Alistair," I say, not really sure of what I'll say next. I wait and feel him hanging on the line. I take a deep breath. "Never mind." I don't want to tell him how I feel.

I want to show him. Or maybe I want him to guess.

After we hang up, I stand at my window and reality sinks into me. Alistair is going to be gone *all* summer. I look around my bedroom and spot the clothes I picked out. Everything seems meaningless now.

"Knock, knock." My mother stands in the doorway. "I thought you'd fancy a milkshake." She walks in, and hands me a tall glass of foamy chocolate milk. "To perk up."

I know I'm going to tell her. She probably knows it too. I'm going to come out to her, and I'm going to do it now.

"He must be feeling a little down about not being allowed to go to the party with you." My mother sits at the edge of my bed and glances around the room. "You keep a very neat place here. Good for you."

I take a deep gulp of the drink and wipe my lips. I don't really know how to say it, where to start.

"Ryde, do you know how much I love you? I love you so much that if you told me you were a serial killer and needed me to hide the bodies, I'd help you."

She gives me a look that makes me feel small and humble. "You understand?"

Her love is so big, it's like standing in front of the ocean with a straw. No matter how much I try, I'll never be able to take all of my mother's love in.

"So, you got something to tell me?"

"Yeah," I breathe out. "I do. But maybe you know it already." I toss the words out in a hurry. "I'm gay."

She reaches out for my hand. "Come here." I sit by her and she pulls my head to her shoulder. "It's okay, Ryde, baby. Everything's gonna be all right. I know it's scary and new, but you'll grow into it and become a fine gay man." She laughs and I laugh too. "Okay?" She kisses my hair and stands. "Don't tell your father just yet. I'll ease him into it in time."

It's so easy with her. But it's not going to be like that for Alistair. "Alistair thinks it's a sin. You know what I mean?"

My mother nods gravely. "They brought him up like that."

"I don't really know how to... I mean, how can I compete with God?"

"You don't. You can't. Look, bend his way a little. Reassure him. He'll come around."

Relief finally comes. "So you're okay with it?"

"I was okay with it from the moment you were born."

"Thank you, Mom." I don't know what to say. She's fantastic. I'm blessed.

She hesitates a moment. "Take it slow with him, all right?"

I can't go any slower than I'm going. I'm practically stopped. But I understand what she means. "He calls the shots," I say.

She laughs again. "Been that way since you were little boys." Then excitement takes a hold of her. "Wait a second. I have a great idea. Dad and me, we're thinking of taking a little time off. Maybe going camping with you and the girls, you know, like we used to. I mean, you're seventeen, and this is probably the last summer we get to *force* you to come. What if I called Alistair's parents and asked them if we can take him along with us—"

"That wouldn't work. They're making him go to that camp again."

"What? I thought—"

"I know. So did I."

"They're really gonna mess that beautiful kid up if they keep at it."

Now I feel like crying. "He has visions, Mom. Says he sees this angel and—
"

"What? What do you mean?"

"Just that. He sees an angel sometimes and it freaks me out the way he believes it. He has these migraines and then, lately, it's like he's a whole other person. He'll go from being sweet to being really dark."

"Migraines can cause that, hon, and especially in teenagers, you know, with your hormones going wild and all, but Ryde, the boy should see a doctor—"

"Sometimes I think he's gonna go...*crazy*." I've just spoken my worst fear and it feels real. "He's always alone in that attic with his scissors and threads, or he's at church being brainwashed."

"Hey, hey, he's got you, doesn't he?" She grabs my hands. "As long as you're near him, you'll keep him grounded." She puts her hands on my face and makes me look at her. "Let me talk to Matilda. Let me see if I can persuade her to change her mind about sending him to that awful camp. She and I get along sometimes. I think she sort of likes me best on the street."

"You write erotica. I doubt she likes you."

"But I'm honest and that counts for a lot."

I look out my window. Alistair's window is dark. "So, we'd go back to the place we used to go, the one with no electricity and no toilets?"

"That's right. If we're gonna camp, we're gonna camp."

I stare at his window, silently calling him forth to it. "What was that place called again?"

"Craving's Creek."

"That's right," I whisper. "Craving's Creek."

I see his window light up.

Chapter Three

The couch springs are broken, so I'm buried deep into it, squeezed between Sheryl and another girl named Natalie. Natalie is minutes away from throwing back the contents of her stomach on my lap. Sheryl is smoking a menthol cigarette, blowing the smoke out in circles.

The party was supposed to be a pool party, but the rain hasn't let up, so we're in Sheryl's basement. There's beer her father bought for us, a case of twelve for fourteen people. Now we're down to six people and I'm the only guy left— Bobby and Luis took off for the waterfront, taking with them the only two girls who could stand. An hour ago, Natalie sneaked in a bottle of peach schnapps and that was a bad idea. The last of the girls are locked up in Sheryl's brother's room and I can hear them all sobbing in there. The party is turning into a drama fest.

There's a terrible peach taste in my mouth and the chip bowl is empty. Time to go.

"I'm gonna get going," I say, looking over at Sheryl.

She puts her hand on my thigh. "After this song. I love this song."

The song is "Black" from Pearl Jam, and I used to love it, but I've killed it by listening to it over and over and over again. *Each man kills the thing he loves*, Wilde once wrote. I think of Alistair and sit up. I'm a little drunker than I thought.

"Ryde," Sheryl says in a strange, dreamy voice. She's not even looking at me, just staring at the washing machine in the corner. "When I turn eighteen, I'm going to Hollywood."

I've known Sheryl since we were in kindergarten. We grew up together. She used to be a bubbly and funny little girl, but she's not anymore. She's thin and moody and always looking to pick a fight with people. She's different from the people here, that's what it is. She's like a cobra trapped in a glass box full of garden snakes. She needs to get out of here or there's going to be some serious damage.

"Will you come visit me?" she asks, putting her cigarette out in an empty beer bottle. "You and Alistair?"

I don't know why she'd mention his name. She never does. He's nothing to her. Invisible. "Sure," I say, turning my beer bottle in my hands. I peel the label.

"You know what they say about peeling off labels, right?"

I look over my shoulder at her. "What?"

"You're horny." She laughs, but her laugh is pathetic. "Come on," she says, getting off the couch. "I'll walk you home." She looks down at Natalie. The girl is sleeping with her mouth open and her long hair half wrapped around her neck like a noose. "This party sucks." Sheryl pulls me up. "Come on, Ryde, let's go walk around in the rain or something." She bangs on her brother's door. "Get outta there!" she hollers to the girls. "My parents want everyone to leave right now." She listens and shrugs.

I follow her up the stairs and quickly say hello to her parents, who are seated at the kitchen table, playing cards. "Where do you think you're going, Mrs. Holly Golightly?" her mother asks.

"Nowhere." Sheryl pushes me out the door. "For a walk." We hurry down the front steps, into the street.

"Who's Holly Something?" I ask, outside.

Sheryl laughs. "*Breakfast at Tiffany's*? Hello?" She slaps my shoulder. "You need to lay off Stephen King." The rain has stopped. "Too bad. I was looking forward to getting wet and wild with you," she says.

I just keep my mouth shut.

We walk around the block and cut through the schoolyard, heading for the park.

The park is dark and deserted. "Let's swing." She sits on a swing and pushes off.

I haven't swung in a long time and the beer makes me a little nauseated. If I keep my eyes focused on the same tree, it's not so bad.

Sheryl is swinging high next to me. "Did you know Alicia has a crush on Alistair?"

I'm glad it's dark. My face feels hot. Alicia is a weird girl in his theater class. But she's cute.

"She asked me for his phone number and she's gonna call him this week, I think."

I'm swinging so hard, I think I might end up busting the chains.

"Don't you think they'd make a cute couple?" Sheryl asks, her voice trailing in the wind. "I mean, they're both so strange. And their names match too. *Alicia and Alistair*. Sounds vaguely romantic."

I abruptly jump off my swing, landing far off the set into the sand. I stand there with my heart beating inside my ears.

Would Alistair go for a girl? He might. He just might.

Sheryl jumps off the swing and digs into her jacket for a cigarette. "Are you pissed or something?"

I look over at her, sneering.

"What's wrong?" She's a good actress. Better than I thought. She's playing me. "Ryde?"

"I gotta go home," I say, taking off for the hole in the fence.

"Wait!" She follows me and grabs my elbow. "Are you jealous or something?"

I lean back from her and stare her straight in the face. I don't care who knows I'm gay anymore. "Tell Alicia she better back off," I say, knowing I've just sold myself out. "Alistair's not interested in her, or anybody else for that matter."

"Yeah, I know…" She lights her cigarette. "That's what I told her."

"Oh." I stare at her for a second.

She smirks and looks down the street at Alistair's house. "He's a little strange, but there's nothing wrong with being a little strange." She takes a drag of her cigarette like she's rehearsing a movie scene. "He's really beautiful too. Too bad he's so terribly shy." She throws her hair back, playing coquette. "I bet he's still a virgin, all innocent and fresh."

"Yeah, well, keep your claws off him."

Sheryl mocks a cry and throws a hand to her forehead. "My dear Ryde, I have no use for boys like him. What could I possibly do with him?"

She steals a laugh out of me. She's pretty good. "I'll see you later," I say, backing away.

When I turn back, I see her swinging slow with her cigarette pressed between her lips. She's still talking, rehearsing a scene for an invisible audience.

I've never done this before, and I'm pretty sure I'll end up falling off this branch and breaking my spine. But I can't risk knocking on Alistair's front door, and his parents would hear the phone if I called. I try throwing pebbles at his window, but he doesn't hear them. It's past midnight and I'm under the flare of the moon, crawling on my stomach on this branch I hope won't crack under my weight. If I can just make it to the end, I'll be within reach of his window.

I slither a few more feet, the bark scratching my stomach through my T-shirt. I can see he's awake. I see him sitting on his bed, bobbing his head. He has his earphones on. Even if I touch his window, he won't hear me.

So I wait and stare at him. After a minute or two, he feels me watching and looks my way. He jumps back like a rabbit spotting a fox and tears his earphones off. "Ryde?" I see him mouth my name. I'm stretched out on the branch, inches away from his window, and about twenty feet off the ground. Suddenly, I don't feel so safe. "Open," I whisper.

He gets out of bed. He's in his white underwear. Alistair is built small, but I realize he's got more muscle than I do. He actually has *abs*. How did that happen? "What if you fall?" he asks me, propping his small window open. There's no way I could ever squeeze myself through that window.

"Can you sneak out?" I don't want to look down anymore. "Out back or something? I wanna talk to you."

He's frowning, obviously disapproving of the situation. "I'll try," he finally says and looks down. "Can you get back down there without falling?"

"Yeah." I start inching myself back on the branch, but the backward motion is much trickier. I see him slipping into his gym pants and that church camp T-shirt with Jesus's famous logo on it. He comes to the window to check on my progress and frowns again. "Careful," he whispers and shuts his light off. I hear the trap door opening and I move a little faster. When I reach the trunk of the tree, I know I'll be all right. I climb down and dust myself off.

We meet in the back of his house, by his father's toolshed. His parents sleep in the room at the front of the house. They probably can't hear us. "You've never done that before," Alistair says. He stands near the shed, his face half-hidden in the shadows. "It's dangerous. Don't do it anymore."

Why do I find him so beautiful? What is it about him anyway? I don't know if I want to kiss him or bite him. And his eyes. His eyes are the reason I get the way I get around him. I can't escape those huge black eyes. I see them when I close my own eyes, night and day. They hold a secret I yearn to know.

"The party was kind of boring," I say, playing it cool. "You wouldn't have liked it anyway."

He just looks at me.

"And on top of that," I add, a little nervously now, "everyone got drunk on Peach liquor and the girls were all crying and stuff. It was pretty lame."

He's still not talking to me. He just stands there, waiting patiently for me to say something real.

"Sheryl and me left and went to the park." Now I see his jawline harden and the fire inside me starts anew. "She wants to go to Hollywood next year."

"With you?" His voice is sharp.

"No, not with me." I touch his hand with a fingertip. "And, anyway, I wouldn't go, even if she asked me to."

He sticks his hand under his arm.

I want him to let his guard down. "My mom says she's gonna talk to your mom about Catholic camp. She wants you to come to camp with us, up north."

Alistair's face finally brightens. "For real?"

"Yeah for real. It would be so cool if you could come. If she said yes, wouldn't that be amazing?"

"She'll say no. I know she will." He looks over my shoulder at the house. "Ryde, I wanna tell you something. Something important I decided this week."

Everything in me stops and listens. "What is it?" I come a little closer to him.

"After graduation, I'm gonna enter the Grand Seminary."

"The what?" I have no idea what he's talking about. I'm going to be a journalist and he's going to be a history teacher. That's what we decided last month.

He's staring at the ground. "The Grand Seminary is where you go when you wanna become a priest," he says, his eyes meeting mine in the dark. "Okay?"

He's nuts. He's completely insane. He's in denial about being gay and using God as some kind of shield to avoid temptation. I want to confront him about it, but if I do, I'll only incense him. "Okay, yeah, fine." I say, calmly. "Sounds good."

"You're fine with it? Really?"

"Hey, it's your life." I'll never let him. I'll blow the Grand Seminary up if I have to. I'll never let him do it. Never. "You wanna marry God and wear black all your life, like you're perpetually attending your own funeral, that's your right."

"It's not like that, and you can't understand. I've been called, Ryde. He's asked me to serve him. And I'm not the only one who's felt him in the house. My mother saw the angel too and—"

"You need to get some fresh air, do you understand me?" I can't take this. What is this? "You need to get out of that attic, away from them, from your mom—"

But he steps back from me and I know I need to stop talking right now.

"Alistair," I whisper, and a shiver runs through me. "Are you fucking serious? What about our plans to go to Europe after we get our diplomas?" I have to say more, but I don't know how he'll react. "What about me? About *us*,

I mean."

"You could become a priest too. You'd be so good at it, and we'd go through the four steps together, at the seminary—"

"Oh, stop. Just stop it. You know I don't even believe in God and all that stuff."

"You do believe in him too. You're just scared."

"And so are you."

"No, I'm not." He raises his chin defiantly and I'm reminded of the first time I saw him, when we were both four years old. Ever since that day, I've been living for him.

"Yes, you are," I say. "You're scared, Alistair." I want to touch him but can't summon the nerve. "You're scared of me and how you feel about me."

"Don't say that."

"But you are. Admit it." Now I've done it and I can't stop here. "Has it ever occurred to you that I don't want you to become a priest or get married or date Alicia or move to Africa or—"

"Well, it's not up to you."

"It's not up to me?" I glare at him. Why am I like this around him? It used to be we'd hang out together and I'd feel peace inside. These days, I'm constantly in turmoil. I could spend twenty-four hours a day with him and still not be satisfied. Can't he see it? I'm obsessed.

"Ryde, don't," he says gently, putting his hand on my arm. "Don't be upset. Please."

Something takes a hold of me and I pounce, stopping real close to him. I'm shaking. "You're not gonna become a priest, do you hear me?" I put my hand on his face and his skin feels hot against my palm. "I won't let you," I whisper and realize I'm pressing my mouth to his. But he's frozen still against me and I make myself move back.

For a moment, we just look at each other. I didn't kiss him.

It wasn't a kiss.

I can see he's breathing hard. I can see he's wired. "Do you know what you just did?" he asks, like he's about to cry.

"Stop. You're not a baby." I rub my finger against my mouth. God, I want to kiss him so hard. I want to kiss him until he chokes. "Don't act so offended."

"I'm not offended."

"Then what are you? Disgusted?" I'm afraid of his answer. "Well, are you?"

"I'm not disgusted or offended! I...I don't know—"

"Goddamn it, Alistair." I close the distance between us and grab him again. I want to shake him. I want to shake God right out of him. "What are you then? Huh? What?" I hold his face between my hands. "What?" I say more softly, leaning my forehead to his. He's breaking me down. I close my eyes. I'm dizzy. I feel sick.

His hand is in my hair. His heart beats like a drum against my chest.

I open my eyes and see him staring right into me. I'm not breathing anymore. I'm locked into his stare, all my doubts vanishing. I kiss him.

He opens his lips and lets me kiss him deep. Our tongues twist together and I'm holding his face, his neck, and my whole body hungers for him. I've never kissed someone like this before. I don't know how we'll ever stop.

But the porch light turns on and that light hits me like a bullet in the head. I literally jump back from him. His mom opens the door. "Alistair? What on earth? What are you doing out here?"

I can't catch my breath. I want to scream. I want to laugh. I want to kiss him again. "I'll see you tomorrow," I say, bolting for the street.

I look back over my shoulder and see him entering his house.

But I don't care how much trouble he's in. Because I kissed him.

Chapter Four

My dad parks the car on Barcelona Street and looks over at me. My sisters were up all night puking. My dad's eyes are glassy and he doesn't look like he'll last very long. "Why don't you go home and sleep, Dad," I say. "I'll do this section and walk home."

"No, no, it's my business. My responsibility." He doesn't sound very convincing. "I can't ask you to do my job for me."

"Go home, Dad." I squeeze his shoulder and pop the door open. He just sits there, beaten. I go around and slide the side door open, grab his and my bag full of empty flasks and the box of business cards. I swing the bags over my shoulders and lean into his window. "I'll be home in three hours."

"You're a good man," my dad says. "I owe you one." He puts the van in gear and gives me a kind look. "Don't go in anybody's house and don't let people give you anything to drink."

"Yep." I smile at him and walk away, lugging the bags and box. It's nice to be on my own this morning. The sun is still low and the heat isn't too bad yet. Besides, this is an old section of town, and the trees here are all tall so there's plenty of shade to walk in. I set off for the first B street at my right. I hope I don't see anybody from school. I really don't want to be seen doing this.

Not that I'm embarrassed or anything.

The houses here are different from the houses on my street. Here, the houses have character and every one of them is unique, like their owners are saying something about themselves. The people here have money. Even their lawns look better. I hope their water is full of crap and my dad makes a killing.

I walk up the first driveway, pink granite of course, and up the front steps. If I did this in Texas, I'd have been shot by now. A dog barks in the window, and I can tell it's a small thing, so I press on and quickly hang a flask on the door handle, then drop a card in their mailbox. I hurry down the steps and back to the safety of the street. People don't like strangers hanging stuff on their doors.

I walk to the second house and do the same thing. The trick is to do the street fast, before people start opening their doors and calling out to me. I don't like to talk to people about water filters. I don't really know anything about them actually.

By the time I'm halfway done with the street, I know people are on to me. I hurry. I don't hang the flasks anymore, but drop them on people's front steps. In two hours, I'll be throwing them on lawns.

Finally, I reach the last house and turn the corner. On the next street, Babylon, I take a break and sit on the curb. It's getting a little hotter and I forgot to bring something to drink, but I'll be all right. I stare at the oil in a rain puddle. It looks like a rainbow. I think of the gay flag.

I think of Alistair.

This morning, when I woke up, I went straight to my window but couldn't see him, and now I have this knot in my stomach because I have a feeling he's freaked out about the kiss. I'm a little freaked out about it too. But probably not in the same way.

He's going to be hiding out in his room until they drive him to that Catholic creep camp. I won't see him anymore. Last night was most probably the last time I saw his face. He's going to hang black curtains in his window and tell his mother never to answer my calls.

But I kissed him anyway. He's a good kisser too.

I have to stop thinking about this or I won't be able to walk right. I grab the bags and box and stretch my legs a little, trying not to think of the way he opened his mouth last night. I want to open everything inside him.

Now I've done it to myself. I shake the thought off and, ignoring the bulging hard-on in my jeans, set off for street number two.

I hear a bike coming up behind me and look over my shoulder. I can't believe it. It's Alistair. He's all flushed like he's been pedaling fast. "Hi," he says, stopping next to me. "Your mom said you were in the B section."

I'm just as out of breath as he is. "Yeah," I blurt out. He came for me. And he's smiling. He looks amazing. I can't believe him. "Your mom know you're out?" I ask him, setting the bags and box down.

He's different. He's radiant. "She's really angry, you know, about—"

"Oh shit, so she saw us?"

"No," he says, and I notice his cheeks darken a little. "She didn't see us 'cause she wasn't wearing her glasses, but that's not what she's angry about." He's standing with his legs spread wide on both sides of the bike, looking as defiant and proud as I've ever seen him. "I'm not allowed to go to church camp. They called her this morning, you know, 'cause I'm gonna be seventeen and all. You can't go to camp if you turn seventeen during the summer." He leans in a little. "So, I'm not going," he whispers.

"You serious?" He's mine now. "We're gonna spend every day together," I say. I make sure no one is watching and come closer to him. I put my hand on his fingers over the handlebar. "Every day."

He bites his lower lip and nods, staring into my eyes. I want to kiss him but not here. We're in the middle of the street, so I force myself back and grin at him instead. "Do you wanna help me with the bottles? We'll finish fast and go down by the riverfront, okay?"

He's helped me before. He knows what to do. I hand him a bag and some cards and watch him walk away. My heart feels like it's going to bust. I love the way he walks. I love his careful steps, the way he places the bottles neatly, label facing forward, always on the first stair, and how gently he opens and shuts mailboxes. Everything about Alistair is light. Like he doesn't want to leave an imprint of himself anywhere, but if he knew how heavy he weighs in my heart, he'd understand he'll never be alone.

I realize I haven't moved yet and he's done five houses already. I strike off for the big brown house on my left, and with Alistair across the street, the job is suddenly a breeze.

Sitting side by side, we skip stones across the water. On the other side of the Saint Lawrence River is Montreal. I rarely get to go into the city, but come September, I'll be in the city every day, at Dawson College. With my grades, I could have gotten into any program I wanted, but I chose literature, because I plan on getting a degree in English or communications or journalism. Or something.

I want to write for a living. And I want to write important articles. Something underground. Counterculture. Antiestablishment. Maybe I'll start my own zine magazine.

Alistair throws another stone and it skips across the water five times, creating ripple after ripple in the river. He's really good at everything. He doesn't notice it though. I look over at his profile in the sun. "You still wanna be a priest?" I nudge his shoulder with mine. "Hm?"

But he doesn't smile or answer my question.

I don't know why I brought it up anyway. "My dad's gonna give me thirty bucks," I say, changing the subject. "Do you wanna go to Miss Candiac and have a pizza?"

Some kids come running by us, chasing a wet dog.

Alistair turns his face to mine. "Do you think I see that angel because of my migraines?"

What do I say? I go for the truth. "Yeah, probably. My mom says it happens and that maybe you should see a doctor."

The dog whips past us again, but backtracks and runs up to Alistair. He's a little brown dog with long, mangy fur. Laughing, Alistair pets him and rubs his pathetic ears back. The dog is ecstatic about it and wags his tail, splashing water over my arms. I don't know why I'm so annoyed. I want to pet the dog but I won't even look at it. Alistair caresses it and I feel this gigantic ball of fury rolling around inside me.

Maybe I'm the one who should see a doctor. "All right, enough already,"

I snap, getting up. I brush the dirt off my pants and look down at him and his new best friend. I've been reduced to being jealous of a mutt.

"Go," Alistair orders the dog softly. "Get." He smiles as the dog runs off. He stands and cocks his head at me. "God is in the little things, Ryde. Remember that."

"Yeah, so I've heard." I crack a smile, but it's not much. "Can we bring these back and collect my money now?"

"*Our* money you mean." He discreetly touches the edge of my hand. "Is your mom gonna talk to my mom soon? About going camping with you guys?"

I'm devouring him with my eyes. I can't believe how much of him I want. "I'll ask her to do it today."

"'Cause I really wanna go there with you," he says, and his eyes tell me he feels everything I'm feeling.

I have to be alone with him. How do I get him alone?

We grab the bags and his bike and start for the parking lot. My knees buckle. His dad is stepping out of his truck, looking like a wrestler about to jump off the ropes. Alistair's father used to be a boxer. He got hit in the head a lot and suffers from brain damage, but no one in the neighborhood really calls it that. He worked on trains all his life and retired last year. Since then, all he ever does is watch television and read the Bible. He's decent to Alistair. Never yells at him or hits him. But he acts like Alistair's broken. I'm not sure what the story is there.

"Where were you?" is the first thing he says as he's coming up on us. He's short and powerful, with eyes as black as his son's. "Father Bilodeau came by to pick you up for choir. Did you forget?"

Alistair looks confused. "Is today Saturday? I thought yesterday was Thursday."

Mr. Genet looks over at me and I see something mean in his eyes. "What is all that?" He nods his chin at the bags. "What are you two doing with that?"

"They're for his father's business," Alistair says. "Remember?"

I'm sweating. I don't feel good. I want to go. "So, um, are you gonna go to choir practice?" I ask Alistair, but I'm careful not to look at him. My voice is small and I try clearing my throat. "I can wait for you. I mean, for the pizza—"

"Put your bike in the back." Mr. Genet eyeballs me. "He doesn't have time for pizza. We have church this afternoon." He fixes the collar on Alistair's polo shirt. "Look at that, you're all dirty now. And you have Destination Unknown tonight."

Destination Unknown is some church thing where the kids meet in the church basement and their youth leader takes them out to a restaurant or someone's house for dinner. It's supposed to be exciting and a surprise, but they usually go for burgers at McDonald's or to one of the old ladies' houses and watch *Mary Poppins*.

He's done Destination Unknown for years. Done it to death.

"Oh, Dad, do I have to go?" Alistair looks over at me, and he's so obvious, it's terrible. "I really don't like Destination Unknown anymore, and the kids there are all much younger than I am." He keeps looking over at me with his big puppy-dog eyes, and I know his father is on to us like a fly on shit. "Please, Dad, can I not do Destination—"

"Get in the car." His father finally turns away, and I'm surprised he's allowing me a moment alone with his precious boy.

When we're alone, Alistair whines. "I...I...I really don't wanna go to—"

"Stop," I whisper, looking over his shoulder at his father, who's staring at us from the driver's seat. "You have to be a little more *subtle* about it. You know, be careful."

"What did I do? What did I say?"

He's so clueless. "Look, go to choir and then fake a migraine or something. I'll come to your window."

His eyes light up. "Okay, I'll do that." He takes a step back. "You promise you'll come?"

If only he knew. "I swear."

He glances back at the truck and steps right up to me. "Will you kiss me again later?" he whispers. "On the mouth, like you did before?"

His words stop my heart. I can't speak. I just nod and stare at his mouth.

He runs off to the truck, trailing his bike through the gravel parking lot, leaving me behind in the dust with another hard-on.

I wipe myself clean with the last of the Kleenex and stuff that mess at the bottom of the small garbage can at the side of my bed. I zip up and try to slow my breathing down. I promise myself not to do it again for another two days.

Maybe not two days, but at least until tonight.

I need a glass of water. I need Alistair's body, mouth, skin. I need to stop jerking off three times a day.

I sit up and pull the sheet off my legs.

My mother knocks on my door. "Ryde? Can I come in? Are you decent?"

I am, but my thoughts never are. "Yeah, come in." I make sure I've left no evidence of my little self-serve marathon.

She enters but stays in the doorway. "Your dad is taking a nap with the girls, but if they're better, we were thinking of going out to dinner. You know, just him and me. Do you mind babysitting?"

"No, I don't mind." Maybe I can convince Alistair to sneak out and come over. "Sure, I'll stay home."

"Oh, you're such a sweetheart." She blows me a kiss. "Look, me and Dad were talking earlier, and seeing how responsible and good you've been lately, we're willing to pay for your license and look at maybe getting you a used car or something."

Now that's the news I've been awaiting patiently. I'm already driving over the Champlain Bridge, into the city, with Alistair sitting next to me. "When?"

"As soon as we get back from camping."

"And when is that?" I hope she hasn't changed her mind about Alistair coming.

"We booked it for next week."

"And what about—I mean, did you talk to Matilda?"

"I'm working on that, okay? She wasn't too hot about the idea, but give me a little time." My mother watches me closely from the door and I feel revealed. "You're pretty crazy about him, huh?"

This is weird.

"Baby, can I just say one thing? I know he's seventeen and all, but his seventeen is more like *fourteen*, don't you think? Just the way he was raised and how much his parents have kept him from really maturing—"

"He's very mature. He's more mature than I am—"

"Why are you getting so defensive, Ryde? You're wiser than he is, and that boy has been gaga over you since the first day he saw you, so you're gonna have to be real careful with all that power you have over him, that's all I mean." She stops. Waits. "Okay?"

"Yeah, okay."

"Now, tell me, have you two been sexual yet?"

"Mom, come on, please, let's not have this talk—"

"Have you?"

I glare at her. "No."

"Okay. Good. You can kiss and fondle each other and do all those wonderful things two guys can do to each other, but don't you go and have complete inter—"

"Mom, please." I hold my hand up. Mercy. No more. "I get it. I understand."

"You're only seventeen, Ryde, and there's so much more to sex than penetration and—"

"Okay, that's it." I lie back and throw a pillow over my head. "Please push this very hard against my face," I cry from under the pillow. "Kill me now."

She laughs and leaves. I wait until the blood vessels in my face shrink back to their normal size and throw the pillow on the floor.

I stand and go to my window. It's four o'clock and he must be back from choir. If I go now, I'll catch him before he heads out again for Destination Very Well Known.

I change into my other jeans and smell my armpits. I roll on some deodorant and throw on a new T-shirt.

When I climb down the stairs to the front door, my feet barely touch the carpet.

His dad's truck is in the front. They're home. I knock on his door again and put my face up against the screen door. I see pots steaming on the stovetop and hear water running in the kitchen. "Mrs. Genet?"

After a while, she comes to the door. She's wearing a new dress, this one ankle length and white with little red dots. Her thin blonde hair is undone, and in the light, I can see bald spots. "I didn't hear you," she says and opens the door.

I'm a little surprised. "Is Alistair here?" I stand in the entrance, but my eyes are steady on those stairs I want to run up. It smells like roasted chicken and thyme. People say Alistair's mother is a really good cook. I wish I were allowed to have dinner here sometimes.

"Would you like some coffee?" She wipes her hands on the stained waist apron she wears when she cooks. "Or a Coke?"

Has she just offered me a beverage? This is a first. "I'm fine, thank you." I check the stairs again. Can't he hear me? The boy's deaf. Or maybe he has those earphones on again. "Can I go up and see him?"

"Not right now."

We stand face-to-face, and I realize she wants to talk to me. The Coke is just an excuse. "Is he all right?" I ask, my eyes straying to those stairs again and again.

"He's had a fit. He's sleeping."

She calls his migraines *fits*. I don't personally like the word. "Oh," I say. Now, if she doesn't let me go up there, I might just have to climb that tree again. "Was it bad?"

"Yes, very. He was quite upset and we had to sedate him."

"Sedate him? What? I don't understand."

"He wasn't himself."

"Well, I...I'd like to see him."

"Not right now." She looks over at the living room and I follow her eyes. The chairs are empty but the television is on. Where is the big guy? Is he upstairs with Alistair? Something feels wrong in this house.

"I'd like to talk to you, Rydell."

"What about?" Helpless, I follow her to the kitchen. It's full of steam and the air is pungent with the smell of chicken fat and herbs. I feel seven feet tall in this kitchen. Everything seems to be built small. I wait to see what she'll do, and when she pulls out a chair, I do too.

"You and Alistair have been friends for a very long time," she begins.

So I don't get a beverage after all.

"And I know he thinks the world of you," she says. "He admires you. Like Paul did our Lord."

I move in my seat. "Which one was Paul again?"

Her eyes narrow. "You don't know your Bible very well, do you?"

"My mom's sorta into Buddha." I know I shouldn't be saying all this, but controversy comes naturally. "And my dad was beaten pretty bad by the priests who taught him at school, so he isn't big on Catholicism." I decide to play it a little safer. "But I respect Jesus, and I always watch his blockbuster movie on Easter Sunday."

She closes her eyes and looks sick for a minute. "Rydell," she whispers, "every word that comes out of your mouth is sacrilegious."

"Really?"

"Yes, and what scares me is that you don't even do it on purpose."

I know she doesn't mean it as a compliment, but I'm genuinely pleased. "I wanna be a journalist and call people out on the crap they do."

"Religious people?"

"Well, if you think about it, most of the crap done on earth is done in the name of God."

She sighs and looks at me like I'm doomed. "Have you ever thought about letting God in? It's very difficult to hold the doors closed on him, and the more you try, the more tired you get. That's what causes depression, anxiety. Even madness sometimes."

I really don't want to talk about this anymore. "I might let God in later. I just have other things on my mind right now."

"Like my son?"

Now is the time for caution and wit, both of which I generally lack. "I do think about him a lot," I say, carefully.

"And those thoughts you have, are they pure thoughts?" She doesn't wait for my answer. "I may be old, but I'm not blind, and I see the way you look at my son and it chills my blood."

"Wait a minute—"

"No, you wait a minute." She takes a short breath. "Listen to me. I'm not even going to quote the Good Book to you. Won't even tell you about a city God destroyed for it festered with sodomites and prostitutes, but I'll talk to you about something you do know. Basic biology." She's enthused, speaking quickly. "You know men and women are created differently, with very different physical bodies, and this is in order to reproduce. This is the only real reason men and women go to bed together. Why they get married. Sexuality is normal and healthy when—"

"That's your opinion, and it's the opinion of a lot of people. I know that, but that doesn't change—"

"Alistair has been chosen, do you understand? His father and I both know it. We've known it since God offered him to us. I never could have children. I was menopausal when I got pregnant with him. It was impossible. A miracle. But his father and I knew he would be different from the time he could speak. He's so gentle and not interested in violent things like the other boys. He likes to make clothes, the way Jesus loved to make furniture. People talk behind his back. They say he's too pretty to be a boy." She leans in and lowers her voice. "They say he's a homosexual. But they don't understand. Jesus was never tempted by women, and He was very beautiful. Our son isn't a vile boy. He's an angel and meant to serve our Lord."

This is real to her. She'd rather believe he's some kind of messiah than gay. For the first time in my life, I'm speechless. I need to get him out of this house. Soon. *Now.* "I think I should go check up on him—"

"Sit down. I wanna say something else."

I lean back in my chair.

"Now, I've been thinking about you and about what Alistair says about you. He thinks you're like Thomas, doubting everything, but that with time and guidance, just like Thomas the apostle, you'll come around and help Alistair in his journey."

"What journey? Where's he going?" I'm humoring her.

"He's going to become a priest, Rydell. And maybe one day, he'll become our supreme leader. He'll be our dear Roman pontiff."

"Alistair...the pope?"

"Yes!" she shouts and I stop breathing. "He's been chosen, do you understand? Chosen! He's seen Him. He's seen Him in his room and I've felt Him here too!"

"Okay. Okay." I look around the kitchen, needing to see real things. We're still on earth. Good. "I won't stand in his way or anything. I mean, you know, if he wants to move into the Vatican and all."

"You don't believe in him."

A cool rage creeps into my voice. "Oh, I believe in him all right."

"Good," she says, more calmly. "Because he seems to care about you most. And I know I have to trust him. The Lord works in mysterious ways. Alistair has chosen you to be his rock, his Peter, and though we really don't understand why, his father and I know keeping him from seeing you will only make him want you more."

In her own way, she's making sense. "All right," I say, getting my wits back. "I can be his friend. That's what you're saying?"

"Don't corrupt him. The body is the soul's temple."

"Didn't Jesus destroy the temple?"

"But he rebuilt a new one, one made out of love and the invisible."

"So maybe Jesus was saying you have to corrupt your body a little, or maybe even corrupt it *a lot*, in order to get to the invisible and—"

"Don't twist the words!"

"It's called *interpretation*."

She stares at me and I wait for a rebuttal. There's none.

"Can he come camping with us next week?" I feel a little drained. "My parents are gonna be there. It's a nice family place. We'll roast marshmallows and play Scrabble."

She smiles a little. "I know it would make him very happy."

"It would."

"What if he has a fit?"

"He won't. He never does when he's with me."

She brings her hands together and watches me.

Well, I think he's coming.

Chapter Five

Sunday morning, and in the kitchen, I find my parents having coffee and toast together. They look relaxed. My dad has a lazy smile on his face, so they must have had a good time last night. The twins are stumbling around the room, running after a frantic fly.

"Thanks so much for babysitting last night." My mother grabs my face and kisses me. "Let me make you some pancakes."

"No, I don't have time." I pour the last of the coffee in my *The Crow* mug and dump too much sugar in there. "I have to leave soon." I look around for the peanut butter.

"Where you going, baby?"

"Church."

My dad squints at me. "What?"

"Yeah, you know, I thought it could be interesting." I swallow some coffee, but my throat is a little tight.

"Interesting? How's that?" My father puts his cup down. "I don't understand."

"Look, it's just to see what's it's like. Sort of like an experiment."

"I'll tell you what it's like—"

"Honey," my mom cuts him off, "don't get so tense."

"No, I wanna know why our seventeen-year-old boy is suddenly interested in joining a group of people who stand around mumbling words written two thousand years ago, clapping their hands and bowing their heads to a statue of a crucified man dressed in a loincloth and looking a little like Robert Plant."

"Larry, we're very well informed of your opinion on religion."

"Dad, listen, I'm not joining the club, just checking it out."

"It's dangerous, Ryde." My father calms down. "Especially at your age. You're still very impressionable. They'll get into your head."

"It's not like that." I knew he'd be like this. He'd be happier if I announced I was joining the circus. "I just wanna see what all the fuss is about."

"Is it...is it because—" But he stops and looks over at my mother. "Is it because you're gay? You think you can pray it away? I'll tell you something right now, you'd be wasting your time."

"I don't wanna pray it away," I say, real low. He knows. My father knows I'm gay.

"And you shouldn't." Awkwardly, he touches my shoulder. "There's nothing wrong with you."

I look at my mother. She's teary-eyed of course. I turn for the sink and put my cup in there. "I'm going to church for him," I say.

"*Him* who?" my father asks.

"Him, Alistair," my mother answers for me. "Larry, are you that clueless?"

"Oh. Oh, I see."

I turn around and face him. "'Cause...I like him, Dad. Well, more than like him." I glance over at my mother. "He's, you know, the one I want."

"Huh," my dad says. "Really? Okay, I didn't know you were into blonds."

I can't help laughing a little. "I guess so."

"All right then, go ahead. Go to church." He drinks his coffee and smiles at me from over the rim of the cup. "Not like I can stop you now anyway." He winks. "Right?"

"No, it's a little too late for that," I say, nervously. "So, can I borrow a tie from you?"

Riding my bike to church, I think of last night and what Sheryl said. She showed up after my parents left and we hung out in the living room, watching *Dirty Dancing* again. She's in love with Patrick Swayze. Last night, we talked about our futures and getting out of this little town. She's very serious about making it as an actress, and her ambition is contagious. I started thinking about university. Now I'm pretty confident I'll make it out there as a journalist. She suggested we write down five goals so we can look at them in ten years and see if we succeeded at attaining any of them.

These were mine.

Graduate from university.

Go to Berlin with Alistair.

Start my own political science magazine.

Move in with Alistair.

Adopt a dog with Alistair.

She cried a little when she read my list and saw her name wasn't exactly in the top five, but now she knows the score. Sheryl says we'll be friends forever, and I think she may be right. She made me promise I'd look out for her, if she ends up an "old, bitter, washed-out, alcoholic actress." We cut our fingers and sealed it in blood. She's my sister now.

When I reach the church, which is in fact a community center, I survey the parking lot. I'm a few minutes late, but the doors are still open. I prop my bike up against the side wall, wipe my hands down the front of my dress pants, and walk up the three steps leading to the open doors. Our town still doesn't have a proper church, so this building is used instead. It's funny because on Friday nights, they hold parties here. Dances for the local teenagers. I wonder if the churchgoers can still smell the leftover musk in the air on Sundays.

I walk in and see people are already seated in the pews, which are, in fact, rows of plastic chairs. There are more people than I thought. The priest, Father Bilodeau, is walking over to the stand. He's wearing a long white cassock that matches his perfectly white hair. He looks a little like the Glad guy. He begins by wishing everyone a good morning. People are shifting in their seats and some are coughing. I look around for that head of blond hair in the pews. I spot him in the first row.

Of course, he *had* to sit in the first row. The Genets are VIPs in church.

As quietly as I can, I head for the front, not looking on either side of me. I find a seat in the first row, on the opposite side of the aisle.

Alistair hasn't seen me yet. He's staring ahead, visibly enthralled.

I listen to whatever Father Bilodeau is droning on about, but Alistair looks so fantastic in his black jacket, I can't stop staring at him. He looks all grown up. Sexy. I clear my throat. Move in my seat. The lady next to me shoots me a cold look, and I lean my elbows on my knees, pretending to be intensely interested in the sermon.

Father Bilodeau is talking about making amends and not being afraid of asking for forgiveness anytime during the day. It's not a bad concept and I can't disagree, but then he starts on the Bible quotes, so I look over at Alistair again. I stare at him hard, waiting. Finally, I see him frown a little and scratch his cheek as if my stare flicked him. He turns his eyes my way and his whole face lights up. For a second I think he's going to jump out of his seat, but I raise my eyebrows at him and press a finger to my lips, curbing his enthusiasm.

He grins from ear to ear and waves at me. He looks over at his mom and nudges her. His excitement is worth this awful tie squeezing my neck. Mrs. Genet looks over at me and her mouth jars open.

Sitting proudly, I wink at her.

She crosses herself and looks back at the makeshift altar.

For the rest of the service, Alistair squirms in his seat like he's got ants in his pants. He keeps looking over at me and smiling. His smile makes me hot and I try to play it cool, but I can barely sit still anymore.

Then everybody is on their feet and I have no idea why. They form two lines in the middle of the aisle. Father Bilodeau stands, holding a silver cup. Two boys, both red-faced and sweating, stand at his side. This is Communion. I've never done it and I know I'm not allowed to. I look around and realize I'm the only one sitting in the pews.

Alistair frowns at me and motions for me to get up.

"I can't," I whisper. "I've never been baptized."

I see curious eyes turn my way and know I've just outed myself as unholy.

Alistair's father pulls him away from my row and pushes him gently into the line. I watch Alistair's face. It's pale and serene like he's thinking of something I can't grasp. For a moment, I feel like I'm trespassing here.

One by one, the people stand before Father Bilodeau and accept the little paper bread disk. Soon, everyone is seated again and praying with their heads bowed. I try to hang my head, but every time I start talking to God, I feel ridiculous. What's wrong with me? Can't I even pretend to pray?

Do I even have a soul? Or am I all brains and guts?

Finally, the service is over, and after Father Bilodeau has blessed the crowd, people begin to file out. As soon as they do, Alistair crosses the aisle over to me. "You came," he says, flushed.

"Had I known how good you look in a jacket, I'd have come sooner."

I've made him blush. "Well, um, do you wanna come with us to lunch?" He looks around for his parents. "I can ask them."

"No, I'd rather not." I make sure no one is watching and touch his arm. "Can you get away later?"

"I think so." He smiles again. "I can't believe you came."

"It was nice. It was all right."

"Well, I gotta go," he says, seeing his father watching. "But I'll call you after lunch."

"How you feeling now? Your headache is gone?"

"Yes." He looks back at his father again. "I'll see you later!" He hurries to the doors.

When I look around, I find everyone is gone.

I'm alone with Father Bilodeau.

I look at him but he turns away from me. Shit, I'm not even worth a sermon.

I'm sitting in the living room, trying to watch this cheesy Sunday afternoon movie, every commercial break a relief. But I can't do anything else. Can't read. Can't move. Can't think. The phone is on my lap and when it finally rings, I jump to my feet and pick up the receiver. "Hey," I say, knowing it's him.

"Hi," he says, full of cheer. "Do you wanna come over now?"

Do I?

"I'll be right there." I throw the phone on the couch and call out to whomever is in the kitchen, "Going to Alistair's!"

I try not to run to his house, but my feet won't allow it. When I come up to his door, he's already opening it. "Hey," he says.

"Hey." I want to slow my breathing down but can't. "Where are you parents?" He never answers the door.

"They went to Sears to buy a microwave."

This is possibly the best news I've heard in a long time. "Oh," I say, leaning back on my heels. "Am I allowed in?"

"Yeah, if we stay in the living room with the curtains open."

I can't stop myself from smiling. "All right then."

Inside, the house is cool and dark. We sit in the armchairs. There's absolutely nothing to do in this house.

"Oh, I wanna show you something." He jumps out of his chair and up the stairs.

I stare at the empty stairs. I want to kiss him again, but it's dangerous kissing him when we're so alone. I don't think I have that kind of self-control.

"Look," he says, returning with a shirt. "It's finished."

The shirt is actually kind of nice. It's navy blue and the collar is not too stiff.

"Do you wanna try it on?" He looks at me expectantly. "I hope it fits."

I pull the shirt on over my T-shirt. It's good. The sleeves are perfect actually.

"Wow, I got it exactly right." Alistair walks around me. "I wasn't sure about the shoulders."

"You got the measurements right," I say, keeping the shirt on. I like it. I like the way it feels on me.

"I know your body by heart," he says, and then steps back as if he's been struck. "I mean, you know, because I see you every day."

It doesn't matter what he will or won't admit because I know it all already.

"So, you like it?" he asks gently and touches the shirt's collar.

"I really do." I put my hands on his neck and bend my face to his. His lips are warm and soft, and he opens his mouth again, pushing his tongue against mine. We kiss harder and deeper than the last time, and he feels so fantastic in my arms. He's holding my waist, and I want to put my hand on his butt. I slide my hand down his lower back, waiting for a sign, my body tuned to his, and when I touch him there, he groans a little, pressing himself harder against me. I feel his hard-on on my thigh. My head is swimming.

I can't. I just can't do this. "Alistair," I say, pulling away. "Let's take it easy, okay?" I caress his reddening cheek. I've never caressed anyone's cheek before. It feels really nice. "All right?"

His black eyes are veiled. "I don't feel good," he says, and I know a migraine is coming. I could make him feel better right now. If I had the guts to unzip his pants and put my mouth on him, he'd probably never have a migraine again. "I need to take my medication before it hits." He walks away from me.

I find him in the bathroom, sitting on the lid. He looks up at me and I stoop down to him, taking his cold hands in mine. "Let's go outside. Let's get some air, okay?" I kiss his hands. I'm kneeling in front of him and kissing his hands.

I think of Jesus. I think of Paul.

I think I'm in love.

Chapter Six

My mom turns the radio up. "Shh," she orders everyone in the minivan. "They're talking about that witch!"

I look over at Alistair. He's leaning forward in his seat, captivated. "What witch?" he asks.

We left for Craving's Creek this morning at seven. We've been in the van for an hour, but I already feel like stretching my legs. The girls are fussy, tired, getting on my nerves. "Shush your mouth," I bark at Winter. "Mom's trying to hear the news."

"Oh," my mom cries out, "that...that...that—"

"Watch it, honey," my dad says, before my mom drops the B bomb.

"How *could* he, Larry, really?"

My dad just safely shakes his head, agreeing with my mother. He's a smart man. Ever since my mother found out about Prince Charles and that Parker woman, she's been the Queen of Indignation. To her, Lady Di is the very embodiment of all womankind, and Prince Charles has become her number one enemy.

"What witch?" Alistair asks again. "In the woods?"

"Don't get her started," I whisper, close to his ear. "Forget about it."

He widens his eyes and nods seriously. Then, he turns back and starts playing with the girls' feet again. He's perky. Excited. Was standing on our porch with his bags ready at precisely 6:40 a.m.

I'm finding out he's definitely a morning person.

I'm not. I only start feeling human around noon. I move in my seat, trying to stretch my right leg under my mother's seat. "Mom, can you put a tape on or something?"

Next to me, Alistair is making faces at the girls, getting them all riled up in their seats. We don't have AC, so the windows are rolled down and the wind is blaring like a siren in my ears, while in the back, the girls are yelping with joy.

Then, over all this, I hear the first notes of "Peace Train". My mom's playing her Cat Stevens tape again. If I hear "Lady D'Arbanville" one more time, I'll jump out the window. "Mom," I try getting her attention over all the noise, "I brought my Oasis tape—"

"Mrs. Kent," Alistair shouts between the front seats. "Would you like an orange?" He's peeling an orange. The smell of it is kind of nice and I watch his fingers tear pieces of the fruit. He brought oranges. He's so sweet, I can't even be in a bad mood properly around him. "Can I give a piece to your sisters?"

"Yeah, sure, why not." I take a slice out of his fingers. "But cut it up in three, like this." Our eyes meet and we stare at each other for a long time. "Stop," I say, smiling. He puts his hand over mine. His fingers are wet with orange juice. I can't help holding his hand, though I really don't want my dad to see.

"So, Alistair," my mother says, turning the music down a little, "you have your own tent? You could have stayed in ours—"

"Um, well, 'cause my father said that—"

"No, no, I understand." She looks over her seat and smiles at him. I quickly move my hand from under his. "I hope it's easy to put up," my mom says, glancing down at our hands.

"Yeah, you just have to pull on something and it explodes into shape."

"Oh, good." She waves at the girls. "Are you two all right back there?"

They scream out their answer. Yes, they're all right.

"I understand it was your birthday yesterday?" My father sounds so official. He's watching the road, but glancing up at Alistair's face in the side mirror. "So, what are you now, sixteen?"

"Seventeen, sir." Alistair sits up straight.

"Don't *sir* him," I say, very low. "It's all right."

"Seventeen, huh?" My father turns to my mother. "You were seventeen when we met."

Now my father has shoved my mother down memory lane, and she begins to tell us about the time they met, but I've heard this story a million times, so I tune out a little. Of course Alistair is listening attentively, leaning in between the front seats again, encouraging my mother to recount every detail of their first date. It's nothing special, but a cute story full of misunderstandings and wrong turns that eventually led to a happily ever after and *me*.

My mother is finishing up. "And when Larry finally told me he wasn't Gerald the rugby player, I didn't even care anymore."

"I'd won her over with my other fine attributes," my dad chimes in, winking at Alistair in the mirror. "You know what I mean?"

"Oh, be quiet." My mother laughs.

"Guys," I say, dryly. "Can you not, *you know*, do that?"

My father looks up in the rearview mirror. "Do what?"

"Oh, never mind him," my mom says. "Ryde's just embarrassed because he thinks only teenagers have libidos."

"What's a libido?" Alistair frowns at me.

I give my mother's seat a little kick. "Mom, why don't you explain it to him?"

"It's nothing, sweetie," she tells him. "Just a word that means a lot of things."

She turns the music up.

It's "Lady D'Arbanville."

"What's a libido?" Alistair whispers, looking at me.

I lean in close to his ear. "It's many things," I explain softly. "It's like a cake, you know? It's layers of things. At the bottom you have desire. Then maybe lust. And on top of that, you have energy, and piled on top of all that, there's the brain and the way it processes all those things."

"Oh, okay." Alistair wets his lips.

My parents are watching the road. My mom looks like she might be falling asleep.

"What?" I whisper, leaning in closer to him.

He's embarrassed. "Ryde," he says into my ear, "I think I have a libido right now."

I burst into laughter, but the seriousness of his expression chastises me. "It's all right," I say, leaning back into my seat. I squeeze his hand. "I like your libido."

But when I turn to look at him again, I see he's bowed his head and is deep in prayer.

It's around noon when we finally drive into the camping grounds. "Look, look," Alistair shouts, waking me up. "*You are now entering Craving's Creek.*" He points at the window.

Groggily, I look out at the sign hanging by the side of the road. "We're here," I say.

On our way, we must have passed miles and miles of farmland. There isn't much around here. Just one small town with a gas station, a grocery store, and of course, a very necessary liquor store. Earlier, we stopped in town to load up on food and wood, and Alistair and I walked around the parking lot, but people were staring at us, so we decided to wait in the van instead. I don't really like the vibe in these small towns. I feel like that clueless city guy in a zombie movie.

We drive through the quiet grounds. Where is everybody?

"Oh, this is it," my mom yells, grabbing my dad's arm. "Number five, right there!"

"Hilary, don't shout in my ear. I see it."

We turn in to a niche in the woods, our new home for the next four days.

"It's beautiful," my mom says, leaning her head out the window. "Look at all those great big pine trees. Oh, and can you smell that, Ryde?"

"What, boredom and mosquitoes?" I smirk and slide the side door open. But she's right; it's beautiful. We're so alone here. There's no one in sight. "It's pretty cool, Mom."

She climbs out and squeezes my arm, resting her head on my shoulder.

"This is gonna be nice. This is gonna be really relaxing. And I'm sure I'll find inspiration for a hot story here."

"Yeah, like Mary Lou meets a lonesome bigfoot with a gentle heart."

My mother slaps my shoulder. "Sounds like a bestseller to me."

"All right, boys," my father calls out, his head in a huge duffel bag. "You're gonna have to gimme a hand with setting up."

I look around for Alistair. "Where's Alistair?"

In the backseat, Summer is crying for my mother. I walk around the van and see Alistair crouching by the back wheel. "Hey, are you okay?" I touch his shoulder. "What are you doing?" There's a small pool of orange vomit a few feet from where I stand. "Did you puke?"

He slowly stands up. His face is very white. His eyes are haunted.

"Are you all right?" I try catching his eye, but he's looking away, at something I can't see. "Alistair? Talk to me."

"The car and the oranges made me sick, I think."

I lead him around the van and find a box of juice for him. "Drink a little."

"Sweetie, are you all right?" My mom is holding both girls on her hips, but managing to help my dad anyway. "You look a little pale."

"He's all right," I answer for him.

"Ryde, you're gonna give your old man a hand here or what?"

I walk over to my dad and pick up my half of the tent. Soon Alistair joins us, and I'm relieved to see the color is back in his face. We help my dad with hammering the picks into the ground.

Under the noon sun, we work together at pitching the tent, and I work fast, knowing the faster we get this done, the sooner I'll be able to take off with Alistair, into the woods, alone.

I can't wait to show him everything. I can't wait to show him the creek. I remember exactly what it looks like. I remember swimming in that crystal yellow water and the sound of the water falling over the jagged rocks.

But when we're finished with setting up the tent, my mother calls us over to the picnic table she's set up there for lunch. "Are you hungry?" I ask Alistair.

He's sweating a little and his face is flushed pink. I can see the wet spots under his arms and I suddenly want to put my face there. I realize there's nothing about him I find repelling. "Yeah," he says, looking over at the table. "I'm hungry."

My mom has covered the table with a plastic, checkered cloth, and there are chips, grapes, watermelon, hot dogs and canned corn. I dig in, hoping I can pace myself.

While my mother hurriedly prepares the girls' plates, my father dumps food into her plate and the chaos we call lunchtime begins. The hot dog is already halfway into my mouth when I hear Alistair speaking gently next to me. With my mouth loaded, I turn to see him talking with his eyes closed and his hands folded together under his chin.

He's praying and I feel like a hog. I chew fast and swallow everything down. My dad keeps eating, but I glare at him. "He's saying grace," I say, between clenched teeth.

My dad eyeballs me, holding the spoon of corn up to his mouth. I silently dare him to.

Beside me, Alistair is getting carried away. "Bless this family for bringing me along on their trip and for this nice weather, this wonderful forest, and for the canned corn…"

I look over at Alistair and back to my father. "Don't you dare, Dad," I say under my breath.

My mother nudges my dad with her shoulder and takes the spoon out of his hand. At last, he concedes and puts his head down. We pretend to pray.

"Amen." Alistair says after a long time and looks around at us with a warm smile.

"Amen," we mutter, all at once.

I pick up my hot dog and catch the look my dad is giving me from across the table. I hold his stare and bite into the hot dog.

He shakes his head at me and tries not to laugh.

The rain beats down on the tent, every stupid drop of it grating my nerves.

It started right after lunch, and it's now four o'clock. Outside, my parents are playing cards under the tarp, and I hear them speaking softly about us kids. That's all they ever talk about, it seems. They sit around and daydream about our futures.

I'm lying on my stomach, trying to write a poem about Alistair. I want it to be a homage to Blake's "Auguries of Innocence", but it's coming out more like a syrupy Bon Jovi song. Beside me, the girls are napping. They lie side by side, sucking on their pacifiers. I watch them sleep for a moment, wondering what they'll be like later.

Alistair says something in his sleep and I look over at him. He still has his earphones on, but the batteries in his Walkman died a few minutes ago. He fell asleep listening to my Weezer tape. He says he likes it, but his parents would never let him keep it. I stare at his face. His mouth.

I lean in and put my face close to his. I breathe deep, taking in his scent. I feel hot and groggy, horny as hell. I press my hand against his heart and feel it beating slow and steady under my fingers. I move my hand down his chest, but make myself stop when I reach his belly. He opens his eyes. "Is it nighttime?" he asks, his eyes still not quite focused.

"No, but it's dark 'cause it's still raining."

"Oh." He's fighting off sleep.

"I wish we could go to the creek," I say. I'm dying to put my head on his chest, but I'm too nervous. Or too proud. "You'll love it once you see it."

"Tell me what it looks like," he says, taking the earphones off. I feel his hand on my arm. "Is it really beautiful?"

I want him to hold me, to put his arm around my shoulder. "Well, we'll have to walk for a long time, at least an hour, and it's through the woods here, going east. The woods are pretty dense, as far as I remember, but then you get to this clearing and cross a little stream, and then there's more woods, and all of a sudden, you hear it."

"Hear what?"

I lower myself a little, my head now at his shoulder.

"What is it that you hear?" he asks, lifting his head to look down at me.

"The water falling over the rocks."

"Oh."

I push myself into the nook of his arm and rest my head on his chest. Immediately, he puts his hand in my hair. I hear him breathing. I close my eyes, knowing this is as close to anyone as I've ever been. I don't ever want to be with anybody else. Is that even possible? To meet the one you want forever at seventeen?

Why do I always have to be so intense?

"What happens after?" he asks.

"After you hear the water, you know you're close, so you keep walking, but a little faster now, and the branches crack under your feet, and over you the sun trickles down into the tall, lean trees, and just when you think that maybe you're lost, that you took a wrong turn somewhere, you brush away the thick foliage and it's right there in front of you."

"What do you do then?" In my hair, his fingers pause.

"Well, you just stand there and take it in. There's nothing else to do for a minute but to just take the beauty in."

"There's no one there."

"No, no one. Just you and beauty standing face-to-face."

"You mean, you and God."

I sigh and look up at him to see his black eyes watching me. "I guess so."

"We'll go there together, right?"

I inch myself up and lean over him. "There's no one I'd ever bring there but you. Don't you know that by now?"

"Promise me?"

I kiss him on the lips. "Yeah." Then on his nose. "I promise."

Outside, my mother calls to us, "Hey, the rain stopped!"

Within seconds, Alistair and I are on our feet.

I sit on the rocks and shake the water out of my ears. Shading my eyes with my hand, I look up the cliff and shout out to him.

But Alistair doesn't hear me. He stands with his toes curled around the edge of the twenty-foot drop, looking down at the turbulent waters below. This is our second day at the creek, and though he must have jumped off that cliff a hundred times already, I still feel that knot in my stomach every time I see his thin white body shooting down feet first into the deep water below. There's a lot of rocks down there.

When he jumps, I hold my breath until I see his blond head popping out of the water. In graceful strokes, he swims back to shore. Back to me. He's a great swimmer, something else I didn't know about him. He pulls himself out of the cold pool of bustling water and sits down next to me. His hair is slicked back and the water drips down his happy face in golden trickles. "I love doing that," he says, smiling from ear to ear.

"I can see that."

Alistair looks around, folding his legs under him. He shivers. His teeth are chattering.

"You cold?"

"No." He turns his eyes to me and smiles. He looks around again. "I love it here."

I push a strand of his pale hair behind his ear and kiss his shoulder. "I knew you would."

I can't believe how little this place has changed. Yesterday, as we were trekking through the woods on our way here, I expected the worst. Polluted waters. Dried-up bushes. Barbed-wire fences. Maybe even warning signs. *Do not swim. Hazardous.*

But the creek is still here. The water is still clear. Everything remains untouched.

Alistair shivers again. We're both in our swim trunks with our discarded T-shirts and shoes scattered around. "Come here," I tell him. "You're freezing." I rub his shoulder and put my arm around him.

"Ryde," he says seriously. "When you go to school in September, in the city, and I go to the Grand Seminary, will you still wanna hang out with me?"

"Hang out with you? Is that what we do?" I can't help being irritated by his question.

"I mean, will we still…be friends?"

"Alistair," I say, impatiently. "Don't ask me stupid questions like that."

He looks back at the water. "Sorry."

I nudge his shoulder with mine. I wish I had a cooler temper. "Hey," I say softly, "we're gonna move in together as soon as I have steady pay, and we'll both work for a while and save up some money and go to Berlin."

"Germany?"

"Yeah, absolutely. There's a real queer culture there, I think, and maybe their mentality is real different from ours."

"Queer? You mean, like weird?"

"No, Alistair. I mean like gay." I watch for his reaction. "You know, like us."

He's ripping at some grass blades between the rocks. He's upset. I understand. But I won't let him put his head in the sand. This is it. This is who we are. He sneaks a look at me. "I can't tell my parents about me, okay?"

"I don't care who you tell. As long as you always tell me who you are."

"And you think I should become a history teacher, instead of a priest?"

If God is indeed watching right now, I'm going on his shit list. "I think you can do much more as a history teacher. For kids, I mean. If you're in a school, you can reach more of them." I can almost feel hell's red gulf of fire licking my toes. "Besides, you know no one really goes to church anymore."

He ponders this for a moment. "I haven't seen the angel since I came here."

"Maybe he's gone." My eyes roam over his back, the nap of his hair. "Maybe he was your guardian angel and his job was to get you here, with me."

"We'll live together?" He's watching me with those big black eyes I can't live without anymore. "You mean, like—"

"Like two people who live together." I run my fingertip down between his shoulder blades. The sun is high and warming his cold skin. He's stopped shivering.

"In the city?"

"Yeah, and we could even have a dog."

"Yeah?" He's seeing it now. He's coming around to it. "I always wanted a dog."

"I know." Gently, I pull him back a little. "You wanna lie down here? The rocks are warm."

We lie on our backs, staring up at the sky. Huge cotton-like clouds form and break apart. I hear the never-ending waterfall and the leaves dancing around us. I reach for his hand. "Do you want us to be together?" I ask, so softly I barely hear my own words.

He turns and looks at me. "Are we alone here?"

I can't look away from him. "Yeah, we are."

"Are you sure?" He looks at the trees behind me. "I feel someone watching."

I cover his eyes with my hand. "Stop. No one's here." With my hand on his eyes, I bend to him and kiss his mouth. "You taste really good," I say. I'm so excited, I don't even know how it is I can still speak. "Kiss me harder, okay?"

His lips part and we kiss. I feel him lifting his hips to mine. Lying over him, I hold his hands above his head. I'm holding him, but it's myself I'm really holding back. I press my body against the length of his, and our hips move in sync. I slip my tongue in and out of his mouth, until all I am is my tongue, and he, an open mouth pulling me in deeper. I'm so hard I can't take it. I roll off him and lie on my back, feeling sick. "I can't stand it," I say, my heart pounding though my chest. I look over at him.

He's breathing fast, staring up at the sky. "Me neither."

"I want to, but I can't." I stare at his profile. His lips are swollen from our violent kiss. "I think I want it too much."

He lifts his head and looks down at himself, at his erection.

"It's beautiful," I whisper, my finger grazing the taut fabric there.

He turns his face to mine. "It is?"

"I want to kiss you there," I say, and my own words burn through me, exciting and dangerous.

His eyes are cloudy. He's watching me.

I lean in closer to him and grab his head, pulling him near. "I'd take you inside my mouth," I whisper, my lips brushing his. "For as long as you need me to."

He makes a sound and I see the bloom of red rising from his neck to his cheeks. His fingers dig into my hand. He stops breathing and opens his eyes. "Oh, wait," he moans, and looks down at himself, quivering all over. "Oh, oh, no." He's watching the wet spot spread in the front of his pale trunks.

I jump to my feet and dive headfirst into the water. The coldness of it almost gives me a heart attack, but I'm thankful for it.

I swim to the bottom and kick back up. I do this for so long, my head feels light.

When the hunger is gone, I climb back up on the rocks and find him lying there, staring at the sky.

I watch him, this man-child, and look around at the woods. "I didn't touch him," I lie under my breath to God, who somehow I feel is always spying on us.

The fire cracks and pops, slowly toasting my face. But I like sitting up close to it, close enough for the heat of the flames to cook my running shoes. I've always been that way.

I suppose that says a lot about me. There's something terrifying when you know your only real limits are those set by natural law. I'd walk through the fire if my body could sustain it without injury. I would. I'd stay there, wrapped in its blue-and-orange arms and have a conversation with earth. Because that's what earth's core is made of, fire. Maybe I just have a little more of it inside my veins than most people. I'm an Aries after all.

"I can't even look at another roasted marshmallow." My mom leans back in her folding chair and looks over at me. "You should stop too or you'll be sick."

She's probably right. But I stuff a melted, blackened marshmallow into my mouth anyway. I dig into the bag and pierce another to my stick. I hold it above the highest flame, watching its skin darken and bubble. I think of my soul, the dark crust around it. And I think about how I made Alistair come this afternoon. The way he moved under me.

"Would you look at those stars?" my mother says, leaning closer to me. Her skin smells like mosquito repellent. "Can you make out a constellation?"

I eat my last marshmallow and look up at the vast sky above us. It's deep black, but splattered with thousands of brilliant white lights. This sky is unknown to me. I've never been under a sky like this before. I may as well be on a whole different planet. "Wow," is all I can say.

Close by, at the picnic table, I hear my father and Alistair talking softly. They've been playing cards and discussing religion all evening. When they first began their discussion, I was tense, listening closely, ready to intervene and take Alistair's defense. But he doesn't need me to. His knowledge of the Bible is much deeper than I thought. This is a side of him I have never really known or acknowledged. My father has met his match tonight. Whatever argument he manages to make, Alistair dismantles. And Alistair does it with poise. He's full of tact. The words he speaks don't sound like they've been drilled into him at all. He understands what he's saying. He's processed these church teachings and made them his own. Out of his mouth, these are no longer dead words written thousands of years ago, but life-affirming lessons with a strong pulse. When Alistair speaks, he isn't a strange seventeen-year-old boy anymore. He transcends all that. It scares me.

There's a part of him that's inaccessible to me.

So I sit here by the fire and watch him through the smoke. What else can I do? I don't have the wisdom to challenge his views. Or maybe I don't even care enough to try. I want him so much, I could take him while he prayed. It doesn't matter to me. He can hand over his soul to God and clean his mind of me, but I'm already inside him, right there, like that giant ball of fire inside the earth's core.

I'm the thing that keeps him together.

"I understand what you're saying, Alistair." My father's voice is a little louder now. And I look over at the table, pricking my ears up. "But I don't think you need to go to a specific place, at a specific time, and follow specific rules in order to be close to God."

"Well, sir, if your hands were where your feet are, you'd be walking upside down."

My father stares at him from over his hand of cards. "I don't know if I follow you."

"It's just that everything in nature is specific." Alistair drops a card on the table and chooses another one. "Everything follows rules. Even chaos. Nature and man are in God's image. Everything is exactly in its place."

"You think organized religion has its place in our time? I'm sorry, but I can't agree. These rules, these specifications every religion insists on, are the very reasons people continue to fight and kill each other. This is *my* rock and this is *my* temple and this is what God looks like and what he said and what he wants."

"It's not trying to follow the rules that causes the fighting." Alistair frowns, and I can see he's deep in thought for a moment. "It's disobeying the first and most important rule God commands us to follow. *Love one another.*"

My father shakes his head. "How old are you again?" He laughs and turns to look at my mother. "Can you believe this kid?"

My mom smiles back at him. "Hey, you're on your own, Larry. You started this conversation."

I stare at Alistair, wanting the contact of his eyes, but my father is already engaging him in another debate, this one about the Vatican and their golden toilets and ties with the mob.

My mother offers me the last of her beer. "It's a few sips," she says under her breath. "If you want it."

I quickly gulp down the warm beer. Now I want more. But my father won't like it.

"I'm glad he came along," my mother says after a while. "He's such a pleasure to be around." She touches my hand on my leg. "Are you two having a good time at the creek?"

I can't stop staring at him. He won't look over at me. I clutch the empty beer bottle. Another beer would be amazing right now.

"You watch him all the time," my mother says quietly. "Like you're afraid he'll disappear."

I finally look at her. "I know," I say. "I try not to."

"He's very attractive. You know his mother used to be devastatingly beautiful before he was born. I guess she wanted him so bad, for so long, she gave him everything she had. Even her beauty." My mother smiles, but there's something bothering her. "There's something about that boy," she says.

I don't like her tone. "What do you mean?"

"I don't mean it in a bad way, Ryde. Just, you know, there's something ephemeral about him. Ever changing."

"Huh?" I'm not sure what she's saying anymore.

"Lasting a very short time." She sits up. "Short lived."

"I know what the word means, Mom, but what—"

"Well, he changes from scene to scene, you know? Like a character the author's not too sure about yet."

I see what she means. I've noticed how Alistair can be childish in one moment, and so poised and mature in the next. And the way he kisses me sometimes... It's almost too much.

"Hey," she says after a minute, "never mind all that. Tell me, what do you wanna do with your life?"

In a serious tone, I explain my goals to her, making sure she knows every single one involves Alistair one way or another. I realize I'm almost ferocious about it. I want her to understand how serious I am about him and our life together. I don't want her to laugh or underplay it. I won't have her teasing me or telling me I might grow out of it.

She listens without saying a word, but her features tense in the light of the fire. "You sound so angry about it," she finally says. "So intense. This isn't war, honey. It's love."

But I do feel at war. With God. His parents. My body. Society. Every time

I kiss him, I'm raising my sword to an invisible throat.

"You know, Ryde, ever since you were a little boy, you were always so serious about things. I remember you used to break all of your wax crayons 'cause you held them so tight all the time. For a while there, me and your dad thought you'd never be able to draw a picture. Do you remember that?"

Vaguely.

"Do you remember the first picture you ever drew without snapping your crayon in two?" She raises her chin at Alistair.

"I drew him?"

"Yeah. You drew a stick man with yellow hair and two black dots for eyes. That's when I knew I'd better start paying attention to the boy."

"You were always nice to him."

"In a way, he's always been family to me. Now more than ever."

I turn my eyes his way again. He's still playing cards, engrossed with his conversation. "Mom," I whisper, "when do you know you're in love?"

She laughs softly. "When you ask your mother that very question."

Chapter Seven

I wake up to the sound of my sisters yelling. They've been in a rotten mood all through this trip. Summer especially. I can tell she hates camping. She's definitely a hotel girl. I sit up and struggle to free myself of the tangled sheets wrapped around my legs. It's hot and stuffy in the tent and my mouth is parched. What time is it anyway? I poke my head out and see my mother cooking up something on the gas stovetop. Even here, in these woods, she still can't get a real break from her domestic life. I crawl out of the tent and look around the site. My dad is trying to wipe Summer's tears while Winter sits mute in her stroller, watching her sister with serious eyes. "Good morning, you little beast," I say, rubbing Winter's dark hair. "Come here." I unstrap her and pick her up, walking around with her while my dad calms Summer down. I poke her in the belly, trying to make her laugh, but Winter is not having any of it and just stares at the woods. "What's wrong?" I ask her, turning her face away. I lean my forehead to hers. "Are you sad? You miss home?"

Winter nods her head and looks back at the woods.

I walk over to Alistair's small tent. "Wake up, sleepyhead," I say.

"He's not in there," my mother says, stirring milk into the eggs. She looks over her shoulder, at my dad. "Maybe you should go looking for him again."

"What?"

"Ouch," Winter cries, squirming. And I realize I'm squeezing her too hard and relax my grip.

"How long have you been up?" I ask my mother. "Maybe he went to the washrooms at the other end of the grounds."

"Your father already checked." My mom dumps some eggs and a slice of white bread on a plate and brings it to my dad. "Go look for him," she tells him again. "I'm starting to worry."

I put Winter in her stroller and grab my sneakers by our tent. "This is messed up. Why didn't you wake me? I mean, how long has he been—"

"Ryde, I've only been up for half an hour." My mother throws her hands up. "He's seventeen years old. I figured he needed some privacy."

"Maybe he went back to the creek." I lace my shoes up and stand. "I'm gonna go check."

"There he is," my father says proudly, as if he's figured all this out for us. "Where were you, young man?"

Alistair stops and smiles, showing us the big plastic bag of water. "This was empty when I woke up," he says. "The pump here doesn't work anymore, so I went to fill it, but it was far and then I stopped a few times because it was really beautiful and I prayed a little."

"Oh," my mother says, sitting by my father at the table. "I hadn't realized we'd emptied our water container last night."

"Well, thanks, Alistair." My father gets up. "Now, I can make some coffee." He looks around. "Anybody want some coffee?"

I raise my hand, but my eyes are on Alistair.

He gives me a small smile and hands my father the water.

"My Good Samaritan," my father says and winks at him.

"You should be careful," my mother says seriously. "I'd rather you didn't go roaming around alone out here. Lots of creeps, I bet."

"Mom, we're in the woods surrounded by farmland. We haven't even seen another human in three days."

"Still, he's my responsibility. Alistair, your parents trust me with you. So, please, don't go anywhere without telling me."

He blushes and sits stiffly across from her. "Yes, ma'am. I'm sorry."

"Oh, baby," she says, tapping his hand, "I didn't mean to sound so serious. I'm not angry with you."

I slide the rest of the eggs onto two plates and bring those along with a loaf of bread to the table. I sit by him and touch his bare thigh under the table. "Eat up."

He casts me a sidelong glance and picks up his fork.

"Are you two gonna go back to the creek today?" My mother obviously feels bad about her little outburst before. "It's gonna be a hot one, I can tell. Last chance to swim, 'cause I wanna be out of here by noon tomorrow."

Alistair lifts his black eyes to her. "If Ryde wants to."

"Oh, I'm sure he does."

He looks over at me. "Do you want to go back there again?"

"Absolutely." Then, nervously but boldly, I lean in and kiss him on the mouth. It's a quick kiss, a peck really. But it's important and it's done. I've just kissed my boyfriend in front of my parents.

"Um, I'm gonna get the girls ready," my father mutters, picking up his plate. He gives me a quick glance. "Make sure you boys are back for dinner 'cause I'm the cook tonight." He squeezes my mother's shoulder before leaving the table with my sisters.

My mother stares at us and there's a mischievous twinkle in her eye.

"What?" I ask her, grinning.

She leans in and takes Alistair's hand in hers, and then mine.

I feel her silent blessing penetrate my skin. And I'm sure Alistair feels it too.

Who needs God when you have a mother?

I'm looking down at the water below. "Oh, God," I moan, hating this feeling. I want to jump. I want to so badly. But every time I think I'm going to do it, I chicken out.

"*God* has nothing to do with it," Alistair says, laughing at me. "This is between you and you." He stands by me, wet and beaming with pride. Of course, he's been jumping off this cliff all morning. He's done it feet first, backward, tried a flip, and finally started diving headlong into the water.

"Yeah, yeah, Mr. Olympic Gold Medal himself." I sniff and look down again. I used to jump off this very rock when I was eight years old. What happened to my courage? "I'm gonna do it, just gimme some space, will you?" I shove him to the side a little. "Back off. Let me assess this."

"Well," he says, stepping back. "While you assess...." He runs and jumps.

And for the hundredth time today, I watch his smooth white body disappear into the bustling waters below. I move closer to the edge, peering down into the cool green pool, waiting for his triumphant face to emerge.

Seconds pass.

I frown, waiting. What is he doing down there? I stare at the water, adrenaline pricking my palms. I watch the water, waiting for it to speak to me.

What have you done with him? I want to ask it.

"Alistair!" I call out, but the noise of the falls drowns my voice. I lean forward, gazing below into the green eye, my heart racing now. "Alistair!" I yell down into the water. "Alistair!"

I wait. Watch the surface for his head.

There's nothing there but a giant void.

He's not coming back up again.

Oh, God, Oh, my fucking God.

I jump.

The air is cold, slapping the soles of my feet. The wind blows upward, into my nose and mouth, and bracing myself, I tighten every muscle in my body, hold my crotch and wait for impact.

I hit the water like a truck. For a moment, I'm so panicked, I'm not sure I'll make it back to the surface. I kick and kick and open my eyes, searching the greenish waters around me. I can't see him. I can't see him. I need air. I need air right now. I swim up and when my head pops out, I gulp air, screaming his name all at once.

"ALISTAIR!" I look around me. I lost him. "ALISTAIR!"

"You did it," he cries out from the bank. "You finally did it!" He crouches down and reaches his hand out to me. "I knew you'd come after me! I knew it!"

I'm going to kill him. I'm going to drown him. "You fucking asshole!" I roar. I'm going to cry. I quickly swim away, to the other bank near the falls. I manage to pull myself out of the water and collapse on the smooth rocks there. I lie face-first, breathing hard and fast, trying not to sob like a child.

"Ryde!" From the other bank, I hear him shout my name over and over again. "Ryde!"

How could he? I could have killed myself jumping off that cliff. I sit up, wipe the water off my face and glare at him from my spot.

He dives in and swims to me. When he reaches the rocks where I sit, he stops and clutches one, carefully watching me. "I'm sorry," he says, out of breath. "It was just for fun."

I try not to look down at him. He's too beautiful.

"I'm sorry," he says again, his cold hand touching my foot. "Please, Ryde, don't be mad at me."

I shoot him a mean glance. "I thought you'd fucking drowned."

"I'm sorry."

I shake my head at him, but I'm trying not to smile.

"I got you pretty good, huh? Can I climb up here with you now?"

"I don't know." I stare at him. "Get up here."

He pulls himself up on the rocks and sits close to me. For a long time, we don't say a word to each other. The sun is high, burning through the foliage around us and streaking the water with silver and gold. A woodpecker is hard at work somewhere, and in the distance, I hear birds calling out. It's quiet here. Wonderful.

"I'm gonna miss this place," Alistair says after a while. "Do you think we'll ever come back here again?"

I look over at him, at his serious face. "I don't know."

"Why do you think they call it that? You know, Craving's Creek?"

I've never asked myself that question. "Maybe it's someone's name. Like Joe Craving or something."

Alistair nods and looks back at the water.

"Or maybe they named it after that waterfall," I say. "See the way it digs into the water, almost like a hand? It can't get enough of it. It's craving more."

"Yes," he whispers. "I see it." He turns to look at me, leafing through the pages of my soul. What is he looking for inside me? What answer does he seek? "Ryde," he says, staring back at the creek. "I love you."

His words are a clean blade stabbing quickly and neatly through my heart. I barely feel the injury, but the cut is deep and permanent nonetheless. Whatever comes now, I'll wear those three words he's just spoken to me like a scar.

I put my hand over his, on his bony knee.

We watch the water perpetually reaching down, and everything that has ever been alive in the world is here with us.

"Let's lie here," he says, after an eternity. We lie on our backs and Alistair rests his head on my shoulder. I curl a strand of his white-blond hair around my finger and close my eyes, but my enormous pride keeps me from saying those three words back to him.

After a moment, he looks up at me. "What do you think your dad is making for supper?"

My heart leaps. "I love you too," I blurt out, almost like a battle cry.

His eyes widen and he settles himself against me again.

"But you knew that already," I say.

"Yes." He giggles against my shoulder.

Soon, we're both drifting off to sleep.

"Ryde, wake up."

I open my eyes.

Alistair looks panicked.

"What?" I rub my eyes. "What is it?" I follow his insistent stare to the woods. A guy is standing there, ten, maybe fifteen feet away from us. He's standing in the bushes. He's very big, has a beard and is wearing a baseball cap. He stands there like a tree. "Get up," I order Alistair, but my eyes never leave the giant man who has yet to move. "Get in the water." I nod my head to the creek. "Swim fast, head to the site and just keep walking."

"No, but Ryde, what about you?"

"Just go!"

The man steps out of the bushes. In two, three steps, he's at our side, within arm's reach.

"Can I help you?" My jaw clicks. "Alistair, get in the water," I tell him again, always keeping my eyes on the man's calm, motionless face.

"Are you all right, sir?" Alistair asks. "Do you need—"

"Get in the water," I order Alistair again, but more violently.

The man moves and I jump between him and Alistair. "What do you want?"

"He's got a sunstroke," Alistair says over my shoulder. "Look at his eyes. Are you okay, sir?"

The man won't look at me. I see it now. He won't look at me.

It's Alistair he's interested in. It's him he wants.

I make a fist and stand tall. "What?"

But I don't exist. He doesn't see or hear me.

"Hey." I can't take this guy. I can't take him. He's too big. If he makes a move, I won't be able to take him. "Get outta here."

Panicked, Alistair grabs my hand from behind. "He was watching us, Ryde," he keeps saying, over and over and over. "He was watching us. He was watching us. All this time. I told you someone was watching us."

"Alistair, get in the fucking water now!" But the man touches my arm. His touch is gentle, like he's making sure I'm real. "What?" I lean back from his big hand. "What?"

The man reaches into his pocket.

I see the black rock in his hand.

His hand flies to me. The pain in my temple knocks me to my knees. I hear my blood. I hear it. My hand is wet with it. I can't see anything through this red film.

Alistair is screaming my name but I'm all right. I'm all right. I just need to get up. I move. I stand. I grab the man's shoulders. I'm shaking him. He's right there in my grip and I yell for Alistair to run. Run. Run. Goddamn it RUN. I'm beating the ground with the man's head. His blood is all over my hands. In my eyes. I can taste it.

It's not his. It's not his blood. It's mine. I'm here. I'm lying here. My hand is beating the ground. My hand is empty. There's no man.

I'm lying here in my own blood.

Alistair?

Through the thin veil of red in my eye, I see him. I see Alistair. He's right there.

He's moving back from me. Moving away so fast. His face jumps up and down between the trees. He seems to be asking me a question.

Why, Ryde? Why?

He's not walking.

He's being carried.

The man is carrying him over his shoulder.

"Alistair…"

Birds flee the safety of their branches, their wings flapping frantically, and I hear him scream. I hear him screaming my name in terror and shock. The sound of his fear makes me weep blood.

Then I hear nothing.

He's gone.

Animus

Chapter Eight

2008

"Ryde, wake up."

I open my eyes.

Sheryl looks panicked.

"What is it?" I blink and try to focus on her face. "What?"

"Where's my phone?" She's tossing things near me. Clothes. Pillows. "Damn it, where's my phone?" she cries.

The taste in my mouth tells me this is going to be the *king* of all hangovers. I already feel the first wave hitting me. Throbbing temples. Pasty mouth. Absolute apathy. "Your phone's ringing," I say, squinting at the dark room around me. I'm home. Good. I slept in my own bed.

"I know my phone is ringing! But where?" Sheryl is starting to come apart. She's going to lose it. "I just know it's Peaches calling!" She rips the blanket off me and digs her hands into my jeans. "Do you have it on you?"

"Hey, hey, hey, watch it there, Missy." I shove her off. "That's not your phone. And please, calm down."

Somewhere in my bedroom, the phone stops ringing.

"I missed her call," Sheryl says, sitting at the edge of the bed, staring blankly at the wall. "I missed it."

"It's okay," I say, carefully. I try sitting up, but only make it halfway. I touch her bare shoulder. She's in that purple bra I hate and her terrible beige underwear. "Peaches is with Michael and Gabe. You'll call her later. It's okay."

"My baby girl is gonna think I don't care about her." Sheryl's shoulders drop and she whimpers a little.

It's the same scenario as last Friday night. We went out, got a little crazy, and she forgot to call her daughter again. But Peaches is five years old and completely content to stay the weekend with her two overwhelmingly doting dads. "Michael's gonna smooth things over with her. You know how he is." Sheryl's ex-husband and his partner Gabe have full custody of Peaches and never expect anything from Sheryl except her answering machine.

Sometimes I think if they expected a little more out of her, she'd fight harder to get her life together.

"Hand me my cigarettes, will you?" She looks over her shoulder at me. "God, you look terrible, hon."

I feel much worse. I reach over and grab her pack of Players light cigarettes off the nightstand, knocking an empty vodka bottle down in the process. "Here." I try sitting up again. "What time did we leave the bar last night?"

She lights her cigarette and turns my way, sitting with her legs curled under her, blowing smoke at me. Her dark roots are coming in through her bleached-blonde locks. I should tell her the Madonna look died when we changed centuries eight years ago. "I don't remember what time it was," she says. Her black eyeliner is smudged. I realize I can see her face now. There's light coming through the dark curtains in my window. It's stopped raining finally. It's been gray and gloomy out there for days. I hate October.

I look down at myself. I slept in my clothes again. "I really lost it last night," I say, as if this is the first time I have woken up in my clothes with no recollection of the evening before. "I don't remember much."

"What else is new?" She closes her eyes for a second. "I need to get cleaned up. I need to go home and do some laundry or something." She gazes around my bedroom, with her cigarette pressed to her lip. "Oh, there's my phone." She plucks it out of the mess of blankets. "I'll call her when get I home," she says in a thin voice. I know she doesn't really want to talk to her daughter right now. It's not because of lack of love, but of too much shame.

"Hey, you don't have to go just now," I tell her. "You can hang out here for a few hours and—"

"No, Ryde, I have to go." Sheryl stands and crushes her cigarette out in the overfilled ashtray on the nightstand. "I have to rehearse my lines. I've got an audition on Monday." She has an audition for a voice-over in some car rental commercial. But I refrain from belittling her work. Used to be, she had real gigs. These days, it's all crap. She looks around for her clothes, and while she dresses, I turn my eyes away, to the window. "What are you gonna do all day?" she asks me. "Don't you have fifty or sixty pages to translate for that yogurt company?"

I haven't even opened that file on my computer and the final document is due on Monday, before noon. "I'll get around to it tonight," I say, knowing that I'll turn it in as I promised. I can't afford to lose any more clients. My rent is due this week and my credit is currently maxed out, but I plan on tending to that situation very soon. Next month.

Sheryl leans over my head and kisses my hair. "Call me later, okay?"

"Yeah, absolutely." I sink back into the pillows.

She stops in my doorway, hesitating.

"What?"

"Are you sure you're okay? You were pretty upset last night."

I started having blackouts about two years ago, after I turned twenty-nine. Of course I worry about it. I know I drink too much. I know it. "I really don't remember," I say. "I mean, my memory of last night sort of stops after that guy, what's his name, Bob or Tom, dropped his beer on my shoes and you grabbed his hair and told him to lick it off."

"Oh my God, Ryde, I'm such a bitch when I drink. Did I really say that to him?"

"I think so, yeah." I rub my eyes. They feel swollen. "Well, how upset was I?"

"Like bawling your eyes out. I just held you for a long time."

"Oh, I'm sorry," I say, embarrassed. How many times has she done that in the last fourteen years? She's been holding me or holding my head over the toilet for as long as I can remember. "I hope I didn't freak you out."

"It was a pretty bad one," she says quietly. "It reminded me of the old days. You know, after... Well, anyway, you got through it."

"What was I saying last night?" I don't particularly want to know. "Was I messed up about Shay?"

Shay.

Oh no. I sit up and rub my hair back. "Oh, shit!" I hate myself. "Shit, shit, shit."

"What?"

"I told him to come by last night. I told him to come around ten and get the rest of his stuff."

"Oh." She sighs. "Well, we were partying pretty hard around ten last night. You never even mentioned it."

"He's gonna fucking hate me."

"Shay already hates you, darling."

"I have to check my messages." I pull the sheets up and wrestle myself out of bed. As I stand, I realize just how dehydrated and starved I am. "I have to check the machine." I pass her in the door and head for the living room. On my desk, the answering machine's red light blinks angrily at me.

"I have to go, Ryde, okay?" Sheryl squeezes my shoulder. "Take a shower. Shave. Clean your apartment."

"Yeah." I stare at the red light, knowing that this time, Shay is not coming back. I don't know how I feel about that anymore. Relieved. Crushed.

Two years of love down the drain. Another one bites the dust.

"Hey," Sheryl says, slipping her leather jacket on in the entrance, "listen, you drew something last night, and you wanted to throw it out, but I picked it out of the bin and it's in your underwear drawer." She opens the door and more light pours in. "I don't think you should ever look at it," she says sadly. "The image you drew is like a nightmare."

"All right," I whisper, eager to be alone.

She blows me a kiss, and her blue eyes tell me she's hurting too. Hurting because tomorrow is Sunday and Sundays are for families and love lives—

everything we've managed to destroy in the last decade. "See you."

After she shuts the world out, I press the Play button on the machine. It tells me I have three new messages.

Shay's gentle and slightly nasal voice fills my living room. I miss him.

On the first message, he sounds tense but still hopeful. *Coming over in about fifteen minutes.* Pause. *Well, um, I'll see you then.* Long pause. *Hope you're home. Ryde? Are you there?* He sighs. Click.

The second message is an hour later, around eleven. *I'm standing here outside your door. Are you home? Ryde? Hello? Pick up.* Angry pause. *Fine, whatever. Thanks.* Pause. *It's raining by the way. I came here in the damn rain.* Click.

I don't bother listening to the third one.

Around three in the afternoon, Shay knocks on my door. Of course, he's come with his bodyguard: his older sister Rochelle. I've cleaned up and am currently on my second glass of tomato juice. I feel fine enough. I flick the television off and throw the remote on the couch. By the door, Shay's two boxes of music, films and books await him. I've organized everything, hoping to make up for last night's mistake.

"Hi," I say, opening the door. The air is cool and smells of dead leaves.

"So, where's his stuff?" Rochelle walks in, bumping my shoulder as she does. She can't stand the sight of me, and I don't blame her. I've put Shay through a lot in the last year. I'm glad she's here for him.

"Right here," I say, showing her the two boxes. But on the porch, Shay won't look at me. "I'm sorry about last night," I tell him, and as I say this, I realize the word *sorry* sounds pathetic coming out of my mouth. I've overused it so much, it doesn't even sound like a word anymore.

Shay's hazel eyes are red rimmed and he looks like he didn't sleep much last night. He nods, crossing his arms over his chest. He's wearing the jacket I bought him when I was in New York last April. He looks so wonderful. Why do lovers always look better to me when they're leaving?

"Shay, check if everything is there." Rochelle is poking around the CDs.

She looks up at her baby brother. "Shay?"

"I put everything in there," I say, stepping back to allow him in. I know he doesn't want to be anywhere near my body right now. "And you know, if anything is missing, I'll drop it off later."

"No," he says, shaking his head. "I'm not doing this again." His black hair needs a cut. But I like it wild and free of hair gel like this. I don't think I've ever told him that.

I don't think I've ever told him much of anything.

"All right, let's go." Rochelle shoves a box at him and grabs the other.

"I'll help you," I say, knowing she won't allow it. "To the car."

She's already halfway down my front steps. Shay has yet to move.

"I'm sorry about last night," I say again. "I went out with—"

"You went out with Sheryl, got wasted and forgot about me." He finally looks at me. I'm going to miss him looking at me. "I know, Ryde. Good-bye."

"Shay, wait, now come on."

"No. I don't wanna talk to you." Briskly, he carries the box off, backing up to the stairs.

I have to say something to him. Anything. "I wish things could have worked out between us," I say, watching him walk away down to his car. "I wish I could have made you happy. Or at least not hate me."

Shay drops the box into the backseat and looks back at me. I see Rochelle say something to him, but he ignores her and walks up the stairs, back to where I stand, knowing I don't deserve even this last effort from him.

"Listen to me." His voice shakes and I hate myself for upsetting him again. "I don't hate you, okay? I could never hate you."

"Shay," Rochelle shouts from the driver's seat. "Let's go."

"Wait a minute!" He glares at her and looks back to me. "I thought that I could help you. I thought that I could heal that wound in you, but I can't, Ryde. I can't. And I'm gonna be thirty next week. *Thirty.* I want normal things. I want what everybody wants. A home. A partner. Things to make sense."

"Shay, look, I know—"

"No, listen to me." He comes closer. "Go back to therapy. You need to push on with that, do you understand? That thing inside you, that thing you never let me see, it's only grown in the last year. And I know you try to numb yourself with the booze, but you're not gonna kill it, Ryde." He touches my hand. "You're gonna kill yourself. And sometimes I think that's what you want."

I blink and look away.

"Is that what you want, Ryde? Is it? Is it?"

I have to reassure him. It's cruel not to ease his mind. "No, Shay," I say gently. "Of course not."

"I never know when you're lying to me." He shuts his eyes and shakes a thought off. He's made his decision. "I have to go now."

This wonderful man loved me as much as he could. As much as I let him. And in this moment, I know he's the last one. I'm done. I can't try anymore. Can't put another man through this again. It's unfair to all of them.

"Please take care of yourself," I whisper, wishing I could feel something. I *should* feel something. But the emptiness inside me swallows it all. "You deserve the best, Shay."

My words don't have the intended effect. Instead, he looks at me like I've just slapped him. "The best? No, Ryde. *We* could have been the best." He hurries down the steps and across the street, to his car.

With resignation, I watch the car drive away. Next door, the neighbors' kids are decorating their front porch with fake spiderwebs and orange lights. Halloween is just around the corner.

But I don't need a holiday for ghosts. I have ghouls to haunt me all year round.

Inside my apartment, I stand in the living room, waiting for a reaction. I could smash something. I could curl up into a ball and weep into my fists. I could pick myself up and get some work done.

I pour myself a double vodka instead. I used to drink it on the rocks, nice and cold, but I don't bother with ice anymore. The drink hits me hard and eases the fire inside me. Under heavy lids, I gaze around at my home. I don't own much. But I don't need much either.

My phone rings and I turn to look at it. Saturdays are always tricky. My mother knows I'm home and she'll keep calling until I answer. But I can't talk to her right now. The machine picks her call up.

Ryde? Honey, are you there? It's me. She coughs. *Hello? Just want to know how your week went. How's Shay doing?* Pause. *Ryde? Are you there? Baby, listen*—her voice drops— *don't forget your father's retirement party is in two weeks. I already got him your gift.* I cringe. *You can just pay me back when you can.* Silence. *Okay, well, call me as soon as you get my message.* Pause. *I love you, baby.*

Click.

Heavily, I walk back to the mantle and pour myself another drink. This will be my last one until eight or nine this evening, I promise myself.

I sit on the couch and watch my reflection staring back at me in the television's black screen. I can't stand myself. I go to my bedroom and crash into bed. I'm thirty-one years old, and I've just lost my ninth boyfriend in eleven years.

Therapy. Pills. Traveling. Boxing. Running. Booze. Sex. Money.

Nothing has ever cured me of Ali—

No.

I won't think about him. Can't think about that.

I look over at my drawers. What did Sheryl say about a drawing? I sit up and the room sways back and forth for a second. Going to have to take it easy today. I reach out and pull my first drawer open.

I feel for a paper and find it. I take it out and stare down at the drawing.

My God.

The world goes as black as Alistair's eyes.

I don't know how much time has passed, but I feel a pillow under my head. The air smells vaguely of disinfectant.

I've blacked out again.

Somewhere inside my mind, I hear my father shouting my name down to me. *Get up,* he keeps screaming, shaking me hard. My mother is yelling for someone in the background to call an ambulance. I know I'm dreaming. Or am I? I want to tell them I'm going to get up in a minute. Just give me a minute. Can they give me a goddamn minute? My dad has stopped shaking me. He's rubbing my hair and speaking softly to me. *I love you. You're okay, Ryde. You're okay. Oh, my God, Ryde, please, be okay.*

I feel something wet on my face. My dad is crying over me. Somewhere, my mother is screaming Alistair's name. Everyone needs to take a breath here. I'm going to open my eyes as soon as I can. I'm tired and I need to sleep it off.

I just want to sleep.

Just want to lie here and not move. Not think. Not be.

Can't they let me?

I've almost made it out of my bleak hospital room when Shay shows up. I knew he would. But Shay isn't alone. He's brought reinforcements again. This time, he's got my shrink, Dr. Scarborough, with him.

Ten hours in the hospital, and they're already prepared to have me committed to the nuthouse. So I had a few too many drinks and passed out in my bathroom?

It happens to the best of us.

I pause halfway between my bed and the door, trapped.

"See," Shay says, turning angrily to Scarborough. "This is what happens when he's left without any supervision. Jesus, I left him last week and already he's—"

"Shay, please." Scarborough touches Shay's shoulder. "Would you give us a moment?"

Shay glares at me, but I know he's trying to be tough. I can see he's holding back the tears. Why did he come here? Why? He left me. I thought the point was for him to erase me from his life, for him to go out there and get himself some "normal".

"Shay, please." Dr. Scarborough's very dark eyes watch me from behind his designer glasses. He's a gentle man of few words, and one of the best headshrinkers in the city, but I have no use for him. He treats patients with post-traumatic stress. I don't have post-traumatic stress. I have an excessive personality and a tendency for self-destruction.

"Fine," Shay finally says. He steps back to the open door and stops, looking gently at me. "Well, are you okay?"

I wish he weren't here asking me that. "Yeah, just had a little too much—"

"A little too much? Ryde, Sheryl found you in the bathroom, with your pants around your ankles, lying face-first in your own vomit. Thank God you never lock your door!"

"Do you mind?" I look at Shay and point to Scarborough. "I'd like to conserve a shred of my dignity."

"You lost that right when you started passing out in your own—"

"Shay," Scarborough interrupts him, "please."

"Oh, fine, I don't give a shit anymore." Shay shakes his head at me. "I'm not gonna do it, Ryde. I'm not gonna be a witness to your slow death. Do you hear me? Whatever happens now, you do it without an audience." He bolts out into the hall.

"Damn it," I say, going for him.

But Scarborough stops me, putting his hands on my shoulders. "No, you can't do that." He gives me a hard look. "The damage is done, Ryde."

I stare at the empty doorway over Scarborough's shoulder, knowing he's right again. I step back and wait for him to deliver his speech.

"I came here in person to let you know that I'm no longer going to be counseling you, Ryde."

What?

I certainly didn't expect this. "Okay," I say, trying to dissimulate my shock. Scarborough has been on my case for two years now. Persistently annoying, he's been the only psychiatrist who's managed to actually get me mildly interested in my mental well-being. So he too is giving up on me. No surprise. "I see."

"No, Ryde, it's not like that," he says softly. "I'm not abandoning you. I just, well, I can't treat you anymore." He lowers his voice, coming closer. He's a beautiful man. Thin and nervous, with jet-black hair and very cold hands. Not my type, but it's not like I haven't thought about it a few times. "I can't help you until you've addressed your drinking problem."

Drinking problem.

"Look," I say, "I know I've been partying a lot lately, but I've been in a bit of a rut, that's all."

He sighs and looks around the room, obviously holding himself back from saying more.

"So, what?" I squint at him. This is a guy who knows a lot of my secrets. "That's it? You've decided I'm a drunk?"

"You're in the first stages of alcoholism, Ryde. You need to seek treatment before you completely ruin your health and every single relationship—"

"Yeah, okay." I laugh at him and his assumptions about me. "Thanks for coming." I grab my jacket on the chair. "And thanks for nothing, by the way."

"Hey, no, please, listen to me—"

"What do you really know about me anyway?" I slip an arm into my jacket, my heart pounding. "Huh? You think you can pass judgment on me?"

"I know you carry an enormous amount of guilt inside you," he says, very carefully. "An amount so huge, it's poisonous. I know you think what happened to Alistair that day—"

"Don't fucking say his name." He's making me sick. I shake it off. "All right," I say, letting the numbness seep back into me, cool and comforting. "Whatever. I don't care. Do you what you need to do. I'll take care of me."

"What happened that day at the creek wasn't your—"

"Jamie," I cut him off, calling him by his first name for the first time since we've met, "I want you to shut up now." I hear the violence in my own voice and try to see his face through the veil of anger in my eyes. "You need to take a step back, all right?" I step past him, heading for the door.

But he dares to put a gentle and very icy hand on my arm. "Ryde," he whispers, "I want you to see something first."

I'm curious. I stop, and for a moment, we stand eye to eye in the doorway. "What?"

I see Scarborough is pretty shaken.

I didn't mean to scare him. "What is it?" I say, more softly.

"You drew something the night before you fell in the bathroom, and when Sheryl and Shay found you, lying unconscious—"

"What do you mean, Shay and Sheryl? My parents found me." I feel strange. Disconnected. I'm having an out-of-body experience. I can't breathe right. "I heard my dad talking to me. He was screaming—"

"You're confusing the past with the present again, Ryde. It's a symptom of your trauma—"

"No, I heard my dad and—"

"Look, you had this in your hand," Scarborough pulls a paper out of his coat pocket. "Look."

I don't want to see it. "It doesn't matter," I say. I need to get out of here. I need some air. "I'm not interested in some stupid drawing I did when I was drunk." I turn away from him.

"Look at it," he cries, stepping in front of me. He's never raised his voice at me before. "Look at it, Ryde." He unfolds the paper, lifting it to my face. "This is what's inside you, do you understand? This is what the boy inside you is yelling out to the grown man you've become. This is what you *know* happened to Alistair. This is what the man did to him."

But I won't look at it. I won't look at it. "Leave me alone," I say, stumbling away.

"Ryde, you can't keep ignoring it!"

I spin around and glare at him. "Who are you to tell me how to deal with it?" I shout, shaking now. "You have no fucking idea what it's like! Just leave me alone!"

Before he can say anything else, I'm running down the hall.

But I saw the drawing. I saw it.

Chapter Nine

I turn my eyes to the front door, trying to focus. What time is it?

Someone persistent is ringing my doorbell.

I look down at the bottle of vodka between my thighs.

I pull myself out of the couch and roll the empty bottle under it. I hear my mother's voice calling my name from behind the door, and Sheryl is with her. Looks like the good women in my life have come to see about me. I haven't answered my phone in two days, not since my last employer fired me.

"Well, hello there," I say, opening the door.

At the sight of me, my mother's face tightens, and I realize I must look pretty bad. "Why didn't you answer your phone," she says, fixing my shirt as if she can tuck my life back into place. "Oh my, would you look at this place?" She smiles nervously and gives Sheryl a discreet look I catch. "You should have seen his room back in the day," she tells Sheryl. "He sure knew how to keep a clean room."

I hate the paleness of her face, her tense smile. She suffers too much. Why can't she just give up on me?

"How you been?" Sheryl asks. Her tired eyes tell me she's not doing too good herself. "We brought you some leftovers." She offers me a bag full of Tupperware.

So I've become an invalid. "You didn't have to. My fridge is full."

"Oh, it's nothing, baby. Just little things from your father's party."

"Yeah, about that—"

"No, it's okay." My mother is staring at the bottles on my mantle. "He understood that you couldn't come. With the way you've been sick lately and everything."

Sick. That's what she calls my binge drinking.

"Hilary," Sheryl says, lighting a cigarette. "Let's sit down. Let's tell him."

They've done this before—these little Monday or Tuesday interventions. "Would you like a coffee before you start?" I ask sarcastically.

"That would be nice."

"No, Hilary," Sheryl says, sitting and staring me deep in the eye. She's never quite looked at me this way before. "Let's just get this over with."

They settle into my couch and I sit in the armchair at their right. But I get up after a second. I need a drink. I go to the mantle and feel their eyes on my neck, but I pour myself a double gin anyway. Vodka or gin is all I can stomach these days. Brown liquor makes me very sick.

When I sit again, glass in hand, they both stare at the drink in my hand, but I bring it to my lips anyway. "What is it?" I ask, calmly enough, before taking a good gulp of the warm gin.

My mother looks over at Sheryl. "I don't know," she whispers as if I'm not in the room with them. "I don't think he's ready to hear this."

"No, it's his *right* to know."

"What's my right to know?" I take another sip but my throat is tight. What is it now?

"Tell him," my mother says, grabbing Sheryl's hand. "Just tell him."

I drain the last of my drink. I'm ready enough.

"Ryde," Sheryl begins in a shaky voice, "your mom and me have been talking about this for days, and we're not sure if we're doing the right thing by telling you, but not telling you would be wrong."

"Man," I say, the tension making me ill, "I can't take the suspense."

"Okay, I'm sorry." Sheryl takes a breath and looks over at my mother and then back to me. "But this is hard, harder than I thought it would be." She reaches out and touches my knee. "Ryde, remember my cousin Dalia, you know, the one who was in our grade?"

"Yeah, what about her?" I'm thinking at the speed of light. What does Dalia have to do with me?

"Well, she's getting married next month to Jonathan, the guy who used to take his penis out in his driveway."

"What?" They're making me crazy here. "Jesus, Sheryl, what are you saying?"

"Calm down. I'm just telling you she's getting married next month and you're probably gonna be invited and all."

I just wait for more.

"And, well," she says, casting a nervous glance my mother's way, "she's gotten really religious in the last years. Her and Jonathan have been going to church and taking it all pretty seriously, so you know, they're gonna have the wedding in church and do the whole white dress thing."

My mother stands and goes to the mantle. She comes back with the bottle of gin and two more glasses. She pours me another ounce. "Baby," she says, taking her glass to her pinched lips. "You know I love you."

I stare at her, bewildered. "Yeah... I love you too, Mom."

Sheryl drinks and sets her glass down. "Ryde, she called me last week to tell me the priest performing her wedding ceremony was someone we know someone from the old neighborhood. This young priest is just freshly out of the seminary."

"No."

"Yes, Ryde. Yes."

"Mom," I hear myself say. "What?"

"It's okay, honey." She gets out of her seat and crouches by me. "It's him, Ryde. It's *him*."

"No, that's impossible."

"Listen to me," Sheryl says, squeezing my knee hard. "You don't have to see him. You don't have to go to the wedding at all."

"Are you sure it's him?" I whisper, my head swimming. "Maybe she made a mistake."

"No, Ryde, no. She told me his name."

Sheryl nods at me, confirming my mother's words. "Hon, listen, the man performing her wedding ceremony is Father *Alistair Genet*," she says. "He's a priest, babe." She blows a curl of smoke out, watching me. "A fucking priest."

I sit in my car and watch the wipers swap rain. I'm drunk.

Too drunk for this.

But I don't care anymore. Through the crack in my window, the wind howls, throwing dead leaves at my windshield. Brutally, dark rain lashes my old, rusty Plymouth Breeze, and every drop warns me, *Don't do it, Ryde.*

The thunder growls, *Leave him alone.* Still, I put the bottle to my lips again and take another long, satisfying swill of the cheap vodka. I know I should stop now. I can barely see straight anymore. I put the cap back on and set the bottle down on the seat next to me. If I get caught sitting here with this open bottle on my seat, I'm going to jail. No two ways about it.

But there's no one on this street, and besides I won't get caught. Not today. Under heavy lids, I watch the church doors through the foggy passenger window. The church is Gothic—gray as the day. I check the time. Sunday Mass should be over by now. Soon, people are going to start filing out.

I look down at the bottle on the seat. Pick it up. Drink a little more.

He's in there, in that gray fortress. My Alistair.

I blink and drink a little more. What am I going to do? What am I going to say to him? I wipe the vodka off my lips, but my hand feels heavy. I don't think I can even get out of this car without falling face-first.

The church doors open, and I lean back in my seat, holding my breath. People are rushing out under their umbrellas, and that's all I can see: a bunch of black umbrellas. No faces. No Alistair.

My vision is blurry. I don't feel good. My heart is beating too fast or too slow. I don't know anymore. I clutch the bottle in my hand and wait. Wait. Wait.

Nothing happens. Everyone is gone.

I drink a little more. This gulp is for courage. Yes, courage to do what I need to do. I grab the bottle, open my car door and sit halfway out. The rain drips onto my shirt, down my neck, and I lean heavily on my open door, trying to climb out of the car with some kind of grace. I barely manage it. I gaze down the long, long path leading up to the church doors. Can I make it? Bottle in hand, I take my first step. Then another. I don't feel the rain anymore. I don't feel anything but this madness throbbing between my temples.

Alistair, Alistair, Alistair—his name is a train going around in my head.

Then, I'm inside the church.

It's dry and very quiet in here. I see blue and red light touching the pews, and look up at the stained-glass windows above me. This is his new attic then. That's what this is.

Now, where's the trap door to him?

I take a step into the aisle, but trip and nearly fall. Where's the priest? Where is the damn priest in this place? I look to my left. There's the confessional. I want to laugh. How convenient. Yes, I'm going to sit in that little brown box with the red leather seat and confess, confess, confess.

Mea culpa. Par ma faute, ma très grande faute.

Leaning my hands against the seats, I make my way to the confessional and slip right in there, like a thief. I slide the door closed and lean back, settling myself comfortably inside the darkness of the small box. I smile and open the bottle. The vodka feels like fire going down my chest. The fire pops and cracks inside me. I haven't felt my core burn this hot since…

I wait.

I don't know how long I've been sitting here when I hear steps. *His* steps. Light. Unsure. Under his feet, the wood barely creaks. I shut my eyes. Everything is spinning. I don't care. I'm smiling in God's personal telephone booth. I hear him walking and then nothing. I can feel him out there. He knows he's not alone anymore.

Someone's watching, he'd said that day.

But I didn't listen because I never listened to him.

I take another sip of the vodka and can't help coughing into my sleeve, but my quiet cough echoes through the church like a scream.

"Hello?" he calls out. His voice is so childlike.

I haven't heard his voice in fourteen miserable years.

"Is anyone here? Hello?"

By the sound of his voice, I know he's seen me enter the confessional and that we're playing again.

Yes, my love. We're all here. God, the Devil, me, you and the monster. I drink again. I can hear him approach. He's standing on the other side of the door. We're in that house again, the one with no roof, playing hide-and-seek.

I hear the door sliding open next to mine. He's slipping into the confessional. I didn't expect it. I drink again. My mind is teetering between now and then.

"In the name of the Father," he says very quietly, "the Son and the Holy Spirit, amen."

I turn my eyes to the grid but can't see him through the lattice.

"In the name of the Father," he says again, this time a little shakily, "the Son and the Holy Spirit, amen."

I close my eyes. "Bless me, Father," I say, slurring my words. "I've sinned." My admission opens a gate inside me and now I can't stop the flood. My pain is like a river, loud and wild, rushing down my veins, knocking everything in its path, crushing my organs, drowning my brain, my heart, and I can't stop it. I can't stop myself from speaking its fury out loud. "I've done terrible things, Father. Terrible. I've done it all. Mortal and venial. Name it, I've done it, and I've done it with no shame at all. I've done it out of spite. Spite for God. And every time I hurt someone, it's him I'm aiming at. " My words spill out of me like rotten things, and I know I'm smiling through it all. "I was born bad. I wanted everything. Questioned everything. Nothing satisfied me. I sought answers to questions I had no right to ask, and God punished me. Oh yes, God punished me for putting my greedy hands on the lamb boy he'd singled out from the rest of his precious fucking herd. He hurt that perfect boy to get to me. God's put me in hell with no chance of parole." I stop. Lift the bottle to my lips and drink. I grin. "You see, Father Genet, I don't even need the Devil anymore. I've got God as my own personal enemy."

I shut my eyes. Swallow the nausea down. I'm too drunk. I need to rest here for a few minutes. I lean my head to the wall and wait.

"You seem to be in a lot of pain," Alistair says after a long pause, but his voice is very thin now. "God...God can help you bear it. If only you ask him to."

"I want nothing from God." I can hardly speak. "I *am* nothing."

Silence.

I try to drink again, but don't have the strength or dexterity anymore. "I took him away from his home," I slur, and I'm crying. I haven't shed a real tear in years. But I taste them now, on my lips. "I took him away 'cause I wanted to have him all to myself. I wanted him to want, love, need only me. Only me." I laugh through the tears. "Only me. How fucking selfish is that?"

"God doesn't condemn love," he says, but I hear the tremor in his voice.

He knows it's me making penance.

Or does he?

"Father," I say, leaning forward, closer to the grid. "Fourteen years ago, I saw the Devil in human form, this giant man with dead-cow eyes and hands as big as shovels, and he came out of the woods, vindictive and greedy, and he took him. He took him away from me. And he hurt him." I'm crying harder now. I feel. Oh yes, thank you, I feel. "He was just a boy, just a boy, and that Devil broke him in the places I wanted to love him, and he raped his body and sliced into his mind and I didn't know where he was because they never told me and the house was for sale and the attic window was black and the curtains never moved and I asked and begged but they never told me where he was and God called him back again after that monster had reached inside him and stabbed his soul like the marshmallow on my stick and it burns me now." I stop. I can't go on. I'm sweating. I'm shaking.

I'm fucking finished.

I hear nothing, not even a breath. I can feel Alistair sitting there like a stone, and I remember the ripples in the water.

What have I done? How could I do this to him?

I lean my head on the wall between us. The rage is gone from me.

I've been exorcised.

"Alistair," I whisper, almost peacefully. "Oh, Alistair."

With a force that causes the confessional to shake, he slides the lattice shut.

The sound of it makes me sit up. I'm frozen and a little soberer. I hear him running. Something falls. A glass or a candleholder, and the sound of it breaks my heart.

Then the church is quiet again and I know he's run out on me. How could I come here and say these things to him? What kind of demon am I anyway? I look down at the bottle in my hand. This is what I've become. I rub my face with my free hand and open the confessional door. The church is empty.

I stand and carefully make my way through the rows, into the aisle. Standing there, I lift my bottle to Christ on the cross. Christ the sufferer. Christ the martyr. I cry out to him. "Think you saved us?"

I stare at Jesus's face, waiting for a sign. May I be struck down for my blasphemous words. May I be killed right here, right now. Put me out of my misery. "What?" I shout defiantly. "What? Huh? What?"

Nothing happens. I wasn't worth a sermon back then, and I'm not worth a thunderbolt today. I sniff and look around the church. It's all a joke, isn't it? I step back to the doors, keeping my eyes on the altar. At my right, there's the holy water basin. I think of the creek. I think of Alistair's white body falling off a cliff.

I slip my last business card out of my wallet and walk back to the confessional, where I leave the card on the bench inside.

As I'm heading back to the doors, I turn to look at the altar one more time and see him.

Alistair is hidden behind the purple curtain, right there, at the front of the church. I see one black eye watching me, an eye as dark as a horror movie, and I see his white-blond hair, combed neatly to the side, and half of his silent mouth. God, he looks the same.

But I also see the black clerical shirt, the white tab collar on his neck.

"Alistair, it's me, I'm sorry—"

He's gone again. I hear him running somewhere in the back of the church, and know I have no right to follow him. Not after the stunt I've just pulled.

I raise my chin to Christ. "All right, old friend, looks like it's me against you again."

Chapter Ten

I rake a nervous hand through my hair and knock on the door again. They're playing music inside the apartment and probably can't hear me. I ring the bell.

Minutes later, Michael opens the door, and I catch the shock in his eyes. "Ryde?" He's staring at me in disbelief. "Holy shit, look at you." He shakes his head and touches my arm. "You look so freaking good." He looks over his shoulder and calls out to his boyfriend. "Gabe!" he yells, "come see how good Ryde looks!"

Seconds later, I'm assaulted by Sheryl and Gabe, who circle me. "Oh, Ryde, you look better than ever." Sheryl hugs me tight. "I was so worried about you," she says into my neck. She leans away from me and brushes my hair back from my forehead. "You did it, hon."

Yeah, I did it.

Three weeks of sobriety. I stopped cold turkey. Alone. No meetings. No counseling. Just me and my will. I turned my phone off and poured every ounce of booze I had down the toilet, and then I waited for the pain, the anxiety, the doubts and the insomnia to show up. And, oh, they came for me, one by one and sometimes all at once, but I greeted them like sisters, and we sat around my apartment in the dark, all of us old friends.

Then one morning, they were gone. I made myself some eggs and cleaned my apartment.

I'm clean and sober for the first time in eleven years. Every minute I'm not drinking, I think of him. It's all for him. All for my Alistair.

"Uncle Ryde," Peaches screams, running into the living room. She's followed by a trail of her little girlfriends. "You're here!"

I scoop her up and kiss her orange hair. I think of my sister Summer. I think of Winter. I think I'm going to have to make some calls this week and start repairing some damage.

"I got you something." I set Peaches down and dig into my pocket for her gift. I have a few translation contracts lined up, and with diligence and honesty, I might just be able to salvage what's left of my translating career. Who knows, I might even try writing again. But first things first. "Here you go."

"You didn't have to," Gabe says, close to my ear. He's a caring and genuine man and I wish I knew him better. Michael is blessed to have him around. They have what Alistair and I could have had.

I watch Peaches tear through the pink wrapping paper. She pops the small velvet box open. Her eyes light up. She's just like her mother, a jewelry girl. "Wow," she says, her face beaming. "For me?"

I place the gold chain around her neck. It has two little golden peaches hanging from it. "So, you're six years old. You're a big girl now."

All her little girlfriends surround her and she's queen for the day.

Later, after the cake has been devoured and the kids have all left, Michael and Gabe put Peaches to bed, while Sheryl and I sit around the kitchen, enjoying the silence. My ears are still ringing from the noise.

"Thank you for coming today," Sheryl says, putting her hand on mine. "I really needed you to."

Lately, she's been trying to be more involved in her daughter's life, but Sheryl struggles with motherhood. Always has. I wish I could help her see the woman she could be. I've been a bad friend to her. I've only led her farther and farther away from herself. "Listen," I say, "I know I've been a nightmare to be around in the last ten years or more, and I really don't know why or how you put up with me for so long, but I want you to know that things are gonna be better from now on." I look her deep in the eye. "Okay? Do you believe me?"

"You look so different," she says, almost sadly. And I know it's a lot for her to take in all at once, this change in me. We're drinking buddies.

She's officially lost her partner in chaos.

"I'm the same, Sheryl, just not drunk."

"Yeah, I know." She looks away, to the window. It's snowing already.

Christmas is coming. Christmas: Jesus's birthday.

Every thought always brings me right back to Alistair.

"So, you went to see him," Sheryl says. "But you never really told me what happened."

"I was wasted. Drunk out of my mind. I said some crazy things. He wouldn't talk to me."

"But you saw him?"

"Not really. We were in the confessional."

She makes a face. "Really? You mean those little booths—"

"Yeah, and I spilled out a lot of profanity and he recognized me and left."

She laughs a little. "Well, sounds like the old days."

I can't believe I'm smiling. I'm genuinely smiling. I feel hope. Maybe there's still a chance.

"What are you gonna do now?" She watches me closely. "I mean, he's a priest, Ryde. A *priest*."

"I know that. I realize that."

"Well?"

"I don't know what I'm gonna do." I sigh and fiddle with the place mat. "I don't know."

"You still love him?"

"It's more than that now."

"What that monster did to him, the way they found him that day, don't you think it's better if you don't insist on seeing him?"

"Better for who? For me? For him?"

"You both suffered so much already. So much. Don't you think maybe seeing you again will only reopen those old wounds in him?"

"I want to open them."

"Why?"

I give her the only answer I can. "Because Alistair's wounds, every last one of them, are *my* wounds too."

She doesn't say anything else.

When I reach the church, I see my car has been towed. No surprise. I owe nine hundred dollars in parking tickets. What a mess I've made of my life. But I'm going to fix it. I'm going to make things right again. Against the cold November wind, I turn my collar up and walk through the open wrought-iron gate fencing the presbytery's lawn. This is where he lives, where he eats his meals and sleeps. Does he have nightmares? Does he dream the things I dream? In my dreams, everything is red and I hear him screaming my name.

But I didn't come to haunt him today.

I shake the snow off my hair and shoulders and ring the bell. Through the large window at my left, I can see someone getting out of his seat. A big man dressed in black.

When he opens the door, I see he's a priest. A tall fellow with small, kind eyes and a freckled nose. He's an older man in his sixties. His dark hair is long and slicked back on his head. "How can I help you?" he asks me, sizing me up. He has the complexion of a heavy drinker.

"Um, I was told Father Genet lives here."

"Yes, indeed." He watches me, waiting.

"Well, is he here?"

"Afraid not." He looks over my shoulder, at the street. "Out to buy some Christmas trinkets and whatnot."

"Okay… I see." I have no idea where to go from here. "I'll come back, I guess."

"Are you a friend of his?" The man's voice is rich and he has a slight east coast accent. "From boyhood, maybe?"

Boyhood. The word touches me deep. Yes, that's what we were then— boys. "I knew him when we were both kids." I offer the man my hand. "I'm Ryde. Ryde Kent."

His eyes narrow slightly. Has Alistair ever mentioned me to him?

"Father Masson is what they call me," the man says, very warmly. "Now come on, no use in freezing your pork chops out here." He opens the door wide.

"Why don't you come in and wait for him? I'm sure he'll be pleased to see your face."

I'm trespassing again. I'm entering Alistair's private sanctuary without his permission. But I want to see where he lives. I want to see his things. Smell him in the air. "That would be very nice, thank you." I step inside the cozy entrance. To my right is a narrow wooden staircase leading up to where I suspect the bedrooms are, and to my left is the living room. There's too much furniture in there, and the walls are loaded with shelves overfilled with books. A corner lamp casts a soft glow around the room, and I catch the scent of ginger coming from the kitchen. In front of me is a long hall, and at the end of it stands a broad-hipped woman with a mass of gray hair on her head. She wipes her hands on her apron, eyeballing me.

Father Masson turns to her. "Good gracious, Frau Eberhart, you're frightening the lad." He leans in closer to my ear. "She's a tough matron, but her cooking makes up for it."

"Hello," I call out to her.

But she only frowns disapprovingly and returns to where she came from. Suddenly, I'm reminded of Matilda, Alistair's mother. What happened to her?

Father Masson nods to the living room. We sit across from each other on matching brown armchairs. He points to the bottles sitting neatly on the table behind us. "Care for a drink?"

"No, thank you." I scratch my head. "I have a drinking problem."

"Very candid of you to say so."

"It's the first time I've said it out loud, actually."

He watches me for a moment. "Congratulations then."

For a few minutes, we discuss the weather, and then move on to the boring topic of my job and family life. I speak freely about the last months because there's something about him that puts me at ease, and slowly, the conversation deepens as we begin to discuss how I first met Alistair. I tell Father Masson about our friendship and the happy days we spent together as boys living out in the 'burbs. I recount our bike rides and adventures in those new houses they never locked up, and as I go on and on, I'm transported into the past, but a golden past—the past I'd forgotten.

There was a time before the creek. Our lives didn't begin on its shore. We were happy once.

"Has he ever told you about any of this?" I ask Father Masson, finishing my tale.

Father Masson hesitates, folding his hands over his large stomach. "Father Genet isn't much of a talker. He's quite reserved, but you must know that, after all."

"Yes, I do."

"And when was the last time you saw him?"

I'm fidgeting a little. "About fourteen years ago," I lie, omitting the part about last Sunday.

"Before he entered the seminary then." Father Masson's small brown eyes catch the light. "Did you know he'd chosen to become a priest?"

"He'd told me about it when we were boys."

"So you weren't surprised."

I have to look away. "I didn't really think he'd actually do it."

"But he has, hasn't he?"

I look back up at him. "Was he a good student? He must have been."

"Our best and brightest." A shadow crosses his eyes. "But he struggled. As do many of our most fervent pupils."

"Struggled?" I echo the word. "With his faith or—"

"He was orphaned in his second year at the seminary. His parents died six months apart from each other. The pressure of his studies and clergy life took a toll on his fragile nervous system." Father Masson pauses, as if he knows he's saying too much.

"Please, go on," I nearly beg him. I'm sitting at the edge of my seat. Oh, Alistair, how much did you endure? "Please."

But he won't say any more. Father Masson blinks and smiles again. "Well, anyway, the poor lad got through it all right, and now he's soon to have his own parish. Mine." He pats my knee. It's a fatherly gesture, but there's a pressure there in his touch. He's hiding something from me. I know it. I feel it. "Now, Ryde, tell me, what made you decide to seek him out after fourteen years?" There's something in his question, something almost threatening.

"Just wanted to say hello to an old friend," I say.

Father Masson stares at me. "Is that so?"

"I… I just want to make sure he's okay, that's all."

"He's with God. Our good Lord is an excellent friend. He could not be in better hands."

"Yes, I suppose so."

"Father Genet was quite spooked last week." Father Masson looks over at the window and back to me. "Seems some lost soul went stumbling into the confessional, some drunkard, saying some hellish things. Of course Father Genet was very upset. Old Eberhart and me thought we'd never get him out of his room again."

My heart is pounding so hard I think he might see it through my shirt. "That's terrible," I mutter.

"Isn't it?" Father Masson asks, and I know he knows it was me.

A gust of cold air sweeps into the warm entrance behind me. Someone has opened the front door.

"Frau Eberhart," Alistair calls out happily, somewhere close, so very close to me. The door slams shut. "I got you those sinful sugar cookies you were praying for all night!" He sounds like a child calling out to his mother. "A whole box!"

I'm frozen still, out of Alistair's sight, but within his earshot. I stare at Father Masson, suddenly terrified. I can't be here. I can't meet Alistair just yet. "I can't," I mouth to the old priest. "Please. I can't."

Father Masson searches my face for an answer to my strange behavior, but finally understands and quickly pulls himself out of his chair, hurrying to the entrance. I see him walk by with Alistair under his large arm, obstructing Alistair's view of me. Heart in mouth, I slither out of the living room just as they're turning the corner of the hall.

I quietly shut the door behind me and run down the path. Though in the snow, my steps land on every one of Alistair's footprints, and for the first time in fourteen years, we're one and the same, if only for an ephemeral moment.

Chapter Eleven

"How about that one," I say, showing him a huge brick house at our left. It's perfect, just the way we like them. Big, insulting, and slightly out of view. "Come on!" I run up the driveway and open the door.

The light is so bright in here I have to shade my eyes. I see a black figure watching us in the corner, but just as my eyes focus on it, it disappears somewhere in the back rooms.

"They don't have a chandelier," Alistair says, but now his eyes widen in terror. "What is it?"

"Wake up! Wake up!"

"Alistair!"

He's slipped off the ledge, onto the stairs.

"RYDE!" he screams, falling, falling, falling.

But I never see him land.

I sit at the bottom of the staircase. Over the stairs, the water falls in great waves of white foam, and I look down at my feet. They're already immersed. The water rises and rises. "What are you doing?" I yell up to him.

He stands with his toes curled around the second-story ledge. There's no railing. There's nothing to hold him back anymore. "Watch me!"

"No, don't, Alistair!"

He jumps.

I'm underwater. I see the stairs, the light dancing on the surface. I'm in the basement. I've fallen through the floor. Where is he? Where is he?

I kick my legs and swim up, but it's too deep. I can't hold my breath any longer.

I can't. I can't.

"Ryde," my father says, crying, touching my head. "You're okay. You're okay, son. Please be okay."

Alistair is looking down at me, reaching his hands down to me. His face is moving back. He's leaving. He's being carried.

The water around me darkens. I can't see. Oh, God, please. I can't see. I can't breathe. The water is red. It's thick. It's turned to blood.

ALISTAIR!

I sit up. Look around.

Where am I?

A shaft of moonlight cuts through the curtains in the window at my left. I know those curtains. I know this room.

"Ryde, sweetie," my mother calls out to me from behind the door. "Are you all right?"

I'm in my old bedroom in my parents' house. Yes, I slept here tonight. I was tired after dinner. Didn't want to take a cab back all the way to Montreal. "Come in," I say, still shaken by my nightmare. The same nightmare I've had for fourteen years.

"I heard you screaming." She quietly walks to the bed and sits by me. In the pale white light, she looks ten years younger. For a second, I wonder if I'm still dreaming this. Am I seventeen again? Is Alistair safe in his attic room at the end of our street, in that little house that doesn't exist anymore?

They tore it down five years ago.

"Ryde, are you awake?" My mother touches my hand on the blanket. "Say something."

"Wait," I say, climbing out of bed. I look through the window. The house is gone. "Yeah," I whisper, "I'm awake."

"You had a nightmare."

I stand in the light of the moon and watch the end of the street. I can almost see us walking down that sidewalk, two boys of summer, talking about our camping trip, dreaming of Craving's Creek. I'm feeling things again, things

I've never allowed myself to feel. Dr. Scarborough says it's part of the healing process, that without the booze to numb my nerves, I'm going to be feeling many disturbing things, and he's asked me to consider medication, just temporarily, to help me get through this.

I don't want pills. I want to feel again. I welcome the emotion.

But it's hard.

"Yeah," I finally say, still staring out the window, as if maybe, just maybe, I can summon the past up, and with it, Alistair. "The same one."

"So you still have them then. I guess I thought maybe you'd stopped having nightmares by now."

I look back at her. What was it like for them? What was it like for my parents after Craving's Creek? I was plunged into an artificial coma for two weeks. Doctors feared the worst—permanent brain damage, loss of speech and sight. For days, my parents didn't know if I'd even open my eyes again. Then, when I finally did, they realized they'd been praying for their son to wake, but were now faced with a stranger instead.

In a way, they'd lost their boy too.

And my mother never wrote again. I remember waking one afternoon to the sound of her screaming. She was smashing things in her bedroom. Her typewriter. Her desk. She'd broken all of her pens and her hands were covered in ink, and she stood there, mad, sobbing, surrounded by shredded manuscripts. *"It was my fault!"* she'd screamed that day.

Alistair was her responsibility and she never forgave herself.

"Mom," I say gently, suddenly understanding the immensity of her own tragedy, "I'm sorry."

She looks at me, confused. This is the moment she's been waiting for, so she waits a little longer for me to finally tell her what she needs to hear, her lips trembling.

"I'm so sorry," I say again, and go to her. "I know I put you and Dad through so much. Too much. And I wish I could just—"

"No, baby, no," she says, and I know she can't take this. She's not ready for more. "It's okay. You're better now. You're coming back to us."

"I am," I say, and the tears come again, surprising me. I let them. I want them. I need these tears. "I'm coming back to myself, but I don't know where he is, and I don't know how to find him. I don't know if I could ever find Alistair again."

"Shh, Ryde, don't." She pulls me close, holding my head to her breast. I haven't allowed her to touch me like this in so long. She's weeping silently into my hair, but I know her mother's heart is rejoicing. "You're my baby boy, my sweet baby boy," she keeps saying.

Where was I going before Craving's Creek? What road? What destiny?

I was cut off. I was shoved into darkness. But I can see now. I can see many paths to take.

"I want to live again, Mom." I lean back from her.

Somewhere inside me, I'm still innocent.

"If you want to live again," my mother says, holding my hands tight, "you have to find a way to incorporate that terrible day into your life. You can't have a before and an after, because life is a continuum that allows us no intermissions. Every moment of your time spent here holds a piece of you, and I want you to be whole again, Ryde. I want you to flow again, steady and deep, like the river you once were."

I stare at her and smile. "You're still a writer."

She blinks, obviously a little surprised.

"Mom," I say, as serious as I've ever been, "I took him to the creek. I insisted he come. There was nothing you could have done to stop me."

"You mean *us*. There was nothing I could have done to stop you and Alistair. Don't you see? Don't you remember, Ryde? He wanted to come. He wanted to be with you. He chose you, Ryde. From the moment he first set his eyes on you, you were his true God."

"Well, I don't think that's true anymore. I think I only represent everything he wants to forget."

"No, you represent the truth. And what is God, if not the one and only truth?"

The truth?

"Mom, the truth is, I'm in love with a priest."

She smiles and shakes her head. "No, baby, you're in love with a man. A flesh-and-blood man."

"I haven't really seen his face yet. I barely know what he looks like now."

"He's beautiful," she whispers. "Probably the most beautiful man I've ever seen."

I frown. "You've seen him?"

She nods.

"When? Where?"

"His father's grave, about five months ago. I go there sometimes." Her voice drops. "Anyway, there was a man there once, this very blond man standing over the grave, and I stayed back, watching him. When he turned to look over his shoulder, I saw his face, and it was Alistair. He was in street clothes, jeans and shirt. He looked like a regular but very beautiful young man. I wanted to say something to him, but he never saw me, and I couldn't even call out his name."

"What did he look like? I mean, his expression."

She thinks about it for a moment. "I don't know... Angry. Distraught."

I've missed so much of Alistair's life. I wasn't there for him in his darkest hour. Does he have any friends? Who is he now?

My mother rubs my shoulder. "No matter how much he's changed, he's still Alistair, the boy you've loved all of your life." Again, she's read my thoughts.

I look out the window, at my old street.

I don't want to live in the past anymore.

I want to think of the future now, but I'm going to need Alistair there next to me to face it.

"Are you girls ready?" I ask my sisters, looking at them from over the kitchen island. "I haven't made pancakes in a while, and I'm not sure I got the mix right." I walk over to the dining room table and set two plates loaded with banana pancakes in front of them. "Go easy on me."

Summer pokes her fork into the thick pancake. "These are huge," she says. "I'll never eat all this."

I pull a chair out for myself and sit with them. I'm nervous. Winter has yet to really look at me. Last night, at dinner, she wouldn't even say a word to me. Have I lost my baby sister? I don't know these two young women. I've been so immersed in my own pain in the last decade that I've missed them growing up. How many parties did I ruin? How many Christmases? I'd show up drunk with whomever I was living with at the time, and by the time dinner was over, I would be thrashed out of my mind, incoherent and arrogant, centered around my own core, a satellite orbiting around its own private planet of pity. At first the girls, when they were young enough to be pacified and manipulated, would be interested in their new brother-in-law, Danny or Thomas, and would laugh at their big brother's antics, but as time went by, their little hearts began to lock me out, and now I don't know if I have the right to ask for my key back.

"So, you're graduating this year," I say awkwardly. I haven't sat at this table for breakfast since I was about their age. "Any idea what program you're going into?" Winter pushes her plate away from her and leaves. I watch her throw her coat on in the entrance. She screams up the stairs to my mother that she's going to the mall.

"Shit," I say, to myself.

Summer raises a red eyebrow and gives me a kind look. "She's just a little upset, but it's not your fault."

"Yeah, it is. Look, Summer, I know this may be too little too late, but I want you to know I quit drinking, and this time it's for good. And I know it wasn't easy for you and Winter to—"

"We're okay."

"I know. I know that. I see that. I mean, wow, you two are doing more than okay. I'm actually in awe. Mom tells me you're both top of your class and that you don't give her any trouble."

"You gave Mom and Dad enough trouble for both of us."

I understand what she means. "I'm sorry," I say. What else can I say?

"But, Ryde, I'm older now, and, well, when I think you were around my age when it happened, I understand it better now. What it did to you."

I have to look away. I'm overwhelmed again.

"And Winter deals with it differently, that's all. But she knows. She knows."

I remember her sitting in her stroller, watching the woods with terrified eyes. "I wish I could have been there for you two, when you needed me."

"I feel the same about you." She hesitates and gets out of her seat. "Can I give you a hug?"

I grab her neck and pull her into my arms, crushing her to my chest. "Everything is gonna be okay now," I say into her hair. "I'm gonna be your brother again."

I just hold her until she's cried her fill. Then, we smile at each other and, embarrassed, dig into the cold pancakes.

"Mom told me he's a priest now," she says, after a long time. "Why would he do that?"

Her question feels fresh and new to me. Probably the only thing I haven't asked myself.

Yes, why?

I have to think about it for a moment. "He grew up religious," I say. "His family went to church all the time, and he was really good at understanding the Bible, you know. Theology was appealing to him. There was something in religion that just resounded with his temperament. It was in his nature to be alone and spend hours deep in thought or prayer. I guess to him, those two things are one and the same. And then, after what...after what happened to him, I think maybe there was nowhere left to run but straight into God's arms. I mean, how could he ever really trust another human being again? No, not Alistair. He was too unprepared for—" But I stop.

"For evil," Summer says, so wisely.

"Yes, for evil."

"What did the man do to him?" She's waited a long time to ask me this question, and she's not a child anymore. She demands her part in this story. "Tell me."

"Everything, Summer. He did everything you can, can't and won't imagine." I've said it out loud. I've said it because it's true and I don't want to deny him those two days anymore. It happened. It happened to Alistair and it's part of him now.

Her face blanches. "How did he get away from him then?"

"They said the man, he was deranged, but no one ever did anything about him. His parents were old, kept him on their land as help, and he'd been arrested before for indecent things. He was fucked-up. Animals disappeared around the adjacent farms, and he did things to them, but after he…after he had his way with Alistair for thirty-two hours, he thought Alistair was dead, and so he just tossed more hay on top of him." I can't go on and stop.

"He took Alistair to his barn?" Summer asks.

"Yes, from the woods. Dragged him there."

"But when they found Alistair, on the road, Mom says he couldn't speak anymore. She says he didn't have any clothes on him, so what happened to him after—"

"I don't know what happened after that." I rub my face and think of vodka. But I won't. I won't. "I was in the hospital when they, I mean, his parents, when they moved up north somewhere with Matilda's older sister, and then there was a 'For Sale' sign on their lawn when I came back home, and no one would tell me where they'd taken him."

"But after that, later, why didn't you try to find him?"

"Because I was a fucking mess, Summer. And I knew I couldn't handle seeing his face. Or maybe I thought he couldn't handle seeing mine."

"What's made you change your mind now?"

I let out a long breath. "Because now the time has finally come when *not* seeing his face has become intolerable to me."

"And what about him?"

"I dream he feels the same."

Chapter Twelve

I stop typing the word "necessary" midway.

I can't write another letter. I can't concentrate on work this afternoon. I have twenty more pages to translate for my new employer, but it'll have to wait. Outside my living room window, just above my desk, snowflakes dance in the wind, and the neighbors' Christmas lights reflect in the glass, red, white and green. I think of churches and stained glass.

It's so quiet here in my empty apartment. I haven't seen any of my old friends in weeks. Sobriety is my only companion these days. Sheryl calls, but still treats me like a strange animal she's not quite sure how to handle anymore. I've been working long hours, trying to get my budget back on track. I don't want to be a thirty-one-year-old boy anymore.

I lean back in my chair and stretch my arms.

I'm ready.

Yes, I'm ready now. I'm going to go to the presbytery and tell Alistair everything.

I stand and turn all my lights off, then grab my coat.

But as I reach for the door handle, the bell rings, startling me.

I pull the door open and there he is.

Alistair.

His beauty shocks me.

God, his face. His face is divinity turned into eyes and mouth.

Alistair steps back and stares at me.

So then, he did find the card I'd left for him that day in the confessional.

"You're here." My voice is shaky. "I was gonna go see you, just now." I let him in and, with my heart pounding, shut the door behind him.

Alistair's white-blond hair is wet around his ears and a strand of it sticks to his shiny forehead. I notice his white tab collar is loose, and his black clerical shirt is soaked around the armpits. But he's wearing jeans instead of his usual black pants. Where's his coat?

"Did you walk here dressed like this? It's freezing out there."

Alistair's black eyes are full of heat and fever. He won't say anything.

I take a step to him. Something in his eyes, his countenance, his strange smile, pulls me to him. "Alistair," I breathe, lifting my hand to his face, but not touching it. It would burn me.

He hasn't blinked yet. His pupils are drowned in a sea of darkness. He's not himself. There's something off with him.

"Are you okay?" I ask, daring to come closer still.

Sweat trickles down his temples, but he doesn't seem to notice it.

"Sit down." I hang my coat on the hook.

He looks around silently.

"Alistair?"

He slowly walks up to me and takes my hand. I don't know what he wants, but I'll do anything, follow him anywhere. He has me now. I can't even look away. "Alistair," I mutter, but he puts his lips on my ear, and they sear my skin. "He wants this," he says, but the words don't sound right. He's repeating them, not saying them. "This is what he wants," he whispers. "Like the horses."

He's out of my hands and running into my bedroom like he's been here before. I hear him in there, laughing. There's a crash. Who is in there? Who am I to him in this moment?

I find him in my bedroom, naked.

What is happening? I want him so much, I don't know if I can take him. He lies over the blanket, with his knees open and his white thighs spread wide. His skin is a white canvas I want to dirty. I move to the bed. My hands shake. "I didn't think you'd want me."

He turns to his stomach, showing me what I've been aching for all my life.

I don't know what game we're playing, but I can't resist him. I can't. I pull my clothes off, and with trembling hands, touch him.

But I've dropped a burning match on kerosene, and when I fall over him, my throat fills with smoke. I can't breathe, can't see. He's inside me. Around me. He's everywhere. The palms of his hands scorch my skin and he's breathing fire into my mouth, but I can't fight it, no, I can't climb out of this engulfing pyre he's thrown me in, because his sex is burning through every layer I have, and I'm down to my bones now—my bones on his bones—and I pound into the heat of him, with nothing to stop me but the fear of losing my mind. This is not us. This is not us.

I want to pull out of him, but he won't let me. He holds me to him, and I don't know how much longer I can go on, but his body is a room with no doors in a house going up in flames. I feel him swell, and I'm caving in, every wall inside me coming down, and then it happens, oh yes, yes, it happens, and he screams while I burst into light, everything around us turning white.

My defenses collapse. My body is dust on his.

I touch his shoulder and feel steam coming off his skin. "Alistair," I whisper into the wetness of his hair.

But he slaps my hand off and jumps out of bed.

I climb out of bed. What is happening? What just happened? "Alistair, wait. Talk to me."

He's dressing, mumbling words under his breath.

I stand there, both victim and accused. "It's okay," I say, softly, meekly. "Please, let's talk."

But before I can react, he's run out of the room, and seconds later, I hear the front door slam shut.

I pull my jeans on and run out of my apartment. The street is empty.

He's gone again.

"Sugar, milk?" Sheryl is anxious, moving fast around her messy kitchen. "I can't remember how you like it."

There are empty beer bottles lying around like relics.

"It must have been quite a party last night," I say. "I'll drink it black, thanks." I motion for her to sit down. She's making me nervous. I'm already a mess. Didn't sleep last night.

She sets our cups down and pulls out a chair across from mine. We sit at her table and I watch her stir her coffee for a long time. Her hair is a little dull under the dim kitchen light, and her pink cotton robe needs to be burned immediately. But she's still beautiful. She has the bone structure of a Golden Era actress.

"Now," she says, looking straight up at me. In her eyes, I see my old friend again. Maybe she's coming around to me after all. "Tell me. Tell me everything."

"It's like I said on the phone. He knocks on my door, right? And I answer, but Alistair looks a little... *flushed*. He doesn't say a word to me. Just takes my hand and, no, wait wait, first he said something about horses, and five minutes later we're in my bed together." I've been replaying yesterday in my mind over and over, searching for a missing clue that could explain Alistair's behavior, but I can't understand it. I just can't figure it out.

"All right, so he's horny. He's a priest, for fuck's sake." She shrugs. "Maybe he was waiting for you or something, building his desire up every day, and then boom, he can't take it anymore and has to have you. He remembers the card you left for him and jumps into a cab and—"

"Yeah, maybe." I'm not convinced. I take a sip of the dark coffee and it helps clear my mind a little. "But... I don't know. It was more than just sexual repression being finally unleashed or whatever."

"You said he was sweating a lot when he showed up."

"He was undone. His collar and his overall attire. He was wearing jeans but his clerical shirt too. Like he was two people at once or something. He wasn't the Alistair I know—"

"The Alistair you know? Ryde, do you hear yourself? You don't *know* him anymore. You haven't seen him since he was seventeen years old. He's a man now.

And probably kind of fucked-up."

"He's not fucked-up." I give her a cold look. "He's recovering."

"Okay, whatever." She leans back, clearly holding her tongue.

"You know, when I was in that confessional that day, vomiting all that evilness out, I think maybe, in some way, I wanted him to know just how dark it gets inside me sometimes, and maybe yesterday was his way of showing me his own personal demon."

"Like a split personality or something?"

I look away, and down into the blackness of my cup.

"Look, Ryde, you know I'm trying my best here to understand you, to support you in all this. But it seems to me you're still on the same path you were when you were drinking."

I look up at her, not sure that I understand.

"Don't you think trying to save Alistair from whatever you think he needs saving from will only lead you to self-destruction, as sure as the vodka would have?"

"I love him."

"You don't know him."

"I *love* him, Sheryl. I can't forget him. Can't back down. Can't stop now."

"You sound like an addict."

"Don't you understand?" I raise my voice. "We were supposed to spend our lives together. That was the plan. You weren't there at the creek. You didn't hear what we promised each other. I swore to him, Sheryl, swore we'd never be apart. So this fucking maniac took him away from me. So what? How long am I gonna let him carry him off? How many more years wasted?"

"Ryde, you're in denial! He's a priest!" She slaps the table. "And I'm sick of playing along with your fantasy! He made his decision. He chose God. Who are you to fuck with that? You're the one who's going to carry him away, just like that maniac. Can't you just let the boy be?"

I'm struck by her words. She's wrong. I drain my coffee and slowly get out of my chair.

"Ryde, wait, listen—"

"I'm sorry you think I'm chasing a fantasy. I'm sorry you don't believe in dreaming anymore. But I do, Sheryl. I do. And I wanna live, and that means trying, goddamn it."

"Oh, I've tried, Ryde. I've tried all my life, and trust me, I know what it's like to dream about someone you can never have."

I stare down at her, see the truth in her eyes.

"Why do you think I married a gay man, Ryde? Do you ever think about that? Because Michael reminded me of you. And look where that got me. Divorced and playing third wheel to him and his perfect husband Gabe."

"Sheryl."

"So, you wanna keep chasing the impossible, go right on ahead. But don't ask me to be there to hold you when everything comes apart. I can't be your platonic wife anymore."

For the first time in my life, I fear I might lose her. "Hey, hey," I say, touching her hair. "Are we still friends? What's going on?"

She puts her hand over mine but won't look at me. "I think I need a break, Ryde. I think I need some space, some time away from you."

"Wait a minute—"

"No, Ryde. Enough. I need to go into detox."

"I can help you with that."

"You don't understand." She moves away from me. "I need to go into detoxification of *you*."

Not much is said between us after that, and before I know it, I'm outside again, in the cold, confused. Why are all these doors closing on me? How much longer until redemption?

As I'm walking down the sidewalk, something hard hits my shoulder, and I spin around angrily. A little boy in a red wool hat is staring at me with wide, dark eyes. "Sorry, mister," he says, obviously trying not to laugh.

Behind me, another boy, his friend, is sculpting a large snowball. "I'm gonna get you so bad!" he yells, running past me.

The boy in the red hat darts off, skidding down the icy sidewalk. "I don't think so!" he screams, laughing now. "You can't even catch me!"

He sounds like a boy I once knew.

I watch them chase each other around, until they've disappeared into the schoolyard at the end of the street. I dust the snow off my shoulder.

Now I know what to do.

Frau Eberhart opens the door but stays behind it, only showing me half of her suspicious face. "Yes, what is it?" She has a strong German accent. "What do you want?"

I raise my chin, trying to be cool and bold. "Is Father Genet here?"

She makes a face, as if disgusted. She shakes her head. She looks over my shoulder and begins to close the door. I insist. "How about Father Masson?"

Defeated, she steps back from the door. She doesn't invite me in, just walks away, down the hall, but I catch her saying something to someone in the living room before she makes it back to her safe haven; her kitchen.

I'm not sure what to do. "Hello?"

"In here, Ryde." Father Masson sounds serious.

I slip my boots off and hang my coat, but my eyes keep straying to those stairs. Two days ago, Alistair was in my bed and we were making love.

Where is he now?

"Hello," I say, entering the quiet living room. "Hope I'm not intruding."

Father Masson sits in an armchair, by the fireplace, reading the Bible. He's obviously deeply immersed, and I decide not to disturb him. I sit in the chair by the window and wait for him to be finished.

After a few minutes, he shuts the big book and sets it down gently on the side table near him. He slips his glasses off. "I had a presentiment I'd see you again."

"I'm very predictable, so I've been told." Is this man my friend or foe? "I was hoping to see Father Genet today. Where is he?"

"I'm sorry he's not here today."

"He's in church then." I'm already getting out of my chair. "I'll—"

"I'm afraid he isn't hearing any confessions today."

So he knows it was me. I'm the drunkard. I feel the heat in my cheeks and hate myself for blushing. "Well, I should get going anyway."

"Sit down, Ryde." Father Masson's voice is firm but kind. "You're safe here."

I don't know what to do, so I sit.

"Now listen," he says, very low, casting a quick glance at the hall, "I want to speak freely with you. Can we drop all pretenses and speak our minds here, as men?"

I acquiesce silently. This man knows Alistair in a way I don't anymore. He can and will give me answers.

"Good," Father Masson says. "Now, let's start at the beginning. Every story has a Genesis, and I'd like to know what yours and Alistair's is."

"Why do you want to know?"

"I'm not the only one who wants to know, and trust me, my dear Ryde, it's much better if I ask the question, not they."

"They?"

He pauses, leans back in his chair. "Do you think a boy like him enters the seminary every day?" he asks after a moment. "What do you suppose the effect of him was on all our old, withering souls? What do you imagine happened when young Alistair Genet, troubled and brilliant as he was and still is, walked down our bare hallways with those luminous black eyes of his fixed to the floor, and his white hair almost a halo over his head? We were smitten. Enthralled. He was our hope. We were looking right at our future, young man. The future of the church itself lives inside him." Father Masson is getting carried away, and I hang on to his every word. "Alistair is the lamb and the shepherd all in one. And this explains his…his troubles."

"His troubles. What *troubles* exactly?"

Father waves my question off. "It's nothing to worry about. He just needs rest and time." He leans in closer, his eyes more menacing now. "But what he especially doesn't need, my good fellow, is old memories to burden him once more. He's on the cusp of greatness, and it's your responsibility, if you care for him, for his fragile mind and heart, to stay where you belong."

"And where is that, huh? Where do I belong?"

"In the past."

We sit face-to-face, silent for a while.

"Ryde," he says at last, "Father Genet is like a son to me." He looks into my eyes and I can see he's being honest. He cares about Alistair. "And believe me, although he suffers greatly at times, and though perhaps it might appear as if he's torn between flesh and faith, he's still so young, still so very, very young. We need, no, we *must* give him time. We must allow God to find His way through him so that He may accomplish His work through our dear Alistair. Do you understand? Even Christ had His demons to fight."

"You're asking me to walk away?"

Father Masson holds his breath, nodding gravely.

"You're asking me to walk away from the man I love more than life itself?"

"Oh, child." Father Masson looks away at the fire. "My dear child. If only you knew how much he needs the church. And the church needs him."

"Fuck the church! *I* need him." I get out of my chair, and before I know it, I'm on bended knee before him. Imploring him. "I need him," I whisper, looking up at his gentle face. "Don't ask me to forsake that. You can't ask me to. You just can't. You have no right."

Father Masson puts a hand on my shoulder. "I know the sacrifice is great, but you'll be rewarded."

"When? When I die? In heaven? Don't you see? I don't care about that. I don't want absolution or eternal life in God's little day care. I want Alistair. Please, I want Alistair."

He frowns, and I can see I've moved him. Yes, I've moved the man inside him, not the priest.

"Please," I say again. "Let him decide. Let me near him. Don't interfere. Don't sway him. Just let him choose what he wants. Give me time. Don't you believe in free will? Doesn't God prefer His servants to come to Him freely?" I let go of his big hands and sit on the floor, by the fire. "Don't you see?" I say again, staring at the flames trapped inside the alcove, "we never had a real chance. Evil broke us apart. And now, after all these years—"

"What evil are you referring to?"

"The man who sequestered Alistair and violated him."

"What are you talking about, child? Father Genet never went through such a thing."

"Yes, he did."

"I'm sure you're mistaken."

He's lying. He won't talk about it, but he's lying to me. I can see it right there in his eyes. "You've messed with his head enough," I say boldly. "Now, it's—"

"Now, it's your turn to fool with him? Is that it?"

"Just let him *know* me again," I say softly. "That's all I ask. Stay back and let us get to know each other again. And if he still chooses God, then I swear to you, I'll walk away."

Father Masson looks over at the Bible on the table. "If only it were that simple."

"But it is. It is."

"Father Genet isn't the man you knew. He's very—" But he stops. He picks the Bible up. "Promise it again."

I put my hand on the Bible. "I promise, if Alistair isn't mine anymore, I'll release him. I'll let him go."

The old priest shakes his head. "It's in God's hands now, lad, what He wants for our dear Alistair."

I step back into the hall. "You're wrong, Father," I say, grabbing my coat. "It's in my hands. Now, tell me where he is."

"He's with Father Cornwell."

"Okay, so who's this Cornwell and where can I find him?"

"Father Cornwell is his spiritual counselor. Father Genet has been a little frazzled for the last few days and was in dire need of some guidance."

"Is this priest a shrink?"

"No, we don't—"

"Right, you don't believe in psychiatry." I slip my coat on. "Will Alistair, will Father Genet, be back later?"

Father Masson sighs. "Yes," he says, clearly annoyed. "Of course."

"Then I'll see you later." I wink at him. "You better get used to me, Father."

It's around eight when I send my latest document and shut my computer off. I've been working for six hours straight, and my eyes are tired from staring at a screen. Used to be, I could work on paper, but these days, everyone is going digital. I don't particularly enjoy my work, but until I find my muse again, this is all I have. In the last years, I've started many different projects, tried numerous things, but never finished anything. Journalism. Teaching English to new immigrants. Cooking school. Bartending. Physical fitness. Boxing. I even thought of joining the army or police force. I trained dogs for a while on this remote farmland for a friend of mine, but dogs don't respond very well to drunken litanies in the middle of the night.

I've been searching for myself, my true self, for so long, I don't think I'm capable of anything else but this search.

But with him at my side…

If only I knew what to say to him. If only I had the wisdom to speak the exact words, those words that could unlock him, I'd take Alistair out of that awful black shirt and white collar and run off somewhere where God couldn't find us again.

Is there such a place?

I stand and throw my coat on. Here I go again, down my street, to the subway station, underground, and out again, emerging from the tunnels below, my heart fluttering with anticipation, because this it. This is the moment of truth. I walk fast, almost furiously, with my hands deep inside my pockets, head down, moving like a train. I need courage. I need determination. Now is not the time for weakness.

The light is on in the presbytery's living room and I see Father Masson's large figure in the chair, by the fireplace. Has he not moved since I left, almost seven hours ago?

I ring the bell. My nerve is failing me.

Through the lace curtain in the glass, I see Frau Eberhart coming to the door. Great. I brace myself for her cold welcome. She gives me the same line, but to my surprise, calls out his name. Then, off she goes.

His feet appear at the top of the stairs, and I step back to the closed door behind me, holding my gloves tight.

Hang on, I tell myself. Just hang on.

Halfway down the stairs, Alistair pauses, seeing me. His dark eyes are clear. His face is serene and calm. "Ryde," he says gently, looking over at the living room. "Hi."

I want to say something but can't make a sound. He's acting like we saw each other yesterday and had a nice time.

Alistair steps down to me and turns to look into the living room. "Father Masson, have you met my friend Ryde?" His voice is childish again. He seems smaller than the last time I saw him.

I hear Father Masson getting out of his chair. He joins us and we exchange banalities for a moment, though I'm transfixed by Alistair. He's fidgeting, keeps pushing a strand of hair behind his ear. Does he remember what we did to each other, only a few days ago? He seems so young this evening. So different from the last time I saw him.

At last, Father Masson retires to the kitchen, leaving Alistair and I alone, but not before casting me a dark look over his shoulder.

"Take off your boots," Alistair says. "Do you wanna sit in there?" He's cheerful.

In the living room, I stare at his every move. The way he walks, touches things, sits. I'm mesmerized, trying to understand how we can be sitting here so politely after what happened between us.

He sits on the edge of the chair, watching me with wide, happy eyes. "I was going to call you, but I've been studying really, really hard this week, and I didn't have the time." He smiles sweetly at me. "I'm glad you came."

"So you still have my number."

He seems confused for a moment. "What?" He giggles. "Of course I have your number. I call you every day."

I search his eyes, his face, but I don't want to risk confronting him. What if I caused some kind of psychological damage? "Well, how have you been?"

He gives me a radiant smile that takes my breath away. "Oh, just great," he says, full of cheer. "How was your summer?"

He doesn't remember. He doesn't remember we made love.

"Oh," he cries, getting out of his chair, "I haven't even offered you anything to drink. Would you like some—"

"I'm fine," I say, not sure how I'll make it through this.

He looks down at me, and for a moment, something dark moves across his eyes. I recognize it, saw it two days ago. It's right there. Yes, right there looking at me.

"Are you two lads up for a game of cards?" Father Masson is standing in the hall. His eyes insist on my face. "Keep this old man company for an hour?"

Alistair blinks and looks over at him. His expression is childish again. "I wouldn't mind," he says. "I always win anyway." He looks down at me. "Do you want to, Ryde?"

How old is he right now?

When are we, in his mind? What does he remember?

"I'd love to," I say, meeting Father Masson's eyes. "Why not."

Alistair looks at me kindly. "Great, it'll be fun."

Father Masson walks to me and takes my arm. I'm thankful for it, because my knees are weak. "Come now, Ryde, let's play cards, shall we?" His touch is firm and I know I can't resist.

Chapter Thirteen

"Dissociative identity disorder."

Though I've said those three words out loud to myself a thousand times today, and have been reading everything on the subject in the last two days, they still sound foreign to me.

On the line, my mother sighs heavily. "Poor thing," she says. "That sweet little boy."

Holding the phone to my ear, I lean my head back on the couch and stare up at my ceiling.

Sybil.

Split personality.

"And what does Dr. Scarborough think?" my mom asks. "What did he say?"

"Many psychiatrists hesitate to diagnose this type of disorder, but Jamie knows it exists, and after what I told him, he thinks it's highly probable Alistair could have developed this disorder as a coping mechanism." What am I saying here? I'm talking about the man I love. "I don't know what to do."

"Oh, baby, I'm sorry. Can we help him? I mean, there must be some kind of cure or treatment or—"

"Therapy. Hypnotherapy. Talk therapy. But he's a priest, Mom, and they don't believe in these things. Shit, they'd call an exorcist before they'd admit their perfect little lamb isn't as virtuous and holy as they need him to be." My head aches. didn't sleep much last night. I'm a mess. "He's blocked out a whole chapter of our lives, years and years. And those years are the years I need him to remember."

"Easy now, Ryde, easy. Take it one step at a time."

"It's so unfair. I finally find him, finally have a chance."

"This is who he is now. This is how he dealt with it, and you have to adapt yourself to that. You have to go along with him. Do you remember what you told me that day, in your bedroom, when I asked you to take it slow with him?"

"Yeah...I remember. I said, 'He calls the shots'."

"Well, let him call the shots again. He'll lead you into his own world, and if he can trust you, maybe, with time, you might be surprised at what a lot of plain old-fashioned love can do for a fractured heart."

Fractured, yes. That's what he is.

Split in two. Or more?

There's that boy I saw two days ago. Lovely and light-footed with a breezy personality. That's who I played cards with all evening. We talked about our old houses and riding our bikes, but his memories of childhood seem to stop there. Then, he skips to the seminary years. And what about the other Alistair I met? Where does he hide and when does he come out to play?

"I think Father Masson, that old priest, I think he's very aware of Alistair's disorder, which he conveniently calls 'troubles'. I think they've seen the other side of him more than once, and are trying to keep the damage to a minimum. That's where that Cornwell guy comes in."

"He needs help. Solid, no-nonsense help." My mother is agitated. "Deep down inside, Alistair must know there's something not quite right with him. He must notice missing hours. Days. He was always such a brilliant child and so insightful too. He must have his moments of lucidity."

I rub my bleary eyes. "This is huge, Mom. So huge. I don't know if I have what it takes."

"You do. You have exactly what it takes."

"You really think so?" I need her now more than ever. I need to know I'm doing the right thing. "What if this is Craving's Creek all over again? What if this is me forcing things?"

"What happened to him is not your fault. Goddamn it, Ryde, when are you gonna stop blaming yourself?"

Her fury stuns me for a moment.

"You boys were innocent. You were swimming in a damn creek!"

"Mom, calm down."

"No, Ryde, I won't calm down. You listen to me. You are not up against God or the Devil, and you don't have to redeem yourself. It's enough already."

"I'm just gonna spend some time with him then, right?"

She takes a deep breath, obviously trying to simmer down. "Yes, that's right. You call him. You spend time with him. You laugh with him. You touch his hand. You show him life outside of those presbytery walls."

"I want him to remember me," I say, trying not to cry.

"That means remembering Craving's Creek."

"Yes. I know."

I shut my eyes, hear him calling out to me from the rocky shore again.

I knew you'd come after me! I knew you could do it!

Can I, Alistair? Can I jump off that cliff again?

The weather is mild for mid-December, and the noon sun feels wonderful on my face, the way it must have felt for Lazarus. Around me, the snow shines so bright, I have to squint to keep from being blinded. I've been living in a tomb of doubt.

I walk slowly, taking my time, letting the fresh air cleanse my dark thoughts out. I've been so consumed with worry in the last week, perpetually obsessing over Alistair's mental state, that I've neglected everything else. I did force myself to work a little, but between my reading up on psychiatry and dissociation disorders, I find myself sitting on my bed for hours, staring out into space, immersed in our past.

And I've been thinking about booze again. A lot.

But I won't bend. I can do this. Man's natural state is sobriety. Alcohol made me an imposter in my own life. I'm through with being a sad clown.

When I reach the presbytery, I stop to look at it. I never imagined I'd ever enter a presbytery, much less feel excited at the prospect.

I wait for Eberhart's stern face to greet me in the glass. Instead, I see Alistair coming down the hall to the entrance. I stiffen up, the anxiety now reaching close to panic. Who is he today? Am I going to meet the child or the lustful succubus? I'm prepared for both.

He pulls the door open, but upon seeing me, his whole face blanches. He puts a hand over his heart and looks like he might faint. "No." He presses his hands to his mouth. "No... *Ryde?*"

"Hey," I say quickly. He's completely shocked. "Did I come at a bad time?" I ask, hoping to give him a clue we've met before now.

I see him thinking, his mind working fast. What if he's seeing me for the first time in fourteen years?

"We were supposed to meet today," I say. "You wanted to pick up a Christmas tree." I'm feeding him the information. I know he needs me to. He looks so lost, so unprepared for this. "I came by a few times. We talked on the phone last night. About the tree."

His whole demeanor changes. "Of course, yes, I remember. I'm sorry, my mind was on something else." His words are well chosen, and now I know he's been in this situation a hundred times before. "Come in," he says, and I notice the tremor in his hand. He's very anxious. I must have been on the phone with Alistair the boy last night. I've never seen this side of him before. I enter and look around for Father Masson or Eberhart. "Are you alone? Is Father Masson here?"

He blinks. He's struggling, trying to keep up a front. "No...he isn't here."

"Alistair," I say, taking a step to him. "Get your coat, okay?" My words are soft. Soothing. "Let's go for a walk. It's really nice out. It's all right. Let's just get out of here."

He hesitates, clearly overwhelmed by my presence. "You look the same," he says quietly and plucks his coat out of the entrance closet. It's a long, black, wool coat with a military cut. "Where are we going?" He's so docile. How far would he follow me?

"Just around the park here." I open the door while he laces his boots up. Outside, we head around the corner, for the park. I'm glad to see there's hardly anyone walking down the path. It's Wednesday. We have the large, quiet park to ourselves. "Are you warm?" I ask him, slowing down a little.

What is he feeling right now?

He seems so perturbed, and I want to ease his mind. He must be trying to figure out how many times we've met. What he's said to me before. Where I was in the last fourteen years.

"It's been nice seeing you again," I say as we come to a bench facing the frozen pond. I gesture for him to sit down. "After all these years, I can't believe the coincidence. You know, you performing the wedding ceremony for Sheryl's cousin and all." I hope I'm helping him, not confusing him more. "When she told me you were a priest, I remembered how we used to talk about it when we were teenagers. Anyway, I'm so happy to have found you again." I dare to look his way. "It's been lonely not knowing you anymore."

So lonely.

At my side, Alistair sits still, watching the pond, drinking in my words. His cheeks color slightly. Yes, things are clearly coming back to him now. "It's been such a long time, Ryde. I wondered where you were, what you'd become."

I try to fill in the holes without being too obvious. "I know, and though we've seen each other a few times since we met a month ago, I feel like we haven't really had a chance to talk alone, just you and me."

"We haven't talked much?" He glances over at me. He's Alistair again. My beautiful and serious Alistair. "Well, how are you? How have you been? *Where* have you been?"

I look away, at the ice. "Shit, I really don't know where to start."

He waits.

Playfully, I nudge his shoulder with mine. "You sure you wanna hear all this? The last ten years have been pretty crazy for me. And you being a priest and all, I'm afraid I might shock the hell out of you." I wink. "You know what I mean?"

He smiles. It's not a child's smile or a seductive grin. Just a smile. "In my line of work," he says, tongue in cheek, "I hear all kinds of things. So, try me."

"All right, but don't say I didn't warn you."

I tell him everything, but start with my first journalism gig, skipping a few years after Craving's Creek. I tell him about the jobs, the partying, the chase, the search, the never-ending thirst for chaos. But I don't mention men and he doesn't ask. I recount my darker times and explain my friendship with Sheryl. Talking about her, I feel guilty, and wonder if I'll see her again. We sit on the bench for a good part of the afternoon, and he listens to my complicated story, my history of drinking, guiding me along with nods and little words of appreciation. To speak with him so openly, to have him so close to me, is thrilling and painful all at once. We missed so much of each other's lives. How I wish he could have been there with me.

"Anyway," I say, coming to the end of it, "I'm sober now, and I think I can stay the course. I really like being in control of my mental faculties again." I'm suddenly embarrassed at everything I've admitted so easily. "I'm thinking of writing again. Not sure what, but I can feel something simmering inside."

"You wanted to be a writer," he says. It's an affirmation but a question too. "We talked about that, I remember."

I look at him, hoping he can see the younger version of me in my face. "I used to write things, little messages, in those houses they were building near our street. Do you remember?"

He frowns and his features strain. "Yes," he says, after a moment. "There was one... I remember it didn't have a chandelier."

I want to grab him and hold him and tell him everything, but he calls the shots. He calls the shots. "No, you're right," I say, steadying myself. "They didn't, and that was the last one we played in. There was a big staircase in it, and you ran up to the second floor—"

"To hide. I wanted to hide from you."

"It was a game."

"It was really exciting," he says, smiling again. "I remember that. We had a lot of fun that day."

"We spent every day together until you moved."

"Yes," he says, but I can see I've confused him. "Right. After I moved to the seminary."

I stand and nod to the path. "You wanna go get that tree now?"

He's relieved I don't press him for more. He stands as well, looking around. "I don't think I have my wallet." He pats himself down. "No, I didn't take it with me."

"Don't worry about it." I walk up to a tall, slightly pathetic pine tree and knock my knuckles against its trunk. "We're gonna cut this one down."

"No, we can't."

"Yeah, of course we can." I shake the tree a little and pretend to assess it. "I never buy my trees." I dig into my coat. "I brought my ax and everything."

"No," he says, laughing, grabbing my sleeve. "You did not."

"I did too." I make a great show of looking for something in my coat. "It's right here."

"Stop it." He laughs louder, pulling on my arm. "You're messing with me."

His hand is on my arm and he hasn't let me go. I stare into his dark eyes, feeling the current between us. "I'm just kidding," I manage to say, quietly.

Alistair's fingers release my sleeve and he gazes around the park. "I haven't been out in so long," he says. "Can you believe I live right next door to this park and this is the first time I've actually walked through it?"

"You were never big on the outdoors." I dust some snow off his shoulder. Any excuse to touch him. "Except for swimming. Do you still swim?"

"No," he says, hauntingly.

I shouldn't have asked him that. For a second, I'm panicked, searching for something to say. Then a young woman walks up to him, unknowingly saving me from disaster. "Father Genet?" She laughs brightly. "Oh, I thought it was you." Alistair immediately recognizes her. He asks about her mother, her brother, clearly remembering her and her family. She's tickled pink at having his attention and keeps glancing over at me. I pretend to be interested in the pigeons nearby, avoiding her inquisitive eyes at all cost. At last, she strolls off, but I catch her looking over her shoulder at me a few times.

"Nice girl," I say, when she's gone.

"Flora?" He smiles. "If you say so."

I like this side of him. "No? Not nice?"

He doesn't say any more about it.

"Come on." I touch his sleeve again. "Let's go get a tree. The biggest one that'll fit in the presbytery's sitting room. It's on Father Masson anyway."

He laughs again. "Oh, I see you haven't changed."

At the kitchen table, Alistair sits by me, his knee almost touching mine under the table. Sweat stands on his face, and his cheeks are pink from exertion. It was quite an adventure trying to get that tree into the house. We nearly gave up, but finally managed it. My hands smell like pine. There's pine needles everywhere.

I look around the presbytery kitchen. I've never been in here before. Eberhart's domain. It's nice. The walls are covered with china plates and the furniture and cabinets are all golden wood and beautifully polished. "Eberhart's gonna flip her lid," I say. "We're gonna have to clean up before she comes back."

Alistair is picking dirt out of his pants. "Oh, she's with her friend for the holidays." He drops a few needles on the table. "I don't even know where the decorations are."

"We'll find them later." I'm looking forward to poking around this old house. "You hungry?"

He thinks about it. "Yes, actually," he says. "I'm starving."

"So, are you the cook when she's out, or what?"

He laughs. "No, I don't even know how to boil water."

"Are you a prince or a priest?" I shake my head at him. I can tell he's a little offended. I like roughing up his black feathers. It reminds me of the way things used to be. "Can I give it a try?" I get out of my seat and go to the fridge. I'm pleased to see it's full. I see various cheeses and cold cuts, but when I catch sight of two eggplants sitting there on the first shelf, I pop the freezer open and find what I'm looking for. "Microwave?" I ask him, showing him a pack of minced veal.

"What are you gonna make with that?"

I wave him off. "Why don't you go clean up and let me handle dinner?" I rummage through the cabinets, hoping to find the other ingredients I need. I look over at him. "Your hair is full of resin."

He runs his hand through his blond hair and hesitates. "Father Masson will be home and—"

"I'll make enough for him." I know this is a lot for Alistair to deal with, but we can do this. We can have dinner together with no major incident. It's just dinner. People do it every day. "I'm sure he'll be happy to join us," I add. "And it's the holidays, right?"

"I suppose that could be all right," he says, standing. "I'll...I'll go take a shower."

I remember his naked body under mine. The curve of his smooth butt. The fine blond down below his navel. I pour myself a glass of water. I need to keep myself in check. "Okay," I say, turning my back to him. Moments later, I hear him walking away.

For the next fifteen minutes, I busy my hands and dirty mind with fixing this meal in a kitchen I don't know. It takes me five minutes just to find the can opener. But when Alistair comes back, I have the sauce going nicely and the eggplant roasting in the oven. I've always been a good cook. I suppose most intense people are. There's something about cooking that makes me feel in control.

"Wow," he says, walking in. "I could smell the food upstairs. It smells really good." His hair is still wet from the shower, slicked to the side, and the scent of soap clings to him. He's wearing a fresh clerical shirt, but I'm pleased to see the white tab collar is missing. "Can I taste this?" He peers into the bubbling tomato sauce.

I hand him the wooden spoon. "Tell me what you think."

He tastes and then rinses the spoon before putting it back into the pot. "Divine," he says, playfully.

"Is there a radio in here?" I check the eggplant and shut the oven door with my hip. "Do you ever listen to music? Or is that not allowed?"

"It's allowed." He pouts. "I'm not a monk."

"No, you're not a monk." I grin at him. "So, radio?"

"We have a CD player and some CDs."

"Well, now we're talking."

He disappears down the hall, and minutes later, I hear the first notes of a CCR song. "Bad Moon Rising." I'm shocked, but choose not to comment. He returns and for the next half hour, we prepare dinner together. When the eggplant has cooled down, I show him how to scrape them clean, and while I mix the meat and sauce filling, he grates the cheese. I watch him out of the corner of my eye, hoping he won't cut his fingers. As the music plays and the heat of the oven fogs the windows, I catch his black eyes looking my way every few seconds. Every time I meet his candid stare, I smile and wait for him to smile back.

I've been offered a gift tonight. A reprieve. There is no past here.

Father Masson has yet to show up.

Alistair sets the table. "I guess he won't be joining us after all," he says, carefully folding napkins. "Sometimes he goes to Marlowe's Tavern for a few pints."

"Yeah?" I slowly slide the gorged eggplant into his plate. "Interesting."

"Oh, he prays about it." Alistair sits and looks down at his full plate. "It's his only vice."

"I thought priests weren't allowed any vices." I sit near him, very conscious I'm walking on thin ice.

"Priests are human." He dips his fork into the steaming meal. "We struggle with staying on God's path too."

"Do you like what you do?" I ask, not looking directly at him.

He thinks for a moment. "It's all I know."

I swallow my mouthful and wish I had a glass of wine to accompany this meal. "Father Masson says you're going to have your own parish. That's a lot of work. Takes a lot of dedication, I bet."

He's eating very slowly and has a tense look on his face. I feel him slipping away from me. "I think I can handle it," he says. "They tell me I just need to pray harder and rest when I can."

Though I want to press on, I wisely decide to change the subject. "Do you like it?" I ask, pointing to his dish.

"Oh, yes, it's so good, Ryde. I'm sorry I didn't say anything."

"It's all right," I say, laughing.

"You don't have a wife?" he asks, speaking the question into his plate. "I don't remember if you mentioned her or not."

"No. I'm gay, Alistair. But I think you know that."

He's flustered, scraping his fork across his plate. "I thought maybe…with time you'd changed your ways." He won't look at me. "It's a sin, Ryde."

I try to catch his eye. "Are we gonna have a religious debate, like we used to?" I lean back in my chair. "'Cause I'm ready for it."

"No." He glances up at me.

"Look," I say, "I know it's a big deal with the church and all, but I am what I am." I take another bite.

I see he's on the cusp of saying something, but can't seem to manage it. So I wait.

"Ryde," he finally says, after a long pause, "I admire your courage. You know who you are. There's something fierce and innocent in that."

"You think?"

"Yes." He looks down into his plate again.

"What is it?"

"You know," he whispers, "I'm the same. I mean—" But he stops.

"You mean you're gay."

He stares into his lap, nodding gravely.

"Okay, so why the long face?" I slide my chair closer to his. "Hm? You think they don't know? Masson, Cornwell, Eberhart, the whole lot of them, you think they don't know?"

"I don't know why I'm telling you this." He scans the room as if looking for someone. Something. "I don't know why I feel like we've—"

"Known each other for years?" I dare to put my hand over his on the table. "Because we have. We just lost a little chunk of time between point A and point B."

"Ryde, I need to know something." He suddenly looks very scared. "It's important. Crucial."

"Ask me anything." I squeeze his hand to reassure him. In the background, the music has stopped. "I swear to you, Alistair, I'll never keep the truth from you, no matter how much it might hurt you."

"You'll think it's strange. You won't understand."

"I *will* understand." I move closer to him. "I swear. Just speak your mind. You can trust me. Please tell me you still trust me."

"Yes, I do. You're the only one I can trust."

"Ask me then."

His face is set in stone. "When was the last time you saw me? And don't lie."

Here we go.

"Last week," I say, my heart starting to pound. "I was here last week."

I hear his sharp intake of air. "What did we do?"

"We played cards with Father Masson."

He blinks, and I see he's holding back from showing any emotion.

"You don't remember, do you?"

He quickly shakes his head, his face turning white. "I can't recall that evening. I thought today was the first time we'd met, but I feel like it wasn't the first time either. I don't know how to explain it. I can't understand what—"

"It happens a lot, doesn't it?"

He grabs both my hands. "Ryde, listen to me, I need help. I need help. You have to help me."

"Hey, hey," I whisper, my stomach turning. "You're okay, Alistair. You're all right." I feel him shaking and I pull him close. "It's okay," I keep saying, for him and for me. "We're gonna figure you out."

"I don't know what's happening to me," he says, his voice breaking. "I think something's wrong with me. I'm crazy, Ryde, do you understand?" He looks up at me and his tears make me want to cry too. "I'm possessed," he says, very quietly, as if confessing something terrible he can't even bear hearing. "A demon is inside me and making me do things."

"Whoa, wait a minute. Wait a minute here." I take his face in my hands. "No, no way. Don't you even think that for *one* second. You hear me? There's not one evil thing about you."

"Help me," he cries. "I don't know what to do. I don't know anymore. Help me. Please, you have to. I'm crazy. Something is happening to me. Please, help me."

"Hey," I say softly and kiss his sweaty forehead. "I'm here, Alistair. I'm here and I'm not gonna let you down."

"I need to show you something." He bolts out of his chair and I hear him run up the stairs.

I take a moment to check myself. I'm overcome with a thousand different sensations. Fear. Relief. And grief too.

I put my face in my hands and try to hold it together. My mother was right. He knows. He knows something is wrong. This is the lucid Alistair, the man who holds the other pieces together. And he's a scholar, a thinker—he's trained to search for the truth.

I think of his plea and the terror in his eyes, and cringe, making my hands into fists. Whatever it takes. I'll do anything.

"This is important," he says, walking back into the kitchen. He's clutching a black leather-bound notebook to his chest. "I have to show you before I forget again." He sits down. "Before I forget again," he repeats, the words sounding like an omen.

I don't want Father Masson to come home now. Please, let the old priest get plastered and fall asleep on his bar stool. "Show me," I say, pressingly. "Now."

"I've been—I've been—I've been—"

"Calm down. Show me."

He nods, getting a hold of himself. "I've been writing in here every day, to remember, to make things make sense." He opens the notebook, his journal. The first thing I notice is the neatness of his tight handwriting. The pages are full from top to bottom. He doesn't indent paragraphs or skip lines. "Everything is in here," he says, staring at the page loaded with blue words. "From the time I wake to the time I go to sleep."

I read a few lines.

6:32 a.m. I wake up. Pray for seventeen minutes. Go to the bathroom. Wash my hands. Father Masson calls up to me and asks if I want fresh coffee or can he just warm up the old one? Frau Eberhart farts in the hallway and covers the smell with her Chantilly perfume. I feel nauseous. I get dressed.

Every detail of his day is in here. It's a minute-by-minute account. "You do this every day?"

He flips through a few pages. "There's nothing in here about you. About the cards."

"Alistair."

"No, I know you're telling me the truth." His dark eyes move over the blank page below. "There are days and days in here of nothingness."

"When I was here, you were different. Do you understand what I mean by that?"

"And look," he says, not hearing me. "This isn't my handwriting." He skips to another page, and I make an effort to dissimulate my shock. "Look at this. Read this." He angrily looks away from the journal. "This is new. These are *new* passages. They weren't there before."

I look down at a random passage of the messy, smudged writing. "When did they first start to appear in your book?"

Though I ask, I have a feeling I know.

"I'm not sure. Maybe a month ago."

Yes, when I first returned to his life. I've woken something inside him. I'm stirring the sediments at the bottom of his mind.

"Did you read this filth?" he asks.

I fix my eyes to the page again and read.

I made him run into the bedroom after me and he fucked me and fucked me and bit me and pulled my hair and he'll burn for it.

I stop. Think of the bottle of whiskey in the living room.

He watches me, expecting an answer.

"Come here." I put my hands on his face. "I love you," I say, because there's nothing else I can or want to say in this moment. I don't care if it's too much too soon. I can't waste one more lousy minute pretending anymore. "I love you," I say again, leaning my forehead to his. "I never stopped."

"No." He shoots back into his seat, pushing my hands off him. "No, no."

"Alistair, stop." I grab his face again. "Stop," I say more softly. "Just stop." I kiss his mouth very gently. "It's me. It's me, Alistair."

He looks at me, his defenses coming down. "Ryde."

"You loved me once. How can I forget that? How can I forget the way you used to kiss me? How much you missed me when I couldn't be close to you? The way you watched my window at night, and the things we swore to each other?"

He frowns, and I see his eyes move to my mouth. "We kissed, and my mother almost caught us."

"I only need to know one thing, okay? Just one thing. Do you *want* to remember us?"

He watches me very seriously. "I don't remember the last time I slept through the night. I don't know where half of last week went because I don't remember Monday, Thursday, and Sunday, and sometimes I don't know where I am, how I got there."

"Hello. Hello," Father Masson calls out from the entrance. "Alistair?"

Alistair's face turns stoic and he stiffens in his chair, pulling back from me. "In here, Father." He quickly stands and rushes out of the kitchen.

For a second, I really hate that old priest. I get out of my seat and lean in the kitchen doorway. "Good evening," I call out to him coolly. "We were just finishing dinner. There's plenty left, if you'd like."

"Oh, well, how nice." He hangs his coat and I notice he's teetering a little. "But Mrs. Allbright was kind enough to feed me this evening." He winks at Alistair. "You know how she is."

Alistair returns his smile, but it's faded, and he stands there, halfway between the kitchen and entrance, looking guiltier than a thief with holes in his pockets. I'm glad to see he's still a terrible liar. "I hope you enjoyed your evening," he mutters.

Father Masson points to Alistair's bare neck. "In a hurry to get dressed, were you?" Then he stops, finally noticing the tree leaning up against the wall. "Will you look at that," he says, grinning madly. "Did you two—"

"We'd thought it would be a nice touch," I say, walking up to them. "You like it then?"

Father Masson circles the tree, his face beaming with joy and drunkenness. "It reminds me of when I was a wee little boy, back in Nova Scotia." He looks over at Alistair. "You've had quite a productive day now, haven't you, my dear child?"

"Yes, Father, I had...we had a really good time."

The old priest's eyes meet mine and I can see he's genuinely pleased. "Well, that's terrific," he says, rubbing Alistair's arm. "I'm very glad to hear it." He hiccups and puts his large hands on his haunches. "Will you look at that tree? Frau Eberhart will be delighted." He looks around the room. "After you clean up in here, of course." He turns to me again. "It's late, isn't it?"

Alistair is quick to get my coat.

I wait until Father Masson has settled in his favorite chair in the living room and lean close to Alistair's ear. "I have to see you again. Tell me when."

He glances over at the living room. "You'll help me, right?"

"Yes, I promise. Don't worry. Please, don't worry."

"Help me get out of this," he says, his eyes wild with truth and urgency.

I'm not sure what he means. "*This?*"

"Yes, this." Alistair presses his mouth to my ear. "The church. Help me leave the church, Ryde."

"Father Genet," Masson scolds from the living room. "You need to get to your sleep, lad."

After Alistair has closed the door, I stand there shaken to the bone.

He wants to leave the church.

Chapter Fourteen

They won't allow me in.

"Let me see him!" I yell again, ready to knock Masson down to the floor if I have to. "Get out of my way."

Another priest, this one younger but sterner, with eyes like an angry eagle, comes to the door. "Let him in before he alerts the whole street," he says, over Father Masson. "Good God!" He walks way, his black cassock swooping the ground like a broken wing. "This is a madhouse!"

Father Masson moves out of my way and puts a hand on my shoulder, slowing me down. "Ryde, please, just hold on before you go up there."

I throw my coat in the corner and quickly remove my boots, looking around for Alistair. For a hint as to what is happening here this evening. "Where is he?"

The other priest returns from the kitchen with a glass of water. He walks past me as if I don't exist, his serious face pulled with worry. He begins to mount the steps.

"What's going on? Who's he?"

"He's Father Cornwell." Masson wipes his brow and I see his hand is not too steady. "Father Genet is having a fit. It happens."

A fit. That's what his mother used to call it. "I wanna see him."

"Wait. Just wait a moment." Masson puts his big hand on my chest, pleading with me. "You can't go up there yet. Can't you see? You can't be around him when he's like this."

"Oh, God, what the fuck is going on!" I bolt past him and he tries to grab me, but I run up the stairs. Out of the corner of my eye, I see Eberhart sitting at the edge of a bed, in what appears to be her bedroom. She's wringing her hands, staring out into space, mumbling words. Praying, I suppose.

"Alistair," I call out to him before I've even reached his door.

But the eagle-eyed priest stands in my way. "Don't. In the name of God, don't."

His tone sends a shiver down my back and stops me in my tracks. "What's wrong with him?" I ask meekly. "Please."

"He's...he's not himself." The priest stands in the half-open door, blocking my view and way. "Your presence here will only make things worse, so please, Ryde, is it?"

"Yeah."

"Please," the priest says, "let me calm him down and I promise you—"

"Father Cornwell," Masson interrupts, his sweaty face appearing at the top of the stairs. He's out of breath from the climb, leaning heavily on the banister. "Don't let him in."

"I have no intention to." Cornwell stops, his face turning red. I see Alistair's black eyes peering at me over his shoulder. I've seen those eyes before. Lustful. Raging. Seductive. I look down and see Alistair's hand cupping the priest's groin. Cornwell blinks and spins around. "Get back in there!" he yells to Alistair.

I dart through the door and into the bedroom. The bed is unmade. The window is wide open, letting a cruel and cold wind into the room. Yet Alistair stands near the bed, shirtless, shining with sweat, clad only in his black pants. His hair is undone, falling into his eyes. He's wild and ready for a fight. I glance over at Cornwell. "I've seen him like this before," I tell him, very quietly. "I know him."

"You know this devil!" Cornwell makes the sign of the cross over Alistair's mocking face. "Stay back, you heathen!"

"Shut up," I shout, stepping between him and Alistair. "Jesus Christ, will you stop that already!" I move carefully to Alistair. "Hey you," I say, though his eyes tell me he's not having any of it. "Remember me?"

Alistair comes closer, very close, peering into my eyes. His stare is mocking and hateful. I can feel his fiery breath on my face. He watches me with a perverse smile for a long time and slowly cocks his head.

"Alistair," I breathe, barely recognizing his expression. "It's me."

He jumps back and shouts a word I can't make out. He leaps to the open window, but I lunge for him, with Cornwell behind me, and grab his arm before he makes it out. I hold him tight as he struggles and kicks my shins, biting down into my arm. "Help me with him!" I scream, trying to keep my grasp on his chest.

Masson and Cornwell grab his legs, and the three of us fight to keep him stable, trying to get him into bed. But he's stronger than we are, cursing and spitting and scratching. "I won't let you go," I say into his ear. "I won't let you go, you hear me?" But he won't stop fighting. His chest is slippery with sweat and I'm losing my grip on him. I can't let him get to that window again. What was he going to do? Would he have jumped? Was he trying to escape? "Alistair!" I cry. "Calm down!"

"Hold him, hold him," Father Cornwell says, struggling hard along with Father Masson, but at last, we manage to lay him down over the messy covers.

Masson puts a hand to Alistair's forehead. "He's burning up again," he says, obviously spent from the exertion.

Cornwell rushes out of the room. "I'll get some medication," he shouts.

In bed, Alistair is still, breathing shallow. His eyes are open, but he isn't looking at us. "Bless this child, Lord," Father Masson says, wiping his brow again. "Bless him. Help him. Oh, please, help him." He bows his head and I see him take Alistair's limp hand in his. "Don't let him perish in the fires of hell."

"Enough of that," I snap. "You're not helping." I stare at Father Masson until he looks up at me. "He needs to see a psychiatrist," I say firmly. "Do you understand? He needs help, and not from you or God, or Cornwell, but from a licensed psychiatrist. Someone who understands this disorder."

"No, no." Father Masson shakes his head, looking down at Alistair's frozen face. "Pray for him. That's what you need to do. Pray for him."

"No. I won't pray." I touch Alistair's white-blond hair. "I'll just love him," I say, for myself more than for Masson.

"You think your love is doing him well?" I turn to see Cornwell standing at the foot of the bed. "Do you?" he asks again.

"Yes, I do," I say lamely. I'm very tired from the physical fight with Alistair. I never thought I'd have to hold him down like that.

"Ever since you came back into his life, Father Genet's condition has deteriorated dramatically."

"That's not true," I argue, though I know I won't win. "I just remind him of some very bad things, but he needs those memories, can't you see? He needs them to be whole again. He's created these personalities, these different Alistairs, as a way to cope with what happened to him when he was seventeen."

"Oh, this story again." Father Masson sighs heavily. "Our good friend Ryde believes Father Genet was attacked," he tells Cornwell. "Sexually."

Cornwell crosses himself and briefly shuts his eyes. I can see he's disturbed and surprised. "He never mentioned any such thing, and I've been his spiritual counselor for seven years."

"You'd have to hypnotize him," I whisper. "But you don't believe in that, do you?"

"Ryde," Father Masson says, carefully. "We know how much you care for him, and how dear he is to you, but Father Genet chose the church and we embrace him, fully, with all of his faults and doubts, and we will conquer this... this—"

"It's called a dissociative personality disorder."

"No." Cornwell comes to the bed and touches Alistair's forehead. "There's nothing wrong with his mind. It's his soul we need to fight for."

I've had it with this. "So far, I've seen three personalities," I explain, ignoring their shocked expressions. "There's the boy." I raise my eyes to Masson. "That's the one you prefer, don't you?"

"I don't know what you're talking about."

"And there's the lucid Alistair. He's the one I knew. The man who's struggling to understand himself and why some parts of his life are hidden from him, and I'm telling you right now, he's on to you. He's on to this whole charade you have going on here."

"Be quiet."

"And then there's the Alistair we fought tonight." I look over at Cornwell. "The one I had sex with last week." I don't know why I said it. But I had to. I just had to.

"Blasphemer!" Cornwell cries, his eyes bulging. "Trickster!"

"No, sorry, but it's true."

"You didn't."

"Yes, I did. And he wanted it. Very much. I didn't know it wasn't him. I mean, I didn't know why he'd let me touch him after all these—"

"Get out!" Cornwell grabs my collar, jerking it hard. "Get out!"

"Let go of me."

"Joe," Father Masson orders Father Cornwell, "let go of the lad."

Surprised, Cornwell releases my collar.

"My head," Alistair says softly. "The light."

"Shut the light," Masson says quickly. "Hurry."

I jump up and do as he says. I hurry back to Alistair's side. "Hey, are you okay?"

"Ryde?"

"You had a fit again," Cornwell says in a hard voice. "Took all your clothes off and messed up the bed." He scolds him like a child. "We had to restrain you. You even opened this window and now the whole house is cold. Frau Eberhart's poor old chest is already giving her enough trouble as it is."

"You must pray now, Alistair. You must pray very hard." Father Masson gives him a sad look.

"Of course," Cornwell says, "you'll have to be confined to this room for a week and there will be no sermon from you—"

"Would you stop it?" I look at Cornwell. "You sound like his dad."

"I'm so sorry," Alistair mumbles, sitting up. "I don't...I don't know what happened. I'm so sorry, Father." He looks up at Cornwell with panicked eyes. "I'll pray. I'll do penance."

This is the trigger. He's a child again, trying to please his parents. How disgusting of them. "Hey, you did nothing wrong," I say to Alistair. "You were just acting up because of your migraine."

"Ryde, you've caused enough trouble here tonight." Cornwell points to the door. "I'd like you to leave, and about what you insinuated before, about Father's Genet's chastity, I'd like to have your word you won't insist on repeating that awful tale to members of our parish."

"What story?" Alistair looks at me expectantly.

"Don't you fucking dare, Cornwell," I say, threateningly and under my breath. "Can't you see he's a boy right now? If you repeat a word of what I said—"

"It's nothing, child," Father Masson says, patting Alistair's leg. "You need to rest." Masson looks into my eyes. "What have you done?"

"What's going on, Ryde? Aren't we friends anymore?"

"Come with me," I say, desperately. "Just come with me, Alistair. Tonight. Let me get you out of here. Out of this bat cave with these vampires."

"Ryde, oh, what are you saying?" He shakes his head, panicked. "You can't talk like that. These are my fathers, my family."

"Come with me. Please."

"You should go now," Cornwell says, justified. "You've done enough harm for one day."

What can I do? What can I say?

Vanquished for now, I bend to Alistair's head and kiss his cheek. "I love you. Remember that."

Alistair looks up at me. He's clearly surprised. "I...I love you too, Ryde," he says, but the words mean nothing to him. He's just a polite boy saying them to a distant relative.

In the door, I give the room a final look. Cloaked in black, the two priests sit at his side, murmuring to him. For a moment, I see only two vultures looking down at a meal of youth.

Then it comes to me.

There's the boy, what the priests believe is Alistair's pure and threatened soul. There's the lewd, sexually charged Alistair—the body he can't inhabit because of his disgust for how it was used. And then there's the lucid Alistair. The thinker. The rational being struggling to keep himself together.

The mind, the spirit and the body.

The Holy Trinity.

Chapter Fifteen

The street is crowded with shoppers scurrying for last-minute Christmas gifts.

My mood is rotten. I haven't slept all night again. All I can think of since last night is Alistair or getting drunk. Pushing through the crowd on the sidewalk, I search for the bright-red neon sign of Marlowe's Tavern. I come to the place soon enough and peer into its dark, wet window. Through the glass, I spot Masson right away. He's sitting at the bar, looking into a pint. Inside the dingy bar, I quickly pick up the scent of old beer and humidity. A few men sit at tables, but none of them even look my way. The barman is a tall, slightly bent man with a gray comb-over and a sullen face. The place is darkly lit, except for the bar, which is loaded with Christmas lights, red and gold. At least they've spared the patrons the usual Christmas songs, and instead the jukebox, an old antique-looking thing, is playing "Mustang Sally".

"Well, this is definitely different from the presbytery," I say right away, slipping into the seat next to Father Masson.

He nods and drinks. I spot the vodka bottle sitting full on the shelf right in front of me. I almost had a drink last night after I got home from the presbytery. But *almost* is good enough for me when it comes down to holding my promise.

Father Masson drains his glass and pushes it out of sight. "Perhaps it wasn't a good idea to meet here," he says, glancing my way. "I forgot about your recent battle with the bottle."

"Don't worry about it. I'm still winning." I motion to the barman and ask him for a glass of Perrier, extra lime. "So," I say to Father Masson, looking him over. He looks as terrible as I do. His eyes are swollen and his clerical shirt is all wrong with its shirttails hanging out. "Is Alistair still sleeping?"

I spoke with Alistair today. He didn't remember last night. He was dead tired though, confused out of his wits. He cried on the phone, begged me to help him. He's afraid of tumors and brain cancer and demons. I told him it was none of those things. I finally said the words to him.

Dissociative personality disorder.

Alistair was shocked, but quickly started asking me questions about it. He took notes, yet I know he's struggling, caught between reason and faith. I don't know how he's going to process all this. I don't know what it would feel like to be so divided. I want to help him.

"Yes, poor lad," Masson says. "Slept all day. Probably won't open an eye till morning."

"Let's get down to it, Father." I sip my cool drink. It's not vodka, but it'll do. "Tell me, have you decided, yes or no?"

He doesn't say anything, just stares at his joined hands on the bar top.

"Yes or no?" I need him on my side. I need him to help me with Alistair. Cornwell is a lost cause. He'll never choose rationality over his esoteric beliefs of demon possession and haunted rooms. But Masson, yes, Masson admits he's been questioning Alistair's mental health for the last two years, and has kept a record of his personality changes and what may trigger them. He's seen the same three I have. I'm here for his word that he'll let me take Alistair out of Cornwell's claws for a while and allow me to slowly introduce the idea of seeing a psychiatrist to him.

Masson finally sighs heavily. "You know his torments could be the work of the Devil, and only God can release him from—"

"Don't start again, and you half believe that yourself. He needs therapy." I dare a look at his face. "You know part of him, the greater part of him, wants to leave the church anyway. You've seen him try to jump out the window last night."

"He wasn't himself."

"Yes, he was. Can't you see? All of his personalities, all of them, are parts of him. Whether he's a child reciting his well-learned prayers to please his father, or a wild sexual beast using his beauty to control us, or Alistair searching for the truth, he's always him. But you don't listen."

"And what do you plan to do, Ryde? Even if you do take him away from the church, from the safety of its bosom, what then? That's all the lad knows. What shall he do with his life then? After your marvelous therapy cures him, what happens to the boy?"

"I don't know… But he'll decide. He'll be capable of deciding, at least."

"And what if this doctor only causes him further damage? What if waking these memories you insist exist, these memories of an event so terrifying, so vile, the boy had to split into different people in order to sustain it, what if they only shatter him into more pieces? Smaller pieces. Aren't you afraid for him, Ryde?"

Of course I'm scared. I don't know if I'm doing the right thing, but Alistair asked me to help him. He begged me. "I need to see this through. I need to spend time alone with him, away from the presbytery, away from you. Cornwell. The parishioners. Everyone. I need to take him back to where we grew up. Can't you give him that?" I turn in my seat and look Masson straight in the eyes. "After everything he's given the church? His youth. His soul. His heart."

"He had such promise for the church. Such promise."

"He can serve God better when he's healed. And who says the only way to God is through rituals and churches? Man, Alistair could do so much more for people out of that damn priest uniform."

"You can't understand. You don't have his faith."

"I don't? How do you think I can sit here in a room full of bottles and stay sober? You think I do this alone?" I shake my head, my own words rattling me. I never thought of that before. Maybe someone up there is giving me strength. "Look, I don't care what you tell people. Tell 'em he's taken some time off. Tell 'em he's visiting a sick relative in the states. Tell 'em what you will, but tomorrow morning, I'm picking him up and he's coming to stay with me for two weeks. Two weeks is all I ask."

"You're arrogant to think two weeks is enough to heal years of—"

"It's a beginning. Weren't you the one who said every story has a Genesis? Well, let us have ours."

Father Masson holds my stare, but I think I'm winning. "Cornwell won't believe it," he says gently. "He'll know I'm lying to cover up for you."

"Well, I'm sure it's not the first lie you'll tell." I look around us. "Unless this is the home of the famous Mrs. Allbright who fixes your meals on Thursday evenings?"

"You don't have to resort to blackmailing, my poor child. I've already made my peace with God."

"Good for you. Now let Alistair make peace with himself."

"Is it true?"

"Is what true?"

"That you and Father Genet, that day, that you—"

"Yes, we were together that way." I won't lie about it. I'm not ashamed. "I didn't know what was happening, but I wanted him so badly. I'd waited for so long." I look into my glass and drain it. "It won't happen again. Not until he's himself." I'm speaking the truth. I've made that decision.

Masson smiles grimly. "I woke up to see him standing at the foot of my bed last night."

"What?" My blood turns.

"Don't fret. I led him back to bed. He was very tame, like a child. As if he wasn't quite sure where he was. Who he was."

"Did he say anything?"

"Yes. He asked me if he could make me a shirt."

I remember Alistair sitting in a pool of light, his fingers working the needle and thread. "He used to sew. He used to make clothes, curtains, quilts. He made me a shirt once. It was blue. It was perfect."

"He never spoke about this at the seminary."

I stand and put a hand on Father Masson's robust shoulder. "See, there are many things you don't know about him."

"If he leaves with you tomorrow morning, will he ever come back to us?"

I step back to the entrance. "It's out of our hands, Father."

Father Masson nods gravely. "Amen."

As I walk away, I hear him ordering another pint of black beer.

Christmas morning, I stand at the presbytery door and give the cab driver a reassuring look. This shouldn't take long, if all goes accordingly. Alistair has agreed to a holiday from the presbytery, the church and all of his priestly responsibilities, which I never ask about.

My mother thinks it's too much, too soon. She keeps telling me I'm going to break more than a wax crayon this time if I insist on drawing Alistair back to life all by myself.

I don't care about any of that. I just want to be alone with him for days and nights. Can't we just be alone? There was always someone watching. Always.

Frau Eberhart pulls the door open. She nods and steps aside to let me in. She pats my arm and pushes a wrapped box into my hands. "Merry Christmas," she says in her thick German accent. "For you. Open."

I'm so shocked, I can't even unwrap the gift.

"Open."

I look around for Masson or Alistair. "*Danke*," I say, hoping the word did indeed mean thanks. "Alistair? Father Genet?"

She nods briskly again and raises a thick and sturdy finger to the stairs. "Making suitcase." She calls out his name, and when she does, I realize how sweet her voice is when she speaks to him. She must really care about Alistair.

I unwrap the gift and find a pair of black wool socks inside. I crack a smile at her. "Very good, thank you." I take a step to her, but she stiffens and tucks a gray strand of hair into her bun.

"You're velcome," she says. She seems on edge, ready to burst into tears.

At last, Alistair comes down to us. He's wearing his priest uniform, complete with annoying white tab collar. His face is very tense. "You're early," he says, setting his suitcase down by the stairs. He looks so nervous, so unsure.

"Father Masson wanted to come down and say hello, but he's deep in prayer."

I have a feeling he's praying for a miracle cure for hangovers.

"The cab is waiting." I look into Alistair's eyes. "Are you ready?"

"Yes." He looks over at Eberhart. "I'll see you in two weeks." He smiles anxiously. "If you need anything or if there should be an emergency, you know how to reach me, of course."

She just watches him with adulating eyes. Then, she grabs his face and kisses his cheeks. She's mumbling words in German, speaking frantically into his ear. Alistair's face reddens and he leans back from her insisting embrace. At last, she lets him go and crosses herself, briefly shutting her eyes. She walks over to the suitcase and brings it closer to the door.

"I guess we should go," I say, a little shaken by her emotional display. "Come on." Alistair is still flushed and seems lost. I pick up his suitcase and open the door. Good, the cab is still there. "Are you coming?" I ask him, my voice betraying the doubt I feel in this moment.

Doubt, the nemesis of faith.

"Yes," he whispers, gazing around the presbytery entrance. "I'm coming."

When I shut the door, I hear Eberhart shout with triumph or joy.

"What did she say to you in there?"

Against the white sky, Alistair's eyes are blacker and brighter than ever. "She said…she said, 'Go and be happy now. Peace be with you'."

Chapter Sixteen

Pressing the phone between my shoulder and cheek, I check my reflection in the bathroom mirror and tighten the knot of my blue tie. Not bad. Not bad at all. I've lost some weight since I stopped boozing, and I look a little like my old self. I can still pass for twenty-seven.

For a brief moment, I think about Shay. About how he's doing. I heard through a friend of ours he's seeing someone. A writer. Another broke freelancer.

Oh, my beautiful Shay, will you ever learn?

"What time will you be here?" my mother asks on the phone. She sounds agitated but still under control. She's been cooking all evening and part of last night. "God, we haven't done a real Christmas dinner in years," she cries. "My kitchen looks like an old Star Trek episode, and the girls aren't helping at all. I forgot you had to actually teach teenagers how to cook before asking them to fry potatoes."

I smile at her good-humored nature and, walking out of the bathroom, glance over to my bedroom door. Alistair is still locked up in there, getting ready with the door closed. "I don't know. We'll probably be there around four." I flick the television off and sit on the edge of the couch. My stomach is all knots.

My mother picks up on my anxiety, though I haven't even said a word about it. "Baby, are you sure he's ready to come over and see all of us? I mean, Ryde, he hasn't even been out of the presbytery for more than a few hours."

"I'm playing it by ear, Mom. Just following my instincts." I rub at my face and check the door again. Still closed. What is he doing in there? "He won't be any more ready tomorrow or the day after. And he says he wants to see you all.

He has such fond memories of you."

"He really doesn't remember anything else then."

"Sometimes I think he does, and that a part of him just plays along. Like there's someone inside him watching all this. That's the guy I need to connect to. The one I love."

"How is he with you?"

"He's…he's very kind and trusting, as if we've never been apart. But there's a part of him I can't access. I feel it when we touch. Well, he doesn't let me touch him much."

"Patience."

I sigh and look at the door again. "I know."

"I sure can't wait to see that boy's beautiful face up close again. I've missed him so much."

We're quiet for a long time, each of us lost in our own pasts.

"So, they just let him leave," she says, after a while. "Just like that."

"Masson and Cornwell know the kind of scandal this could cause. Shit, a priest with a severe mental disorder? You know the kind of headlines that would make these days? A *gay* priest for that matter." I look over at the bedroom door once more and lower my voice. "Bottom line is, Jamie says we need to get him into therapy very quickly before he does any harm to himself." A chill runs through me. I hate the very thought of Alistair hurting himself, but that's why he's here.

"What about your work? What does your bank account look like right now?"

I laugh. "It reads the same as a thermometer hanging somewhere in a Siberian gulag."

"Well, don't worry about that." She's using her serious, accounting tone, and I love her more than ever. "Your dad and I stuffed a little Christmas cheer into an envelope for you."

"Oh, Mom, you didn't have to. I'll get by. I've got some work lined up next week."

"Hush now." She sighs. "We're proud of you, that's all. Now, hurry up and get over here, you two. I can hardly sit still."

"I love you," I say, and feel it deep inside. "You're the best, Mom."

After we've hung up, I knock on the bedroom door. "Alistair? Can I come in?"

"Yes," he calls out. I find him standing by the window with his back to me. "Are you all right?"

He stares out the window with a strained expression. "I don't have any shirts for dinner parties."

"Let me get a good look at you."

He turns around and opens his hands. "Black. All black."

"Yeah, I see that. Well, do you wanna go as a priest or as a person?"

"A priest is a person. They're not mutually exclusive."

I touch his black shirt. "Black is so serious. It's Christmas."

"I haven't worn anything but black shirts for as long as I can remember."

I slide my closet door open. I'm not a dressy type of guy, but I do own a few shirts, except I'm six inches taller than he is, and my shoulders are much wider.

"I have this." He's looking into his open suitcase on the bed. "My mother sent it to me before she died." He plucks out a white shirt and carefully slips it out of its plastic case. "Never wore it."

"Put it on, Genet."

He smirks and shakes his head at me. "Fine, but leave."

I rummage through my closet for a decent black tie and hand it to him. "I'll be in the living room."

I pace and wait. I've been trying to be cool with him. We'll get through it. But really, I have no idea what I'm doing. I took him out of the presbytery and away from everything he knows and he just followed me, never really put up a fight. It's like he doesn't have a genuine idea of who he is and what he wants. What is best for him.

I know. I know what is best for him. *Me.*

But am I enough?

The door opens and I spin around, catching sight of the most beautiful man I've ever seen. Out of his priest clothes, Alistair's classical beauty is unleashed, powerful, almost sinful. "No?" he asks, wide-eyed. "Terrible, right?"

I know I'm standing there with my mouth hanging open. "You look stunning," I finally say, walking to him. I put my hand on his face and he doesn't recoil from the touch. He leans his face into my palm and stares into my eyes. "Sometimes," he says, "when you look at me like that, I feel like you see something in me I thought only God could."

I kiss him on the lips, and for the first time since we've met again, he kisses me back. But he quickly pulls away, obviously a little frazzled about it.

"Alistair," I say gently, taking his hand. "A kiss is safe with me. Always."

He understands. His face brightens. "Do we leave soon? I can't wait to see your parents again. And our old street. Your house and—"

"We can leave right now if you want to. But listen to me. If any time during this trip, if you start feeling anxious or if you remember something, or maybe want to leave because—"

"I'll be okay, Ryde." He smiles reassuringly. "I'll be with you."

How I wish it were that easy.

"Turn right here," I tell the cab driver, a man with the verbal skills of a talk show radio host. He hasn't stopped talking since we left my apartment. At least the man kept my mind off what lies ahead: my first sober Christmas dinner.

And Alistair's return to our old neighborhood after fourteen years of absence.

"Very beautiful street," the driver says, his smart eyes meeting mine in the rearview mirror. "Many trees and decorations."

I agree and look over at Alistair. He's been very quiet in the last minutes. He's staring out at the mounds of snow lining the street, *our* street, and at the houses' windows, which are glittering with lights. "I remember this," he says, almost to himself. "My old house was here."

Now I'm starting to lose my nerve. Was this a good idea?

The driver pulls up into my parents' driveway and I see my sisters spying out at us through the living room window. The Christmas tree is huge and where it always used to be. I check the meter and pay the driver anxiously. "Thanks so much. Merry Christmas."

After the taxi has driven off, Alistair and I stand in the driveway, face-to-face. "You look really nice, Ryde," he whispers. "You're handsome."

Handsome.

I take his hand in mine. "How you feeling?"

He looks around at the front yard, the steps, the street, the house. He frowns. "Have you ever had surgery?"

"Yeah," I say, very low. Surgery on my brain. But he doesn't know I spent months in the hospital after Craving's Creek. I haven't told him about that yet. "I had my tonsils taken out," I lie.

"They operated on me and removed my appendix when I was twenty-three. When I touch my stomach, there's this kind of numbness." He stares at the end of the street, where his house used to stand. "It's the vague memory of the knife," he says. "We remember everything. Everything is inscribed in our cells. We have our own scriptures, but I guess scientists call it DNA."

I never saw it like that. "Is that how you feel right now? Is something in you remembering?"

"Ryde," my father calls out, interrupting us. He's standing in the open door. "You boys coming in or what?" He grins and motions for us to come up. He's had a few gin and tonics, I can tell.

It feels strange and good to hug my father. "Hey, Dad," I say, leaning away from him. "How you been?"

"Never better." He lets go of my shoulders and looks over at Alistair. "Wow, would you look at you. It's good to see you, son. Very good."

My nerves are so raw, I feel like sobbing. I swallow it all down and we enter the warm house. It looks like a Christmas movie in here. As we're hanging our coats, Summer and Winter greet us. Summer is the first to welcome Alistair. She looks beautiful in her green satin top and elegant black pants. Winter is more reserved, wearing a black blouse with a touch of white on the collar. Her dark hair is pulled up into a high ponytail and she isn't wearing any makeup or jewelry. "Hi," she says, shaking Alistair's hand. "Nice to meet you."

"We've met before, Winter," he says, as if they're alone in the room together. "I remember you." He holds her hand for a long time. "You're stunning now."

My standoffish sister is flustered. "Well, I was just a baby back then," she mutters, clearly affected by Alistair's beauty and presence. So then, there is one thing my sister and I have in common. We both like blonds.

We stand around the entrance for a while, the four of us chatting about the snowstorm we had this week and the girls' trip to Paris coming up in March, and I'm feeling more and more at ease. But then my mother appears at the end of the hall and everyone stops talking, stops moving. I don't even think we're breathing. We all know what this moment means for her. For Alistair.

"Hi, Mom," I say, after a few long seconds of silence. She hasn't moved from her spot. "You remember Alistair."

She only stares at him from the end of the short hall. I turn to see Alistair staring right back at her. Summer and Winter feel the emotion in the room and step back a little, retreating to the staircase.

"Hello, Mrs. Kent." Alistair takes a step forward.

But my mother hides her face and runs off, back into the kitchen. "I'm so sorry," she cries. "Just give me a second!"

"Hold on, okay?" I pat his shoulder and dash for the kitchen. I find my mother in my father's arms, her face buried into his shirt. "Mom—"

"Just give her a second," my father says, stroking my mother's hair. "It's all right, darling," he keeps telling her. "It's all right."

"I never thought I'd see him again," she says into my father's neck. "Never thought he'd make it past his twentieth birthday. Always thought he'd end his life." She pulls back and wipes her eyes, her nose. "But he made it. He made it. And I don't know how."

"God helped me." Alistair is standing near us, a few steps away. "God saw me through."

"Oh, Alistair, my sweet little boy." She smiles through her tears. "Come here, please."

Finally, they hug, and I have to look away or I'll be a mess. I run myself a glass of water and drink slowly, looking out the small kitchen window above the sink. My father puts his hand on my shoulder. "How you been holding up?" he asks, close to my ear.

I turn and face him. We haven't really talked in the last years. It was my drinking. I know that. He couldn't stomach it. Couldn't stand to watch me throw my life away. Yet he never said anything derogatory to me. And I understand his way. My father didn't say much to me, but he didn't have to. He always taught me by example. He didn't tell me how to be a man. He showed me.

"I haven't had a drink in months."

His eyes sparkle with pride and relief. "I knew you'd come to that."

"Did you? Did you always believe?"

"Yeah. Every second of the day. But I won't lie to you. It was tough, Ryde. It was tough for all of us."

"I'm sorry."

"That's yesterday." He goes to the fridge and pulls out two Cokes. He opens the cans and hands one to me. "Cheers."

Alistair and my mother are still whispering to each other, touching like old lovers. She can't keep her hands off his face, and he's radiant, basking in her attention and motherly affection.

The girls come storming into the kitchen. "When do we eat?" they ask in unison.

My mother ushers us out of the kitchen, but takes hold of Alistair's arm. "You stay and help me," she says with a wink. "We have a lot of catching up to do."

I give her a discreet look, hoping she'll catch its meaning. I don't want her to bring up anything that might rattle him right now.

She nods seriously. Of course, she understands. She's the only one who ever did.

"Will you two be all right in your old room?" My mothers hands me a pile of blankets. "We can make up a bed for him in the guest room. You know, if you think he'll be more—"

"This is fine." I look back into my bedroom. Alistair is standing at my window, looking out. "Dinner was so fantastic, Mom." I squeeze her hand. "It was exactly the way I wanted it to be. Thank you."

"He seemed to have such a good time." She peers over my shoulder at him. "Then slowly his mood changed, didn't it?"

We had a great dinner. Conversation was easy and warm. But somewhere between the last course and dessert, Alistair began to retreat into himself. I could see it happening. I'd catch him staring off into space, his eyes vacant. He couldn't follow the conversation. Then he disappeared into the washroom for a long time, and when I went to check up on him, I found him having an anxiety attack. He was shaking and confused, didn't know what he was doing in my house. My father fixed him a stiff drink and we moved to the living room, where we exchanged a few gifts, and slowly, Alistair seemed to come back to us.

The evening has taken its toll on his nerves and I don't feel too steady either. I need rest. I need quiet. I need to think.

"We'll be all right." I take the blankets from her. "It's been a long day. Wake me up tomorrow morning, okay? I wanna help you clean up."

"Don't worry about that." She looks into the room again. "Good night, Alistair."

He doesn't hear her. "Good night, Mom." I hug her and watch her walk away to her bedroom, where my father is already passed out and snoring loudly. I shut the door behind me and drop the sheets on my old bed. It's a double bed, but worn down, and I have a feeling we'll both be waking up sore tomorrow morning. "I'm gonna take a quick shower," I whisper.

He doesn't hear me or acknowledge my voice.

"Alistair?" I go to him and stand at his side. I follow his gaze to the end of the street. "They tore it down a few years ago. Your house used to be—"

"Do you see him there?"

"Who?" A chill runs down my back. "See who?"

He lifts his chin, showing me, but I don't see what he means.

"Look, do you see him there? Right there, in the window." He slowly and hesitantly raises his hand and waves at someone. He smiles. "Hm, he sees me too." He waves again, this time more confidently. "Hello, little boy," he says to the invisible.

I decide to play along. "What's he doing there?" I look out the window at the dark street and try to see what he sees. His house maybe. That yellow window shining like a tiny third eye. "What's he look like? I can't see him very well."

Alistair stares unflinchingly, as if afraid to blink. "He's just a boy. A little boy."

"Do you think he's okay?" I want to touch him but don't.

"Yeah, he's okay. Just can't sleep. His mother left for church."

"Where's his father?"

"In his shower, washing everything off."

I feel my heart begin to pound. I need help with him. What if I say the wrong thing? For a moment, I debate on calling Jamie at home. But it's one o'clock in the morning on Christmas. "Do you think we should ask the little boy to come over?"

"No." Alistair's voice is suddenly hard. "Leave him there. He's been really bad. He's punished."

"How can he be bad when he's just a little boy?"

"Because he's a fucking little tramp." He turns his eyes to mine and I see the fire in them. "Leave him there. Let him rot."

I can handle this. This is the man I love. I know him. I know who he is. "Whatever you say. Guess you're the boss, right?" Trying to hide my anxiety, I turn for the bed and start making it. What do I do? What do I say?

Alistair is right at my back, his hand sliding down over my crotch. "Are you scared?"

I don't move. I'm not going to do this, not going to make love with him when he's like this. "Hey, my parents are right in the next room."

"So what?" He bites my shoulder and grabs my chest, squeezing my nipples hard.

"Whoa, there, cowboy." I turn around and push him gently off me. "Take it easy."

He laughs, throwing his head back. Then he unfastens his tie and slips it off, watching me with a coy smile. He slowly unbuttons his shirt and slides it off his white shoulders. His eyes are mean, full of defiance. "Like what you see? Get your rocks off by fucking the priest?"

"Stop it," I mutter, looking away.

"You don't want me to stop." I hear his belt. His zipper. "All you want is to be inside the priest."

I don't know what I'm doing but I follow my instincts. I turn around and face him. He's naked, a sliver of light touching him. He takes my breath away, but I won't let him see it. "I'm not interested in the priest," I say, as bravely as I can. "Or you for that matter. Or the little boy rotting in that house." I see the change in his face and press on. "Right now, what I want is for you to lie down with me here, Alistair." Then I realize every time I've seen this personality— the seductive and spiteful Alistair—he's never said but a few words. But he's speaking to me now. That must mean something. Improvement. "You're very beautiful," I say, touching his face. He grabs my hand and tugs it down to his crotch. "No," I say, moving my hand away. "I don't want that." I touch his face again. "No. Okay? No."

He laughs again, but his eyes have lost their hateful glow, and he seems confused. So lost. He moves back from me. I watch him, waiting. He's walking around the room, mumbling words to himself. I can't make out what he's saying. Then, he stops and glares at me.

He stretches his arms out, making his body into a cross.

And I see he's my drawing. That's what I drew.

I drew him crucified, but not to a cross. No, I drew him crucified to a man. I remember drawing it that night, furiously. Yes I drew a boy too, a boy looking up at Alistair the Raped and Crucified. A boy holding on to his bloody ankles. And there was another man on my drawing—a silent black figure watching it all from afar. The priest. The witness.

Alistair's eyes are turned upward now at the ceiling. He's posing for me. I watch him, wanting to yell for help, but I'm too transfixed by the pain on his face. He seems to be telling me everything in this moment, everything that happened to him in that barn. It's all there on his contorted face, and I almost feel my own loins being split with violence. The silver of light shines on his body, and I can see every invisible wound that monster inflicted on him.

It's too much for me. I can't. I can't take it.

Broken, I sit on the edge of the bed and hide my face in my hands.

He's making sounds. Moans and groans. I can't look. I don't have it in me to look.

Then I hear a thump and my hands fall at my sides. He's kneeling, facing me with his head bowed. "Forgive me, Father, for I have sinned," he repeats over and over. "Forgive me, Father, for I have sinned." His voice is full of torment. "Forgive me, Father, for I have sinned—"

"Oh, God, Alistair, stop." I put my hands on his head. "Please, stop. It's okay. It's all right." But he keeps going. Chanting the prayer like a lament, louder and louder. He's going to wake my parents. My sisters will hear him. "Baby, hey, come on now, it's okay." I stroke his pale hair. "Shh, you're forgiven. You're forgiven."

After a moment, his voice loses its strength and his words begin to get tangled. He looks up at me and I see the panic in his eyes. He glances down at himself and back to me. "What?"

"No, it's okay." I take him by the shoulders. "We're okay."

"I'm naked, Ryde." He covers himself with a hand. "What?"

"No, look, it was a lot for you to see my family again, to see my house. Your old street—"

"Oh, I can't." He looks around, despairing. "I can't do this anymore. No, I can't. I don't want to. I can't live like this."

"Don't you give up on me. You can't. You don't have the right." I lean my head to his. "You have no idea the progress that you're making. Please, Alistair, please. Let me help you. Let me take you to see a doctor."

"A psychiatrist? No, Ryde. I don't want to." He stands and looks around for his clothes. "Don't make me. They'll put me away. They'll give me medication and it'll make me worse, I know it."

"Calm down." I hand him his underwear. "Don't get worked up again or you'll have another—"

"Another fit!" he yells and covers his mouth. "Oh, I'm sorry. I'm so sorry."

"Jesus Christ, Alistair!" I grab his head again, forcing eye contact. "You're gonna be okay, do you hear me? Look at me."

He shakes his head. "No, no, I can't. I'm crazy—I'm crazy."

"You're not crazy. You've been hurt real bad and we just need to fix you."

"You can't fix me, Ryde. Can't you see?"

"I don't care."

"You say this now, but how long can you love a man like me?"

"Put me to the test. You put God to the test every day, and He loves you, right? He pushes on, doesn't He? So, you put me to the test and see how I compare."

He stares at me for a long time. "Oh, Ryde," he says at last. "What happened to me when we were young? You know, don't you?"

"Of course I know. But I don't wanna talk about it right now. Not right now. Please, baby, let's just lie down and try to sleep. I'm done. I'm beat."

"I know. You're only human."

"Come here." I lie down and pull him to me. "Let me hold you. Let me give you a little human touch." I try to be humorous, but I can barely manage a wink.

In bed, he nestles close to me. He's naked from the waist up, and the feel of his skin on mine is my private version of heaven. "What am I gonna do if I leave the church?" he asks.

"You've already left the church. You're lying half-naked in my arms."

"Ryde, you know we'll never be able to have sex. You know that, right?"

I shut my eyes and think about the afternoon we spent in my bed together. "Never is a big word."

"Because I'm dead from the waist down," he whispers. "You have to know that. I've never had…I can't…I mean, I don't get aroused."

I stroke his hair, holding him tight against me. "That's bullshit."

"You don't believe me." He looks up at me. "I should know if I'm impotent or not."

"Alistair, I just need you to trust me, okay? Just trust me. There's nothing wrong with you mechanically. It's just in here." I rub his head.

"Why was I naked? Tell me."

"You wanted to have sex."

"I've done it before, haven't I?"

I freeze up, not sure of what to say.

"It was you then."

"What do you mean?"

He puts his head on my shoulder again. "Don't get upset, all right? One day, about a month or two months ago, I woke up from a nap and I was sore inside. There was, well, there was, you know, sperm *inside* me."

"Well, who the hell d'you think it was?"

"Father Cornwell."

"What?" I sit up. "You tell me right now, did that old fucker ever get in your pants?"

"No, no, no. I just thought… I don't know. I don't know what I thought."

"Man, I need a drink. A shrink. *Something*."

"Stop it." He gently pulls me down again. "Calm down… But tell me, was it you?"

"Of course it was me." I put my arm around him. "Yes, it was me," I say, more softly. "And it was you too, but just a different you. So see, don't talk to me about impotence, Alistair."

"I'm so confused," he says, into my neck. "I'm so tired, so sick of it all."

He's crying again and his tears only strengthen my resolve. I'm going to get him through this. "I want it to stop. Just please make it stop. I can't go on like this, Ryde. I just can't. It's not a life. I don't know how to make things make sense anymore."

"I'm here," I whisper, and spend the night holding him, listening to his heartbreaking prayers.

Finally, when the sun starts to rise, I turn to see him sleeping, his eyes jumping under their lids.

But I can't rest.

I'm sitting at the kitchen table, drowsy and bleary-eyed, trying to work. Everyone is still asleep in the house, including Alistair. It's ten o'clock, but I haven't slept since yesterday. I've cleaned up the dining room and kitchen, and I'm on my fourth coffee. What am I going to do about Alistair? If he refuses to see a doctor, I won't be able to hold him together for much longer. This disorder is wearing him down. I'm afraid for him.

Terrified actually.

I'm alone against all of his demons, and there are many. What about mine?

Next to my laptop, my cell phone rings. When I see Sheryl's number flashing on the screen, I jump out of my chair and quickly answer her.

"Hi there," she says, right away. "Did I wake you?"

"Sheryl, I'm so sorry about the things I said."

"No, Ryde, I'm the one who's sorry. I should have been so much more supportive, but you know I was scared. I didn't know if we could make it sober together, but I didn't even try."

"I missed you so much. You have no idea."

"I missed you too." In the background, I hear Peaches talking.

"How's the little princess doing?"

"Oh, she was so spoiled yesterday. My parents went a little nuts."

"You went to your parents?" Sheryl hasn't done a family gathering in years. She and her mother have been estranged since Peaches's birth.

"Yes. I'm in their house right now actually. Me and Peaches slept in my old bed last night."

"Really? Shit, guess where I am?"

"No, really?"

"Yeah, I'm right across from your house." I walk to the front door and open it. The morning is white, crisp, sunny. "Hello there." Across the street, Peaches and Sheryl stand in the open door. Peaches screams out to me. I hang up and put my boots and coat on, crossing over to them. When I come up the steps, I pause, overcome with relief and emotion. This is my blood sister. My Sheryl. "Hey," I say, climbing the last step.

Peaches jumps into my arms. "Uncle Ryde!"

Sheryl tucks a strand of her hair behind her ear and watches on. She's in her pink flannel robe, and though she isn't wearing any makeup, she looks better than ever. Fresh and rested. "How you been, handsome?" She touches the edge of my coat. "You look amazing. Tired, but amazing."

We hug for a long time, not saying a word.

"So, how was dinner with the family?" she asks, stepping out of my arms. Peaches runs back inside for her boots and coat.

"It was good. Nice. You know, pretty sane." I scratch my head. "Alistair came too."

"Really now. So you and him...it's official? You're dating a priest?"

"Pretty much, yeah." I laugh and grab Peaches as she runs out. "Why don't we make a snowman with the little princess and I'll catch you up on everything, all right?"

She cocks a brow. "All right. Lemme get my coat and cigarettes. 'Cause I have a feeling this is gonna be intense."

"Hello?" I walk into the quiet house. "Where's everybody?" I check my watch. It's noon. They can't be sleeping still. "Mom?" As I take my coat off, through the window, I see the morbidly obese snowman Sheryl and I built with Peaches's help. The man looks a little like Don Corleone with a cowboy hat.

Peaches wanted a cowboy snowman. We even put Sheryl's old Screaming Eagle red leather boots on him.

"Hello?" I enter the silent kitchen. Seconds later, I catch sight of Summer, Winter and Alistair in the backyard. They're sitting in their coats, chatting around the snow-covered table. I slide the patio door open. "What are you guys doing out here?"

Alistair smiles at me. "Talking."

"I see." I wink at Summer. "Where's Mom and Dad?"

Winter looks over at me. She's wearing a black bomber jacket. "Boxing Day. You know how they get."

"Wait a minute, isn't that my jacket you have on? I had one just like it when I was seventeen."

"Yeah," she says, looking down at it. "I found it in your closet last year."

"Well, it looks good on you. You can have it."

"Looks like she already owns it." Alistair laughs. "Where were you?"

"Across the street, at Sheryl's place. She's visiting her parents, and her daughter is with her too. Do you remember Sheryl?"

Alistair thinks for a few seconds. "Yes, I remember her. She was a dramatic kind of girl with a lot of friends and she used to throw parties."

"She still does."

"You dated her."

My sisters look up at me, both of them surprised.

"No, Alistair. I never dated Sheryl. Or any girl for that matter."

"Oh." He searches the snow for an answer. A memory.

"She'd love to see you again. She was wondering about lunch. Could be nice to go out for brunch, no?"

"I was thinking we'd do something else."

"Whatever you want," I say, seeing the worried look on his face.

Winter stands and walks past me into the house. "I'm a little cold. Aren't you cold, Sum?" She squeezes my arm. "By the way," she says into my ear, "don't let this one get away. He's amazing. Lucky you."

My sisters are really coming around. When they've gone back inside, I step out on the terrace and shut the door behind me.

"You're in your socks." Alistair points to my feet. "You'll get sick. Put some shoes on."

I pull up a chair next to his and sit. "Gimme your hands." I take his hands and gently put them on my thighs. "There. Now I'm hot."

He looks down at his hands on my thighs and moves them a little higher, high enough to send a shockwave of desire through me. "Ryde," he says, looking into my eyes, "I want to get better." He leans in and kisses me on the mouth. His lips taste like coffee. "I wanna be with you, Ryde. I want us to be together again."

"And I wanna be with you. So much."

"I'm really scared."

"I know, baby, I know."

His hands move up a little more. "I don't think I'm meant to be a priest, but I don't think I know anything about myself, really."

"Do you love me?" I ask, querying him with serious eyes.

"Yes, I do. I love you with all my soul."

"Okay, so that's one thing you know about yourself."

"You're right." He leans back. "I want to see him. I want to see Dr. Scarborough."

I wasn't prepared for this. This is huge. "Are you sure? Positive?"

"I want to see him." Alistair nods seriously and looks away at the yard. "Today."

"Today?"

"Yes, today. Can you arrange it? I'm lucid. I'm myself. I don't know how long that will last."

I stand. Take my phone out. "Let me call him."

Alistair blinks. "Thank you," he whispers.

Jamie answers on the second ring. "Ryde? Are you okay?" In the back, I can hear voices. He's at home with his family.

Alistair looks over at me. In his eyes, I see urgency and desperation. I see hope too.

"Dr. Scarborough," I say, taking Alistair's cold hand in mine, "I'm calling about Alistair."

"So, this is it. He wants to see me."

"Yes."

Jamie takes a short breath on the line. "Then meet me at my clinic in an hour. Let's not waste this opportunity."

Corpus Corporis

Chapter Seventeen

Inside the waiting room, I stand at the window, looking down at the vast and green terrain surrounding the Glasshouse Mental Institution. This hospital is enormous, built like a fortress full of labyrinths. Jamie's office is on the seventh floor in the left wing, and I've been coming here so often in the last three months, it's starting to feel like home.

This is Alistair's thirteenth appointment with Jamie. We always come on Sunday mornings, like Mass, when the PTSD clinic is closed. Jamie has had the kindness and generosity to offer Alistair his help free of charge, and this for as long as it takes. In exchange, he's asked if he may eventually use his notes and recordings of their sessions to write about Alistair's case some time in the future. We have both agreed to that.

I trust Jamie. But more importantly, Alistair feels safe with him. The sessions usually last about an hour, and during those sixty minutes, I stand at the window or sit and wring my hands, waiting.

Waiting.

At last, the door opens and Jamie steps out. He leaves the door ajar, and I see Alistair sitting with his head in his hands, recovering from whatever intense emotions he put himself through again today. He's so strong, so determined to heal. I don't know how he does it. I'd have had a mental breakdown by now. But not Alistair. No, he comes here every Sunday, dressed in his priest clothes, which he still refuses to stop wearing on Sundays, and sits in that chair, facing Jamie. Facing the whole of his dismantled life.

"How are you?" Jamie asks me, very quietly so as not to disturb Alistair.

"I'm all right." I look over his shoulder at the man I adore. "So, what's going on today?"

Jamie moves away from the door. He sighs and rubs his chin for a moment, clearly gathering his thoughts. These sessions with Alistair are taking their toll on him too. "We made a lot of progress today," he says finally. "We touched on some very painful things, and he was lucid through most of it, until Alistair-Child took over, and then I had to pull back a little."

We've named the three Alistairs: Alistair-Child, Alistair-Priest and Alistair-Dare. Jamie believes there isn't an Alistair-Man the way I thought there was. He believes the lucid Alistair is still a fabricated personality, not quite true, and that the real Alistair is beginning to show. Jamie has helped me see just how fragile Alistair is, and how he uses his intelligence to create this lucid, truth-searching man in order to hide the real damage inside him.

I used to be very confused about it when we started therapy, but I'm not anymore. I understand the disorder much better now. It's like playing hide-and-seek again. And I'm getting very perspicacious when it comes to discerning whom I'm talking to when I'm alone with him.

"I've upped the dosage on his medication, because I found him a little more anxious these last two weeks and I don't want him regressing. Not now." Jamie looks back at the door. "Not when we're getting so close to Craving's Creek."

I bite my lip. Check on Alistair again.

"Ryde, how are you these days?"

I look back at Jamie's concerned face. "What, do I look that bad?"

"No, but like I told you the other day, you have your own coping mechanisms well in place, and sometimes I think this might be a little too much for you to handle."

"I'm okay." Am I? I don't really know anymore. I still have my head and I'm still sober. I must be doing something right. "Yesterday," I say, "we were in bed together, and I felt like maybe I was finally connecting with him, 'cause he wasn't so guarded, and we came so close to…you know. But then, I don't know, it just went to shit."

"I know it's tough, Ryde, but you have to be patient. Okay? It'll come to that, one day. It'll happen."

"I know I sound like that's the only thing on my mind, like I'm doing this just so I can have sex with him, but it's—"

"Oh, come on, I don't think that at all." Jamie laughs quietly, but his face turns serious again. "Look, you want what all of us want. Your needs are completely normal and healthy, all right?"

"Then I think, when it does happen, I'll fuck up. I'll be so goddamn nervous, it'll be a disaster."

"Hey, hey, don't do that to yourself." He squeezes my shoulder. "Take it one step at a time, okay?"

I nod and look over his shoulder. Through the crack in the door, I see Alistair is up now and staring out the window. I want to go to him. I want to put my arms around him. "Doc," I say, my mouth feeling dry, "he's been talking about going back there. You know, going back to the creek."

Jamie looks over at his office. "I don't recommend it, Ryde. I really don't."

"It's gonna be up to him." I dread that day more than I do my own death. "When he says he's ready, I'm gonna have to follow him there. That's the way it works between us. He jumps, I jump."

"He's not ready yet."

"But it's coming to that, isn't it?"

Jamie sighs and looks back at me. "Yes, it's coming to that."

"What does he remember? Tell me."

"You know I can't discuss that with you."

"Jamie, tell me. Now."

He comes closer to me. "He remembers the barn," he whispers into my ear. "Hay in his mouth, the smell of horses. Pain. Lots of pain. That's where we stop. We always stop there."

I have to look away at the window to get my bearings back.

"Ryde?" Alistair is standing in the doorway. "What's wrong?" He takes a few steps to me.

"Nothing, baby, nothing." I take his hand and kiss it. "How you feeling?"

His face is very pale and his eyes are haunted still. "Just tired. And I have a headache."

"Let's go home." I grab his jacket and mine. "We'll see you next week, Jamie."

Jamie accompanies us to the door. "Alistair, call me on Wednesday, please."

Without a word, Alistair throws his arms around Jamie's neck and hugs him. "Thank you," he says, and quickly walks away to the elevator doors.

"He has faith in you," I say to Jamie, rubbing his shoulder.

"And I in him." Jamie turns away and quietly shuts his door.

"Can I put another marshmallow here?" Peaches is already pushing the pink marshmallow into the pink icing on the cake. My birthday cake looks like something you'd serve at a sweet sixteen party to a room full of cheerleaders.

It's the gayest cake I've ever seen and I think I love it. "Yeah, go for it." I ruffle her hair. "If you can find room on that thing." I check the stovetop to see everything is simmering nicely and going as planned.

"I'm finished," Peaches says, stepping back from the table to admire her work. "Do you like it, Uncle Ryde?"

"I think I'm gonna marry it."

She laughs and runs out of the kitchen. I stir the creamy white sauce and taste it again. It's good. Real good. I could probably make a living out of cooking. Maybe I'll give that a try someday.

"Oh, it smells like bacon so bad in here." Sheryl pinches my butt. "We're all gonna get enormous because of you. You've been cooking decadent meals, Ryde. I might move in if you keep feeding me like this."

"Taste this." I raise the spoon to her mouth. "And tell me I don't have a gift."

"Oh, you have more than one gift." She laughs and gropes my crotch.

I grab my glass of water and hold it over her head, threateningly. "I think you need to be put out, Miss Sheryl."

She laughs and pulls on my belt, and I chase her around the kitchen with the water, both of us screaming like kids. I finally have her cornered when Alistair walks in. "Grab her," I tell him.

He laughs, shaking his head. "I wouldn't dare."

"Oh no?" Sheryl turns to him and gives him a seductive grin. "Too bashful, are we?" She slowly walks to him, swinging her hips, and takes a hold of his shirt. She kisses him on the mouth and leans back. "I'll be your Mary Magdalene, Alistair," she says, very dramatically. I burst out laughing and watch the color rise in his cheeks. Sheryl laughs and fixes his shirt. "I'm just fooling with you, sweetheart."

"I know," he mutters. "You enjoy making me blush."

"She sure does."

He steps up to her and gently, almost ceremoniously, puts his hand on her forehead. "Because you have a giving heart and a wounded soul," he says, and I see Sheryl's bold smile slowly fading away. She's moved by his words. His touch. "Bless you," Alistair murmurs to her and walks away to the fridge.

She looks at me with her mouth a little open.

What can I say? The man is spectacular that way. Alistair has these moments of intense spirituality.

He pours himself a glass of ginger ale and looks at us. "What?"

"Nothing, you're just really intense." Sheryl has recomposed herself. "You gave me chills just now. Maybe it's those black eyes of yours."

"My words would mean nothing to you if you didn't already believe them."

She casts me a quick glance and looks back at him. "You think so? Funny, because I don't think much of myself most of the time."

"Well, God thinks a lot of you. You're His daughter, His beautiful little child."

"Alistair, I don't wanna insult you, but I don't care about God. I really don't believe in Him at all."

"And that's fine. Because He believes in you." He takes a sip of his drink and watches her.

"You mean to tell me you really, truly, believe that there's this…this man or spirit in the sky who created this world in seven days and sat back to watch us mess up, and then, when things were really too much for Him, sent down His only son to die for our sins?"

"Well, Sheryl, do you mean to tell me that you really believe that you and Michael, two ordinary people with broken hearts and unhappy lives, got together one night and created this beautiful, perfect and pure child out of almost nothing?"

Sheryl holds his eyes, her breath getting caught in her throat.

"Do you really believe you're responsible for that miracle?"

I'm dumbfounded.

"Wow," Sheryl says, smirking. "You're so good at this, you could almost be a priest."

He smiles and looks over at me. "Your sauce."

"Oh, shit." I turn the burner off and move the pot off it. "Shit."

He looks over my shoulder at the browning sauce. "You can still save it, right?"

"Yeah," I grumble. "Pass the milk."

They both watch me pour and stir milk into the sauce. Sheryl is still quite moved by their little showdown and staring at the whiteness in the pot. Alistair touches my shoulder. "See, you saved it."

Sheryl's eyes meet mine over the pot, and I know what she's thinking.

But I still don't have the answer to that question.

In the door, Alistair and I watch my parents walking down to their car. "Thanks again," I call out to them. I'm glad they were here tonight.

"Happy birthday," my mother says for the thousandth time this evening, blowing me a kiss. "You two have a good night."

I watch their car until it disappears at the end of my street. The sky is pink and orange at the horizon, and there's a semblance of spring in the air. We've survived another Montreal winter.

Alistair walks back in and I shut the front door. We're alone again. Sheryl and Peaches left just after cake. Tomorrow is a school day, and Sheryl has to be on set. She's been cast for a recurring role in a television series called *The Prophet*, and if the network likes the pilot and picks it up, she might be working a steady gig and making interesting money. I'm rooting for her. We all are. She deserves a break.

"Did you have a good birthday?" Alistair sits on the couch and looks up at me. He's been very calm lately. So much better. Sometimes I get nervous, wondering when it'll all come apart.

"I did. I had a wonderful birthday." I sit by him. "And you know what's cool about it? I'll actually remember it tomorrow."

"Do you miss the drinking?"

"Yeah, I do." I lean back and stare at him. "Probably the same way you miss the church sometimes."

He silently acquiesces.

"Thanks for wearing jeans and a shirt." I tug at his pale blue shirt. "I love you in casual clothes."

"I don't know how I feel about it."

We're speaking so softly, sitting very close, and I put my hand on his leg, just above his knee. "It's like everything else in life. You get used to it."

"Maybe I don't wanna get used to it. Maybe Father Masson is right. I belong with them, at the presbytery."

"Has he been calling you again?" I have to be careful. Now is not the time for an argument. "I really wish he'd respect the promise he made me."

"He made a promise to God, first and foremost." Alistair's voice is tense. "And so did I."

"Okay. All right." I move my hand away and pick up the remote. I turn the television on. We've talked about this too many times. I'm not doing this again tonight. "You wanna go back to the church, then by all means, go back to the church."

"Maybe I should."

I feel my jaw click, but keep my eyes steady on the stupid television. It's on the Comedy Network channel. Some stand-up comic is doing his routine. The laughter grinds my nerves, but I refuse to change the channel or turn the volume down. "Maybe that's what you want," I say, out of anger but mostly desperation.

If I lose Alistair this time, I won't survive it. I can't live a day without him. He's everything to me. Everything.

"Is that what *you* want?" he asks in a small voice.

I turn to look at him over my shoulder. "Are you crazy—" But too late, I've said the word.

Crazy.

"Yes, I am, according to my psychiatrist."

"Alistair, don't even—"

"Don't even what?" He makes a move to get up, but I hold him back.

"Wait, wait," I plead with him. "Please, hold on."

"Let go of me." He pushes my hand off him and stands, looking down at me. "How long are we gonna do this? How long are we gonna pretend I'm a normal man?"

"I don't know!" I don't know why I'm yelling. I jump out of my seat and stand face-to-face with him. "I have no fucking idea, okay? Okay? I don't know!" I kick the coffee table and our empty coffee cups go flying. "What the fuck do I know about this, Alistair?"

"And you think I do?" He's never shouted at me before. "You think I like lying down with you every night like a corpse?"

"No, come on, now." I come closer to him. "We're not doing this," I say, very gently, calming down. "Let's take it easy. Take a breath."

He looks like he's going to weep. He nods and crosses his arms over his chest, staring down at the floor.

"Listen to me," I say, pulling his hand out from under his arm. "The shit that we've been through, it's fucking colossal. Jesus, I've seen guys break up over one of them buying the wrong kind of bread, so look at me." I lift his face to mine. "Look at me. We're not like everybody else. Don't talk to me about normal. I don't want normal. I don't need normal. I only want you. Just you." I kiss his lips. "All right? Okay?"

"Sometimes... No, never mind."

"Sometimes, what? Tell me."

"Ryde, sometimes I think you chasing me like this makes me run off in the wrong direction."

"Is that what you think? That I'm chasing you?" But I am. I am. That's all I've ever done was chase him.

"I don't know," he says, pushing his face into my shirt. "I don't know. I can't talk. Can't think. Can't stand the sound of our voices."

I hold him and rock him, but I want him. I want to make love to him. How? How do I begin? I kiss him on the neck, breathing his name inside his ear, but he's so stiff in my arms, and I don't have it in me. I can't break through. We've waited too long. The ice is too thick between us now.

He moves out of my arms and looks at me. "I wanna try," he says, his eyes burning with love for me. "Do you wanna try?"

"Yeah, if you want to." I can barely get the words out. "Because you know I want to."

"Let's go to bed. No more talking. No more thinking." He turns the TV off and enters our bedroom.

Inside, I find him sitting on the edge of the bed. I kneel in front of him, put my hands on his thighs. I kiss his mouth. His neck. I move my hands up. Carefully, aware of his every breath, I lay him down and move my hand over his stomach, kissing him, but his lips are sealed and his body is closed to me. "Let it go. Relax," I whisper, my fingers reaching to touch his belt.

The touch seems to burn him like a hot coal, and he sits up, curling his legs under him. "No, don't touch me there."

I shut my eyes, hear the blood in my ears. I need to get a hold of myself. I'm too wired. Too crazed. "Okay," I hear myself say. With effort, I get up and go to the bathroom. I shut myself in. Something wild comes over me and I grab the towel off the rack and whip it against the wall, over and over, but it won't do. It won't fucking do. And I look around, seeing nothing, just white and my contorted face in the mirror. I hate myself. Hate everything about me. I watch my reflection, seeing the disgust in my own eyes, and I make a fist, raising it to the mirror, knowing I'm going to punch it, yes, I'm going to slam my fist into it, and there's going to be blood and pain, but I deserve it. I deserve it. I step back and swing my fist through the air, but Alistair screams my name as if he can see me through the door. "Ryde, no!" His cry stops me. I stare at the man in the mirror.

"Ryde, open the door. Open the door."

I blink and look at the door, still shocked. I unlock it.

"What were you doing? What were you gonna do?"

"Nothing... I don't know." I'm vanquished. I feel demolished. "It's okay, don't worry."

"No, come here." He stands in front of me, blocking my passage. "I'm sorry, Ryde." He puts his cold hands on my face. "Please, don't look at me like that. Like it's over. Like you're giving up." I can't make myself move or care. I'm out of fuel. Out of ideas.

"Ryde...please. Please."

I wish I could ease his mind or say something comforting, but all I'm capable of is standing here mute.

He grabs my hand and guides me back to the bedroom, but all the while, he's talking to himself, mumbling words under his breath. Gently, he unfastens my shirt. He unzips my jeans and pushes me down on the bed. I can't feel anything anymore. Something is broken inside. I know he's taking my socks off, and still muttering to himself. I want to sit up. Want to tell him I'll be all right in a few minutes, but I just lie there, in my underwear, while he fusses with the blankets, trying to get me under them.

"I pushed you to the limit, yes," I hear him say. "Too far. I took it too far." He's undressing, getting into bed. "The fear. Always the fear." I don't know what he's saying. He's naked now. I see his pale skin in the moonlight.

I close my eyes. Feel dead. What's wrong with me?

"Too much stress. Too much talking. Too much remembering." He kisses my naked shoulder. His lips are hot and so soft on my skin. "It's like hell. Like hell on earth. Yes. Hell. Hell. Hell." He's kissing my face, my mouth. "Playing with Lucifer in the desert, running around a bush in flames." His hand moves over my chest, down my stomach. "There's no sense in it, but there's no escaping it. Drowning in the Lethe River, sinking into oblivion. No pain. No pleasure. Nothing." His tongue glides down and into my navel. "Oh, God, yes, the flesh is the flesh, is the only thing he left us." His lips skim my dick and I hear myself groan in a dream. "Unison, yes, unison," he whispers. "Unison is God's word." He takes me deep into his mouth. I grip his hair, looking down and into his black eyes. Is it really him loving me? "Alistair," I whisper, "are you here?"

He stops and looks up at me. "Yes, I am…and I want this." His stare meets mine, and in his eyes, I see doubt and fear, but lust too.

Oh, such lust.

Then I know he's here with me. "Are you sure?" I ask anyway.

Alistair kisses my inner thigh. "This is our communion," he whispers. His lips are soft on my skin.

I close my eyes and run my fingers into his pale blond hair, feeling whole for the first time in fourteen years.

Chapter Eighteen

When I open my eyes, I see an empty pillow.

"Baby?" I'm already out of bed and jumping into my jeans. "Alistair?"

The apartment is so quiet. The silence makes me sick. Golden light filters through the curtains in the living room window and I know he's gone. I don't know why I know. I check the kitchen anyway, but he's gone.

He made me come in his mouth and now he's gone.

Like a man walking into a sickroom, I enter the bedroom and slowly open the first drawer. It's empty. I stand before the closet and stare at the eleven bare hangers hanging there.

I throw on a sweater and pull some socks on.

I grab my wallet, my phone, my keys.

In the subway, I'm the living dead leaning on a pole, watching my ashen face flashing back at me every time we enter a tunnel.

The taste of him is still on my tongue. I think I'm going to go insane. This is it. This is where my sanity gets off. I've reached the last stop.

Outside, it's sunny and warm and I know God is content. Yes, He has His white lamb back.

I knock on the presbytery door and wonder how it is I can still stand. I'm so sad I can't even cry.

No one answers me. I bang on the door. "Masson!" I scream. "I fucking hate your guts!" I lean my head on the door, babbling words. *Please. Alistair. Please. Open. It's me.*

I stare at the door and walk away. I wipe my eyes with my jacket sleeve and walk up the steps to the church doors. Inside, the beautiful light washes over me like water.

Seconds later, Alistair appears. He's wearing a white cassock. Father Masson is right behind him. "Oh, hello, Ryde," Masson calls out to me.

I shake my head at him. *Why?* I asked him silently.

"Ryde, what are you doing here?" Alistair happily waves at me from the altar. "How did you get in?"

"The doors were unlocked." He's gone. My lover is gone again. All there is now is this child. "I just... I wanted to say hello." I stuff my hands into my pockets. "Do you have Mass?"

Father Masson says something into Alistair's ear and comes down to me. "Father Genet showed up this morning," he says when he's reached me. He's careful not to speak too loudly. "He was very upset, and so full of grief."

"Was he himself?" I check over Masson's shoulder. Alistair is busy with a young boy. An altar boy?

"Yes, he was himself. He was lucid, knew what he'd done with you."

"Help me." I look into his eyes. "Help me. Please."

Father Masson grabs my arm. "Get a hold of yourself."

"No! Help me!" I implore him. "Now, help me."

Masson looks back at Alistair. "He's a child right now. What can I do?"

"Let me take him to Jamie, to his doctor."

"And you think he'll allow it? Ask him. Go ahead."

"Alistair," I yell out to him. "Come here, I wanna talk to you."

He looks at me, confused, then begins walking softly down the aisle. "Yes?"

"Listen to me," I say, trying to keep the madness from showing on my face. "I need you to come with me."

"Where?" He looks at Masson.

"Home. Our home."

"What?" He steps back a little.

"Alistair, now, come on, I know you know what I'm taking about, but you're just scared, and this," I open my arms, "this church, this place, it's your hiding spot, can't you see that? Every time you come close to—"

"Father," he whispers, his eyes widening, "what does he want?"

"It's all right, lad. Ryde is a little drunk again. Do you remember the confessional?"

"Jesus fucking Christ!" I grab Masson's collar, shaking him. "I should kill you right now. I should put your fat face in that goddamn holy water basin and drown you."

"Help us!" Alistair stumbles back, tripping on his cassock, running off to the back of the church, screaming for help. Masson shoves me off him and shakes his head at me. He's upset, terrified. "This is God's house," he screams. "And you come here to defile it!"

"Gimme my boyfriend back," I yell, grabbing him again. "Gimme my goddamn boyfriend back!"

A man appears at the front, followed by another. "Hey, you there!"

"Robert, get this man out of here," Father Masson says, winded, and fixes his white tab collar. "He's threatened to kidnap Father Genet. He's obsessed with the boy."

"He's not a boy, you asshole. He's a man. He's thirty-one years old."

"Get out."

"Sir," the man, Robert, says, moving closer. "This is a church. This is a sacred place."

"Fuck sanctity and fuck *you*!" I step back to the doors, but I'm still hoping to see Alistair's face half-hidden in those purple curtains. How could he forget last night? How could he forget me? "You have no idea what you're doing. You think I'm defiling this place?" I stare into Masson's red face. "No, *you're* defiling him. Us. Our love. That's what's sacred. And that's *your* sin against us." I open the doors and turn around again. "Well, what the fuck are you doing still standing there, huh? Go see him. Go reassure him, if you care about him so much."

"What are you going to do?"

"Me? I'm gonna call the archbishop and let him know you have a mentally ill priest hiding out here, but first, I'm gonna get drunk."

"Ryde, no—"

"I'll see you in hell, Masson."

Calmly, I line up three empty shot glasses on my coffee table.

I pour vodka into each glass and stare down at them. This is going to be good.

This is going to be my own private heaven and to hell with everybody else.

"In the name of the Father," I say, picking up the first shot, but I'm crying again like a boy. Like a stupid, wounded kid. And the tears run down my face into my mouth. I try to drink, but the sob in my throat makes me spit the vodka out, and it trickles down my chin along with the tears and spit. "And of the Son," I say, crying harder. I want Alistair. I failed him. I let him down again. I bring the glass to my lips, but my useless hand is shaking too hard, and the vodka spills out and down my fingers. "And the Holy Spirit." I reach for the last shot, but knock it down instead. Dazed, I watch the vodka trickling over the glass table, to the floor—each lost drop reminding me of the creek. Of its never-ending fall.

When will I stop falling from grace?

The vodka bottle seems to be staring at me. "You want me?" I ask it. "Do you, you deceiving shit?" I watch it. It's beautiful, lean and white and full of promises. "Yeah, well," I say, grabbing it by the neck. "I don't want you anymore." I go to the kitchen and stuff the bottle between two bags of frozen corn. "There, this is your new coffin." I shut the freezer door and lean my head on it. "Enjoy it, motherfucker."

Oh, that was close. I shut my eyes. So very, very close.

Back in the living room, I look around my empty apartment, and for the first time in my life, I wonder if I'll make it through the day without hurting myself. I sit and pull my phone out of my pants.

Sheryl picks up on the first ring. "Hey, you," she says, cheerfully. "What's up?"

I lie down on the couch, curling into a ball. "Sheryl," I say in a broken voice. "I need you to come over. I don't think I can hold on."

"Don't move. Don't do anything. Just stay there." I hear her say something to someone. "I'll be right there, Ryde. Just don't drink, honey. Don't you dare do it."

Three days later, Sheryl parks the car in front of my apartment building and puts her hand over mine. "Are you sure you're gonna be okay all alone?"

I've been staying at her house for three days. I can't ask for any more of her attention or time. "Yeah, I'll be all right." I lean in and kiss her cheek. The last days have brought us closer than ever. She'd work during the day, but called me every hour, and in the evenings, we cooked together and talked. We talked until things started making sense in my mind again. I have a plan now. With Jamie's help, I'm going to file a formal complaint with the archbishop, and together, Jamie and I are going to build a case against Masson and Cornwell and the whole damn seminary.

But my plan, as well laid as it is, is missing one key thing: Alistair's choice.

"Call me, okay?" Sheryl hugs me tight. "Tonight."

"You know, I don't even know how to thank you, I mean, for everything, for every minute you've spent."

"I love you, Ryde." She kisses me on the lips and it's nice. "Go."

"Yeah, here I go." I pop the door open and look out. Three days, but it feels so much longer. I step up the stairs and open my mailbox. There's nothing there but bills. I wave at Sheryl and watch her drive away.

Inside the apartment, I check my machine. I have a few new messages. Two from my mother, one from my current employer, and the last is from my bank. My account has been suspended.

Depressed, I lie down on my couch and flick the television on. I don't want to deal with anything just now. The world can wait.

Listening to the news, I drift to sleep.

Something wakes me, and I sit up, blinking at my dark living room. The television is still on, and in the corner, I see the time: nine o'clock. I try to remember when I fell asleep.

What woke me up?

Then I hear a knock. Someone is at my door.

I stand and stare at the door as if it might speak to me. Is it him? Is it?

"Ryde?"

I fly to the door and pull it open.

"Now, listen to me—listen—you have to listen." Alistair walks into my apartment, not even looking at me. He's in a T-shirt, and his hair is wild, and he's pacing the room, speaking very fast. "I wrote today, I wrote everything, like I always do, and I wrote and wrote, about Eberhart leaving the presbytery to go back to Germany to be with her brother, and I wrote about the broken window in the school where they asked me to come and help them with making the lunches on Friday and then I checked the date and I saw the—I saw—I saw the—"

"Hey, hey." I touch his arm. God, he's here. He's really here. "Slow down." I smile at him and take his face in my hands. "Hi...how are you?"

He leans his forehead to mine. "Oh, Ryde, I saw the missing pages. It's three days. Three days, right?"

"Yeah." I shut my eyes.

"I'm sorry," he whispers, kissing my face. "Why didn't you come find me?"

"Don't you think I tried?" I move away from him, the emotion rising in me again. "I woke up the next morning, after we made love, and you were gone. You'd vanished, Alistair. And I went to church and there you were. But you were that kid again, that little boy who doesn't know we're lovers and doesn't—"

"You think I do it on purpose?" He cocks his head, watching me. "Do you?"

"Jamie says part of you knows what the other parts are doing, all the time. That your brain can't possibly —"

"Maybe he's right. Maybe I'm just the biggest trickster, liar, and coward that ever—"

"Stop, no, that's not what I'm saying." I go for his hand. "You're here, okay? You're here and that's all that matters to me right now." I put my arms around him and hold him close. "It was so fucked-up, Alistair, and I was real messed up about it, and I bought some vodka."

"No, Ryde, no."

"I didn't drink. I didn't do it."

"Oh, thank God." He crosses himself. "Bless you."

I can't help smiling. I tug at his T-shirt. "Look at you. No black shirt. No white collar."

He looks down at himself as if seeing his casual clothes for the first time.

"What's going on?"

"Well, Ryde, I've left the church."

"What?"

"Yes, yes. I went to see Mignacca this morning. The archbishop. And I told him everything. I told him about my disorder, my therapy. Our love affair."

"You just went there in your Levi's jeans and white Gap T-shirt and sat in his office and told him everything?"

"Yes," Alistair says, and I suddenly see a young man standing there in my living room. Not a priest or a boy, but a beautiful gay man with the cleverest black eyes I've ever seen. "So, you know," he adds, "he asked me if I wanted to repent and seek help. He begged me to accept to be transferred far away from here, far away from *you*. Of course, I told him I wouldn't. I even admitted I was seeing a shrink.." Alistair nods to himself, clearly just comprehending what he's done. "Took me seven years to enter priesthood and seven minutes to leave it."

"Shit." I frown, waiting for more.

"I'm not a priest anymore."

I can't help laughing. "Just like that."

He smirks. "Yes," he says, sarcastically. "*Just like that.* You know, all it took was a serious mental disorder, and for me to break every single one of my vows."

This time, I can't help laughing loudly.

"You think it's funny?" He slaps my arm. Hard. "I have nothing."

"No, you have me." I grab his hands and squeeze them. "But most importantly, you have yourself."

"Parts of myself. What am I going to do?"

"I don't know."

He steps up to me and gives me a defiant look. "Yes, you do. You know exactly what's left to do."

I know what he means. He means going back to Craving's Creek. "No, no way." I walk away, heading for the bedroom.

But Alistair follows me there. "Yes, Ryde, yes. Don't you see? I've left the church, I've done my part, but you need to do yours. You need to take me back there and show me. Show me."

"So I can lose you again? No."

"If you don't take me back there, then I'll go alone." He means it. I can see it in his eyes. "I'm brave enough."

"I know you are." I remember the cliff, the way he used to jump into the creek without fear or hesitation. "I'm the one who's scared, Alistair. I don't have your faith."

"I have enough faith for both of us. Don't you know that by now?"

I stare at him for a long time. This man I worship. Can he sustain it? Can he swim in Craving's Creek again?

"Yes or no, Ryde. Tell me now. Will you take me there one last time?"

I touch a strand of his hair. "I will, but not now, okay? If you wanna do it right, then we have to wait until summer. Until the second week of July. That's the time we went, fifteen years ago. You wanna do it right, don't you?"

His black eyes are full of urgency. "You promise me. Promise me we'll go."

"I swear."

"Promise to God."

"I don't believe in God."

"Then swear on my life."

"Goddamn it, Alistair."

"Swear it, Ryde." He puts my hand on his head. "On my life. *For* my life. I want it back. I want my life back, Ryde. Please."

There's nothing I wouldn't do for him. Nothing. "I swear on your life, Alistair Genet. I'll take you back to Craving's Creek for your birthday. But I just hope we fucking survive it this time."

Chapter Nineteen

Jamie pries the window open. "It's hot in here," he says, letting a breeze into his stuffy office. He goes to the sink and washes his hands again. I didn't know this before, but Jamie suffers from obsessive compulsive disorder. He's been battling this disorder all his life. He also has panic attacks. The fact that the man treating my boyfriend suffers from OCD should worry me, but instead, it only makes me trust him even more.

It explains Jamie's compassion and patience with Alistair.

"Do you want a glass of water?" he asks me, looking over his shoulder. "Or tea maybe?"

"No thanks." I watch him. His movements are nervous. He's clearly on edge today. I wonder if I'm allowed to ask our psychiatrist if *he* needs to talk. "You okay, Jamie?"

He adjusts his glasses and gives me a quick nod. He wipes his hands on his sleek black pants and checks the open door again. "You think he's all right?"

I look over at the open door, out at the waiting room. Alistair is on my phone, talking with his new boss. He's just started this job last week, at the National Archives, and so far, he seems to be adjusting to his new environment quite well. "He's fine," I say, looking back at Jamie. "You're the one who looks a little anxious, I have to say."

"So, you think he's ready to work those thirty hours a week?"

"He enjoys it. He comes home with a sense of accomplishment."

"His progress is unbelievable." Jamie sips his water, watching the door again. "Almost too unbelievable."

"You think he's gonna come apart?" I lean in. "Tell me. Is that what's on your mind?"

Jamie sighs, looking back at me. "He's very intelligent. And he has so much faith. If anyone can pull through something like this, he can. That being said, I still think Craving's Creek is a bad idea."

We leave next week. July thirteenth. Though I've tried to dissuade him by every possible means, Alistair won't change his mind. He's determined to go through with this. "He's convinced himself it's the only way."

"Yes, well, maybe that's the one thing you guys have going for you. Because if he's convinced it's the only way to heal, then that belief in itself could be enough."

"What do you mean?" I check the door again and catch Alistair's eye. I wink at him, and though he's still engrossed in his conversation, he gives me a beautiful smile anyway. I love him in blue jeans. He takes my breath away.

"I mean," Jamie explains, "sort of the way we use placebos with certain patients and convince them they're getting the real thing, and because they believe they are indeed being medicated, they start showing signs of improvement."

"Hm, kinda like a priest performing an exorcism on someone who believes he's possessed."

"Do they still do that?" Jamie smiles and drinks again. "It'd be nice if the church started opening a psychiatry journal once in a while. You know, see what we quacks are up to these days."

"Look," I say, more seriously, "don't think I'm not scared about going back there with him, but it's too late now. I'm already strapped in for this ride."

"You keep thinking about him, about his reaction, but Ryde, what about yours? What happens when you both begin to regress, and the past starts mixing in with the present, and you're both out there, in the woods, playing this game of hide-and-seek with yourselves?"

"I don't know."

"You know I'm going to be away from Montreal, but I want you to call me, day or night, if something—"

"Jamie, you need a fucking vacation." I laugh and shake my head at him. "All right?"

He rubs his eyes under his glasses. "I think you're right. I don't remember what the inside of my house looks like. I'm here seven days a week." He smiles and winks at me.

When Alistair walks back in, we both turn to look up at him.

"Sorry about that," he says, sitting next to me and picking up my hand. "There was a lot of confusion over the schedules, but we worked it out."

Jamie stands and retrieves his notepad from his desk.

"All right, well," I say, making a move to get up. "That's my cue."

"No, Ryde." Jamie motions for me to sit again. "I think you should stay. I think we should spend this last session together before you leave for your trip."

I look over at Alistair. "Yeah? No?"

"That's fine."

Jamie sits and crosses his long legs. He glances down at his notes, then puts the pad down on the table between us. "Forget the notes. Forget last week. I want to talk about Craving's Creek. I want you to tell me what you expect to feel down there, Alistair. And you too, Ryde."

"I don't know," I say, scratching my head and looking over at Alistair. "I expect to feel a lot of shitty things."

Jamie waits, saying nothing. He stares at Alistair expectantly.

Alistair turns his eyes to the window. "I don't know what I'm going to feel."

"You're returning to the place where you were abducted, Alistair." Jamie speaks coldly and with no emotion showing through at all. I know this is part of the therapy, because we've discussed it last month. From now on, Alistair is ready to hear the truth of what happened to him, though he doesn't remember it. "The place where you were raped and beaten for thirty-two hours."

I hate this so much. I have to dig my nails into the palm of my hand to keep from saying anything.

"The place where you were left for dead in a stack of hay."

Alistair looks back at Jamie. I immediately see the change in his face. He's switched. "You should have seen the mess he made," he almost growls. "Blood and shit everywhere." He licks his lips. "Nasty," he hisses.

"He's switched," I mutter, looking at Jamie in a panic. "You made him—"

"No, I don't want to talk you," Jamie says. He leans in a little, holding Alistair's furious stare. "I want to talk to Alistair. We don't need *you* right now. We're fine. We're just talking. We don't need you."

I'm transfixed, not breathing, watching them.

Alistair shakes his head. "The horses could smell it. They wanted the boy too."

But Jamie looks away from Alistair and picks up his notes, nonchalantly. He scribbles something, and clears his throat. "We don't need you," he says again, not looking up. "But thank you for coming."

"He needs me," Alistair says, his voice straining with anger. "He's fucking useless, the priest. Praying praying praying praying, Oh God, help me, Oh God, make me good, Oh God, oh God, I'm so bad, so bad."

"He's not a priest anymore." Jamie won't look at him. "The priest is gone."

I go for Alistair's hand, but Jamie raises his hand. "Don't touch him."

Beside me, Alistair is breathing hard and starting to sweat.

"Let me get him some water," I say, getting out of my seat.

"No." Again Jamie motions for me to sit still and be quiet. He glances up at Alistair. "I want to talk to you. Will you talk to me?"

"No," Alistair says quietly, shaking his head. "No. No."

"Baby," I whisper, seeing him coming around to us again, "hey, that was very short. You switched in a few minutes."

"You're going back to the place where you were abducted," Jamie says, as if nothing happened. His tone is cool and calm. "Back to the place where you were raped and beaten for thirty-two hours." He puts his notes down. "Back to where you were left for dead in the hay."

Alistair is shaking. He has tremors in his hands. "Yes," he says, but his voice is weak.

"You're going back to that place."

"Yes," he says, more strongly. "I'm going back."

Jamie's dark eyes peer into Alistair's face. Now I see the emotion in Jamie's eyes, and know this was probably the toughest he's ever been with a patient. "Okay, Alistair," he says, and crouches down by him. He rubs Alistair's hair back from his sweaty forehead. "You're amazing." He stands and recomposes himself, going to the sink to wash his hands again.

Alistair leans back on the chair, staring blankly at the ceiling. He's exhausted. "I heard myself speaking," he says without looking at either one of us. "I heard the words I said."

"You mean—"

"Yes, Ryde." He turns his eyes to me. "I heard my voice saying those things."

"You were present." Jamie is trying not to let his excitement show. "You were here with us." He bites his lip, obviously thinking of the next stage. "Look," he finally says, sitting across from us again, "whatever happens now, you both need to stay focused on each other. Craving's Creek isn't just a place anymore. It's a space in time where you both left a part of yourselves, and it's going to take both of you to find those boys again." He pauses. "You have what it takes."

"And if we don't?"

"You're always doubting," Alistair says, frowning at me. "Doubting Thomas you are."

"I don't doubt you, or me, just—"

"God."

"I don't believe in Him, remember?"

Alistair sighs and looks away. "Yes, you remind me every day."

"Hey," I say, squeezing his knee. "We don't need God, okay? We have each other."

He smirks. "My mother was right about you."

"Yeah, she was." I nudge his shoulder. "But that's the reason you love me."

"Blasphemy, all of it." Alistair is trying not to smile.

Jamie picks up his notes. "So, I'll see you when you two get back?" he asks, more seriously.

Alistair gives me a long and probing look.

"Yeah," I say, taking his hand. "Absolutely."

But I wonder, how do you return from a place you never left?

Chapter Twenty

Sheryl and Peaches stand back, giving my mother and I some room. "You have to call me," my mother says again, her fingers digging into my arm. "I won't be able to wait for four days without hearing from you."

"He can't call you, Mrs. Kent," Alistair says, standing by the van—a Dodge minivan he insisted we rent for the trip. "We're not bringing cell phones, remember? We didn't have them in 1994."

My mother briefly shuts her eyes, obviously holding back from arguing with him. She knows it would be pointless anyway.

He's planned everything. Every detail has been thought of. We'll be recreating the trip, almost minute by minute. He's made me write everything I remember in his journal, and that's the schedule we'll be following.

"It's seven a.m.," he says, checking his watch. "We have to go now."

I give my mother a helpless look and kiss her cheek. "Don't worry," I say, close to her ear, "it'll be all right."

She doesn't believe in this. She thinks it's masochistic and dangerous. "I love you," she says at last, and steps back to where Sheryl and Peaches wait, looking like they're waiting for their turn at the casket.

"This isn't a funeral," I say, not too convincingly. "Come on, people, somebody gimme a smile here." I gesture for Peaches to come closer. "You, come here and give your old uncle a hug."

She jumps into my arms, but Alistair is getting impatient. "We have to go now," he says, opening the passenger door. "It's five past seven."

My mother grabs his arm and pulls him close, clutching his head. "You don't have to do this, sweetie," she says. "There are so many other roads to take."

He pulls himself out of her embrace, his eyes clouded with sadness, and puts his hand over her head. "You were always like a mother to me," he says. "Have faith in me, please. I need you to."

I watch my mother's face. She's understanding things.

Sheryl hugs me, and for a moment, I don't think she'll let me go. "When you came back that time, you were never the same, and I lost my friend, Ryde… I lost my best friend." She leans back and looks me deep in the eye. "Don't do it to me again, you hear me?" She looks at Alistair. "And you, Alistair Genet, the strange boy no one really knew, I'll see you in four days, Blondie. All right?" She winks, but her face is white.

"Let's go," Alistair says, climbing into the passenger seat. He shuts the door and rolls up his window. He's ready. There's no turning back now.

I walk around the hood and catch him staring out into space. I get into the driver's seat and shut the door, looking over at him. "This isn't the way you were when we left that morning. And where's your orange?"

He turns his black eyes to mine and pulls an orange out of his bag.

"Good." I put the van in reverse. "Now smile. You were happy. You were excited."

My mother and Sheryl wave us off, and slowly, I drive out and into the street. "Open the glove compartment, please."

Alistair pops the compartment open. "What do you need?"

"My mother's Cat Stevens CD."

He finds it and slides into the CD player. "Which one? Number three?"

"Yep."

When I hear the first notes of "Lady D'Arbanville," my heart leaps and something moves inside me, like an eye opening deep inside my gut. I have butterflies in my stomach. That song. That fucking song. I haven't heard it in fifteen years.

Driving out of the city, I keep glancing over at him. He's tapping his foot, fiddling with his orange. When he finally begins to peel it, the scent of it, sweet and tangy, fills the car, and again, the memories of that morning seem to be knocking on a door in my mind. I turn to look at him again.

His hair seems to have paled in the last hour. His face is open and full of curiosity as he looks out the window, at the road. He sits with one leg curled under his chin, holding his knee, and I notice the tear there in his blue jeans. He pops a piece of orange into his mouth and looks over at me. His radiant smile blows my mind.

"Want some?" he asks, bringing a piece of orange to my lips. "Open up."

The taste of the fruit awakens another memory, and I have to blink the emotion away and focus on the road.

Then, Alistair puts his hand over mine on the wheel.

His fingers are wet with orange juice.

The sound of dry pine needles and gravel under the van's wheels makes me anxious.

Camping.

I haven't even looked at a picture of a tent in fifteen years. I can't go into a store if they sell camping gear. The very smell of mosquito repellent makes me sick.

But I'm here. I'm here.

"Is this the one?" Alistair looks out his window. "Are you sure?"

"Yeah, number five. This is the one." I carefully drive the minivan between two trees and turn the engine off. "You all right?"

He chews on his lip and shrugs. "So far, so good." He opens his door and steps out.

I sit in my seat with this enormous knot in my stomach, watching him through the windshield. He's walking around the site, which hasn't changed much since we were here last, poking at things: trees, the picnic table, the blackened bricks of the fire pit. I slip my hand into my pocket and touch my phone for reassurance. I know I shouldn't have lied about it, but there was no way I was coming out here without my phone.

"What are you doing?"

I quickly take my hand out of my pocket and open my door. "Just taking a minute."

He walks to me and gently presses his hand to my chest. He rarely touches me unless we're making love, and when he does touch me in these little unexpected moments, it always makes my heart stop and start again. "Are you okay?" He brushes something off my shirt.

A simple touch from him makes me feel like I could do anything. I could cut down these trees around us and build him a house. But I'll start with setting up the tent instead. "You wanna give me hand with putting up the tent?"

It took a lot of arguing and begging in the last month, but he finally agreed we'd share a tent, though we hadn't shared one fifteen years ago. I was uncompromising on that point. And to his credit, Alistair is capable of reason when I'm threatening to go completely ballistic if he doesn't give in to me.

"Was it over here?"

"Yeah, right there." I start unloading the back of the van. I nod my head to the grocery bags. "Just organize the kitchen area for us, will you?"

"Yes, sir." He grabs a bag from the back. "Corn, hot dogs and watermelon, right?"

"That sounds kinda gross to me right now. Let's make some sandwiches—" I stop.

Because he's not listening to me anymore. He's staring at the woods, frozen. "Alistair?"

He gags and holds his stomach, bending in two. "I don't feel good," he moans, and gags again.

I rub his shoulder. "Sit down."

He doesn't make it to the picnic table. He stops and gags again, and then throws up an orange mess into the pine needles near the fire pit while I watch, helpless, rubbing his shoulder. "Okay?" I ask when I see the color slowly returning to his face. "It's over?"

He nods and looks down at the mess. "The oranges made me sick, I think."

"Yeah," I whisper, looking around us at the woods, the empty road, the darkening sky above. "Come on." I take him to the table and force him down on the bench. "Just sit here for a few minutes."

"No, I'm okay. I wanna help you with the tent."

I stare up at the threatening clouds. Is God here with us today? Is He watching this, sitting there in the front row, enjoying the little rerun show we're putting on for him?

"It's going to rain," Alistair says, his dark eyes searching the heavens. "It's going to pour out here."

Yes, he's right. Fuck it. Let it be done.

"No," Alistair groans, laughing behind his paperback book. "Stop it, Ryde."

But I don't listen to him. Instead, I lift the bottom of his shirt and kiss him there, on the fine golden below his navel. The rain beats hard on the tent, and we have absolutely nothing to do. I'm delighted with this. I run my hand down his thigh and then up again, teasing him. I glance up—he's still reading, but I feel the swell of his erection under my palm. I kiss the bulge in his jeans, hard, harder, and feel him raising his hips to meet my eager mouth. "That's all you ever think about," he says, but there's a smile in his voice, and I know he wouldn't want it any other way. I unfasten the button of his jeans and slowly pull his zipper down. When my lips touch his bare skin, the book goes flying. I'm starting to understand the way he works. It takes a long time to light his fire, but once he's lit, he burns like no other man I've ever touched. I fall over him and kiss him deep, looking down at his beautiful face. We make love in the only way he allows it, with our mouths and hands, but I ache for him. I want him far inside me.

"Alistair," I whisper, and against the sound of the rain and wind, I whisper what I want from him, into his ear, his hair. *Do it to me. Everything. Now.* I watch the lust swell inside his eyes as he stares down at me, unsure, but I guide his hand down and feel his fingertips discovering me.

I turn to my stomach and let the air out of my lungs. He enters me like a sinner entering his home again, and he takes me slow, deep, but then faster, harder, and I feel everything. Everything. Because I'm sober. I'm sober and feeling again for the first time in years, and I moan, grunt, can't keep control—my body is awake in a way I've never allowed it to be. He's unstoppable, insatiable, going and going, pounding into me like he's in it for blood, revenge, murder.

Hours later, when we stop, we're both in tears, sweating and clinging to each other. There's nothing to say.

His body has told me everything.

I hold him against me and fall asleep with my face in his white-blond hair.

"Over here," I call out to him, through the trees. "It's here. We're here." I push the branches obstructing my view of the creek, my heart racing with anticipation. "Come on!" I scream, looking over my shoulder. Where is he? He was right behind me. "Alistair?" I have to see. Have to see the fall. Is it still here? I can't hear anything.

I look around. Where are the birds?

"Alistair!" I step through the thick foliage, my eyes searching for the fall.

But the creek is dry, empty and ringed with dead leaves and dirt. I shiver, watching the trees around me. No animal lives here.

Nothing lives here.

The silence cries out to me, and I spin around, suddenly aware of the absence around me.

Absence. Nothingness.

"Alistair," I call out again, weakly, my own voice echoing back to me.

Then I see him.

He stands on the cliff, toes curled around the edge, looking down into the dirt.

"No!" I wave my arm through the air. "Don't jump! There's nothing there! Alistair!"

He lifts his face and I see he's smiling down at me. "Yes, there is, Ryde. There is. You're such a doubting Thomas!"

"No! God, No!"

I sit up, frantic, and look around the tent. "No," I hear myself say, but realize I'm awake. I rub at my face with both hands and crawl to the tent's opening. Still frazzled, I fuss with the zipper and finally poke my head out to see Alistair sitting by the fire pit, his face flickering in the flames. "You're awake," he says. "I thought you'd sleep until tomorrow morning."

The sky is ink black, speckled with shimmering stars. "What time is it?" I ask, stepping out of the stuffy tent. "Why didn't you wake me?"

"It's around ten." He stands and walks to me. "Why would I wake you?"

"Because you're out here alone and—"

"I'm not alone, Ryde." He kisses my mouth. He tastes like sugar. "God is with me."

"Have you been eating marshmallows?"

"Yes. Half the bag actually." He laughs and sits by the fire again, showing me the empty folding chair at his side. "Come sit with me?"

I plop down next to him and think of beer. A cold one would be so fantastic right now.

"You were moaning before, in your sleep. Did you have a nightmare?"

"Yeah." I lean in and warm my cold hands at the fire. I look over at him. "Have you just been sitting here all this time?"

"Yes."

"Praying, I guess." I look back at the fire.

"Sometimes I wish you'd pray with me." He digs for another marshmallow and sticks one on his thin branch. "We do everything together. And don't you think two people who make love the way we just made love should be able to pray together?" He brings the marshmallow up to the flames and I watch its white skin melt, brown and bubble.

"See that marshmallow," I say. "That's my so-called soul, babe. Roasting nicely for you. And you wouldn't enjoy me any other way, now would you?"

He takes the stick out of the flames and shakes it hard, sending the marshmallow flying somewhere into the woods.

"So what's that supposed to mean? You've just tossed my soul to the wolves."

He won't speak to me and stares at the orange flames dancing in the pit.

"Oh, come on, Alistair, I'm just fucking with you."

"I need you to—" He stops, pouting and looking into the fire still. "Never mind."

"You need me to what?" I touch his hand on his knee.

He shoots me a desperate look. "I need you to pray for me too sometimes."

I lose the smile. Look down at my feet.

"I'm here, Ryde, I'm doing this, and I'm facing all of these memories, and I'm scared, you know. I'm scared."

"But I'm right here with you."

"Yes, but you weren't there. You weren't there when I was—"

"No, I know. I know that." I squeeze his fingers. "And I'm sorry I'm being so obstinate about the whole God thing, okay? I'll pray, all right? I'll pray with you right now if you want me to."

"You will?"

"Yeah, say something. Get me started. How does this thing work?"

"You just close your eyes and talk to God."

I stare at him. How? How do you just close your eyes and talk to nothing inside your head? But I'll try. I'll do it for him. I shut my eyes and wait for him to begin.

I hear him speaking softly and crack an eye open, peeking at him. He sees me and frowns. "You're not even trying."

"No, no, I am. I swear, I am."

"You don't even know how to pray. How's that possible? Don't you feel anything inside?"

"Yeah, I do feel, all right? But I'm a rational person, Alistair. I don't need to—"

"Rational? Is that all there is to you, rationality? Well, Ryde, there's a lot more to life than being rational and…and, and if you could just—"

"If I could what? Get on my knees and pray like a good little boy? No, babe, I'd rather get on my knees and suck your dick."

"Oh, now you're just being vile!" He bolts out of his chair.

"Wait, wait." Now I've done it. "Hey, come on, don't—"

"You know what? I'm going to bed." He angrily jerks the tent open and shuts himself in. "Good night, Mr. Rationality."

Hating myself for upsetting him tonight of all nights, I put the fire out and grab some food and a water bottle. When I crawl into the tent, I find him lying on his side, facing away from me. He's cracked a light stick and the tent is glowing pink. "I'm sorry," I whisper into his ear. "I'm a lost case."

He sighs heavily. "Those are God's favorite kind of souls."

"Well, He can chew on me later." I kiss his shoulder. "I brought some food. Let's have an indoor picnic."

He turns to face me and I see the pain in his eyes.

It kills me. "Oh, Alistair, don't look at me like that, please."

He pushes his face into my hand. "How come I don't remember anything, Ryde? How can I be here, and do all the things we did all those years ago, and not remember those thirty-two hours of hurt? I can't even remember what he looked like, what he did to me. To *me*, Ryde. My body." He shuts his eyes tight. "Me," he says again, over and over. "Me. My body."

"Why do you want to remember? Why? I'm trying to understand it, but—"

"Because there's a boy inside me and he keeps running around empty rooms, calling out to be found."

I rub his hair back, gently. "Okay, you call the shots. You've always called the shots. Tomorrow, we go to the creek. You're gonna jump off that cliff, and fear or not, I'm gonna jump right after you."

"Tell me what it looks like," he whispers, nestling against me. "The creek. Is it beautiful?"

"Yeah…it's perfect."

"Tell me how we get there, to that place."

"Well, you have to walk for a while, through the woods here, at our left, and then you come to a clearing, and you start wondering if—"

"If you made a wrong turn somewhere."

"Yes," I say, my heart speeding. He remembers this. "But just when you think you're lost—"

"You step through some thick bushes and you see it."

"Yeah, you see it, baby. And it's beautiful and you just stand there."

"Just you and beauty, face-to-face."

"No," I say, tears stinging my eyes. "Not beauty, Alistair. *God.* You stand there face-to-face with God."

We're both standing on the edge of the cliff, looking down into the turbulent waters.

Somehow, the cliff seems much higher than I remember it.

"Are you sure this is where I jumped?" Alistair is gazing down into the water. His face is a little pale. "I don't think I could have."

"No, you did." I stare at the rocks below and then at that long, foamy fall gushing down into the creek. "A hundred times at least."

"Hm." He frowns. "Seems a little reckless."

"See, that's what I tried telling you fifteen years ago." I pull him back a little. "Look, bottom line, I'm not letting you jump off this cliff today, all right?"

He looks at me. Smiles.

"Alistair, I'm warning you. Don't you even think about it."

"Or what?" He steps back a few feet and stands on one foot, pulling his shoe off.

"No, no, no, you don't." I show him the fall, the rocks. "You're not a limber little kid anymore."

"Who says I'm not limber?" He jerks his belt off and drops his jeans. Staring boldly at me, he slips his T-shirt over his head and tosses it to the side. He stands there, glorious and defiant—my man.

"Will you come after me?" He stands back on a heel and I see he's summoning up his courage.

"Come on," I whine. Yes, I'm scared. I'm not jumping off that damn cliff. "Baby, don't make me."

"Fuck it," he says, cursing for the first time since I've known him, and his whole face hardens—he jumps. He doesn't make a sound on his way down, falling straight and almost silently into the water below. I nearly rip my shirt and jeans off—oh this is it, this is it—I'm going in. I look down again, standing there in my briefs, shivering and waiting for his head to pop out of the water.

But I know it will. Here he comes. Yes, there he is. He waves at me and laughs, throwing his head back and screaming like a madman. "HOLY SHIT!" he yells, against the sound of the wild fall.

I laugh hard, with relief and sheer joy.

"Ryde!" he calls out to me. "Come on, your turn!"

I'm right there on the edge, so close, leaning in, feeling the coolness of the fall.

I quit drinking, now didn't I? I did that. *Me.* I found Alistair again. I brought him back to life. I did it.

I can jump off this cliff.

The emptiness under my feet shocks me. I'm falling, falling so fast, and there's nothing to stop me, but he's down there, my Alistair. It's going to be all right.

I hit the water hard, a little harder than I was prepared for, and the burn in my chest chokes me for a moment, but I swim and kick, staring at the murky surface above. When my head breaks through it, I let out a cry of victory.

"You did it!" Alistair grabs my shoulder, nearly pulling me down again.

"Oh, my God," I say, suddenly understanding what I've just done. I look up to the cliff and shake my head. "Jesus," I moan. "I'm not doing that again."

"Me neither," he says, seriously. "I scraped my thigh along a rock there. One inch to the left, and I would have landed straight on it."

"Are you bleeding?" I touch his thigh under the water.

"I'm okay but let's swim back." In long, steady strides, he swims back to the rocky shore, and I follow him. We pull ourselves out of the water and sit on the smooth, warm rocks.

For a moment, we both sit there, catching our breaths and staring at the cliff. After a minute, I nudge his shoulder with mine and wink at him. "That was kind of fun actually." He laughs at me and shakes his head. I put my arm around his shoulder. "So, how do you feel? Does any of this feel familiar?"

"I don't know," he whispers, looking down at his knees. "Maybe, some of it." He looks around at our surroundings, the creek, the woods. "It's a strange feeling. It's like…it's like I'm dreaming."

"Have you ever dreamed of this place, I mean, after?"

"No. But I think if I ever did, I'd wake up remembering it."

"I only remember it in dreams."

He turns and looks at me. He's never quite looked at me like this before. "Ryde," he says, "do you know how much I love you?"

I hold my breath, feel his words deep inside me.

"You found me again," he whispers. "You never gave up on me. After everything I put you through, after all those years, all that time between us, you never gave up. You loved me without expecting anything of me. You loved me like a mother loves her son. Like a brother loves his brother. You loved me in the dark, through the madness and chaos, but not once, not *once,* did you ask anything of me."

I don't know what to say. He's never said any of this to me before. But it feels good. Oh, it feels so good.

"Ryde, you're my gift. My God-given gift." He turns his eyes back the creek. "And maybe that's all I need to remember. Maybe that's enough."

I lean my head to his bare shoulder. We're here. We've made it this far.

"We'll be together forever, right?" He holds my hand in his. "We'll never be apart again."

I turn his face to mine. The sun is on his white-blond hair, and a memory of him, sitting in his attic, sewing that shirt, comes over me. He's my cloak. The only garment I ever needed. "Forever," I whisper back to him. "Now lie down with me."

We lie back on the warm rocks, staring up at the forget-me-not-blue sky.

"I think I'm gonna fall asleep," he says, pressing his face into my neck. "You don't mind, do you?"

No, I don't mind.

But this time, I'm going to stay awake.

"Ryde, wake up."

But I wasn't sleeping at all.

I turn to look at him. He's still lying on his side, but looking at the woods behind me. "Wake up," he says again. "Wake up."

"What is it?"

But I know. I *know.*

I glance over my shoulder, at the trees. "What? Tell me."

Alistair is on his feet. He stands there, breathing hard, watching something, someone in the trees. His eyes are glazed. Is he even awake? "What does he want?" he whispers.

I need Jamie. I need to call Jamie. I glance up at the cliff. My phone is up there, in my jeans.

"What does that man want?" Alistair asks again, in a very thin voice. He's terrified. "Ryde—"

"He wants you." I don't know what I'm doing, what I'm saying. But the truth is all I know. The only thing I don't have to remember. "He wants you, Alistair. He wants to drag you through the woods and take you to his barn and hurt you."

"No," he cries, shaking his head. "No!" Before I can grab him, he strikes off for the woods behind us. I see him bolt through the bushes, unaware of them it seems, running straight into the forest.

"Oh, fuck!" I scream, bolting after him.

The branches whip at my face, my chest, my thighs, but I can't slow down, because I see him gaining speed, and if I trip or fall, I'll lose him. I shout his name, crying out for him to wait, but he only runs faster, jumping over dead trunks, skidding and slipping across the pine needles and leaves, running, running, but he keeps looking back, over his shoulder, and I catch the terror in his eye. Is he running away from me? What am I to him in this moment? "Alistair," I try again, my voice booming through the silent woods. "It's me, stop!"

He won't stop. He's running away and toward something. So I run. But I run better now, steadier. My breathing is slowing down, as my body remembers those mornings of sprinting around the vacant soccer field near my house, when it was just me racing against me. The air burns my lungs and the needles hurt my bare soles, but I can take it. I can run like this forever. I listen to my breaths—even and perfectly paced—my feet landing and lifting from the ground, and I follow him.

We run through the woods, out into the clearing. The light surprises me. But he's still running, speeding now, glancing over his shoulder at me, his bloody bare feet barely touching the grass. Where is he going? "Wait," I scream, losing my rhythm, feeling the fatigue in my legs. I can't catch him. I can't get to him. I push myself to sprint and get close to him, so close, but he yells and races away from me again.

We jump over train tracks and I see a road up ahead. A road. Cars. Trucks. I need to get to him. I have to stop him from dashing across that road. I dig into the last of my reserves and push harder, and I come close again, within arm's reach. I could grab him now. I could tackle him to the ground, and knock him out if I have to, but as I reach out to him, something stops me from touching him. Why am I chasing him? Why?

He doesn't need me to catch him. He doesn't want me to.

Understanding, I run up to him again, and with time, begin matching his stride. He looks over at me, but allows me to run by him. We run straight and steadily, and I turn to see his eyes locked on something somewhere out in a distance. I jog by him, keeping time with his steps.

Side by side. That's all he's ever needed from me.

We run together now, through the clearing, to the road, and then he stops.

"Alistair?" I'm so out of breath, I can hardly get a word out. "Look at me."

"Oh, God," he cries, falling to his knees, staring at something far away. His eyes are wild and filling with tears. "Oh, God," he moans now, shaking his head. "No." The tears run down his face. "No. No."

I don't know what to do. I follow his stare, searching the land for what he's seeing.

I see it. I see that fucking barn. "Oh, baby," I say, staring at the old barn far off across the road. "No, don't—"

"No!" he screams and jumps to his feet again. He's pacing, yelling, talking to himself with his head bowed, and I stand there, helpless, watching him come apart. His voice keeps changing. His tone is furious and then full of terror, and I see he's a child and a man, all at once, but this is bad, this is so bad. I have to stop this. "Please," I whisper, but he doesn't hear me. He's running around in circles, and screaming words out, words I can't understand, and then he starts hitting himself. Slapping his naked chest, pulling on his hair. How do I stop this? He's hurting himself, but I can't get through to him. He won't hear me. Won't look at me. "Come on, Alistair, please, don't." I try for his arm, but he pulls away and I know he'll take off if I grab him again.

"No!" he yells again, holding the sides of his head as if his mind is ripping apart. "No, I can't. I can't. I don't want to, please! I can't. I can't." He keeps repeating those two words, running around in a circle. "I can't. I can't. I can't—"

"Jesus Christ," I cry, looking at the field around us. There's no one here. "Help me. God, someone help me." I can't stand it. Can't just stand here and watch him come apart. I'm losing him again. He's slipping away from me. "Please, please."

Alistair is tearing at his hair and mumbling words under his breath, shaking his head, and I know he's lost. He's lost now. Somewhere between here and there, now and then. He's trapped in his own nightmare, and I can't reach him anymore. I don't have what it takes. I don't have the words anymore.

"GOD!" I yell and kick the dirt. "Fucking help me! What the fuck do You want? Help him!" I don't know what I'm doing. I'm on my knees. "Oh, please," I say into my hands. "Please, help him." I'm praying. I'm praying. "Lord, please, please. Make him stop. Give him peace. Please, I'll do anything. Anything. Just give him peace. Please." There's total darkness around me. I see nothing. Hear nothing. Just my voice praying. "Give him peace. Let him rest. Cut it out of him. Cut that thing out of him. You only have the power to make rotten things good things again. Cut it out of him. I beg you, Lord. I know You hear me. You hear me. Give him—"

"Ryde."

"I'll do anything. I'll renounce anything."

"Ryde." A hand on my shoulder. "Hey."

"Give him peace. Fall over him like that shirt he made me. He's Your son. Your boy. Please—"

"Ryde… Shh."

I open my eyes. Look up at Alistair's face. His cheek is bleeding. His nose is bleeding. His chest is red with imprints of his hand. His legs are badly cut. But he's all right. He's looking right at me.

"Do you know what you just did?" he asks, sniffling blood and tears.

"Oh, Jesus," I say, breaking down. I hide my face in my hands and just let it go. I sob into my hands, silently, deeply, and it feels good.

I hear him next to me. He's on his knees now. "Lord, allow Your healing hand to heal me."

I look over at him, calming down.

"Teach me," he whispers with his head bowed. "Oh, Lord, teach me to reach out to You in all my needs, and help me to lead others to You by my example."

"Yes," I hear myself say. Whatever.

He's all right. He's mine again.

"Lord, may I serve You with all my strength. Touch gently this life You have created, now and forever." He puts his hand on my shoulder. "Amen."

I stare at the barn. "Amen," I echo.

We don't move for a long time. I feel the sun on my back, a gentle and merciful wind blowing through the leaves of grass around us.

At last, Alistair stands and helps me up. I wipe the blood off his cheeks, his neck. I rub his hair back and look him deep in the eye. "Okay?"

He smiles a little. He's still shaking. Still recovering.

"Which way?" I take his hand in mine. We're half-naked. A little ruined, but alive.

Alive.

"Let's walk down that road," he says, his voice still a little broken. "Back over there."

I gaze down the road. "It's the long way."

"Yes, I know." He smiles again, and this time, his black eyes shine.

"All right then." I pull on his hand. "I'm right there with you."

We walk along the road, in the ditch, out of view and in contemplative silence. Ahead, the road stretches for what appears to be forever, and my feet hurt, but I don't care.

Then he stops. He looks back and over his shoulder. He's looking at the barn. It's an old, decrepit thing and now forever fenced in. Alistair stares at it, and slowly, very gently, he waves. "Good-bye."

I'm going to miss that little boy.

But I've missed him all my life. Somewhere down this long road, I'll think of him, standing in that tiny window, and I'll know then, yes, I'll know my mother was right.

Life is a continuum. It allows for no intermissions.

Today, on this road we stand, Alistair's real recovery begins. I'm going to be with him, side by side, every step of the way.

"I love you," I say and look over at him.

He nods and smiles brightly.

I laugh. "But you knew that already, didn't you?"

We walk faster, over the train tracks again, but our steps are lighter now. The sun is setting. Everything is receding. Soon, the sky will be black once more, splattered with stars, but I'll know that sky, because I've seen it before.

Then Alistair stops again. "Hey, look," he says.

I look up at the sign he's showing me.

You are now entering Craving's Creek.

About the Author

Mel Bossa is the author of *Split* and *In His Secret Life*, both Lambda Award finalists, as well as numerous other books and short stories. She lives in Montreal's gay village, where she volunteers for a crisis center. As a queer Franco-Italian feminist raised in a patriarchal society, she's felt like the Other for a great part of her life and finds peace in dreaming up worlds where grace wins over fear.

It's not the size of the dog in the fight, it's the size of the fight in the dog.

Tap Out
© *2015 Cat Grant*

As a child, Tom Delaney did the best he could to protect his mother from his abusive father, but her eventual suicide left him a guarded and wary man who's still carrying around a metric ton of baggage.

At Bannon's Gym, Tom learned how to take back his power, and found love with fellow mixed martial arts fighter Travis Gallagher. Yet Tom can't bring himself to take their relationship to the next level. Not if moving in together means leaving behind Gloria, his surrogate mom, who's desperately ill.

When Gloria's son, Eddie, hires an out-of-work nurse to care for Gloria, Tom is out of excuses—and afraid he's being pushed out of his family of choice. That fear explodes in a violent sparring session that leaves Travis with a broken nose and Tom on the brink of getting booted out of Bannon's Gym for good.

When tragedy strikes, Tom realizes it'll take more than fists to conquer his fears, or he risks losing everything—his fighting career, his family, and the man he loves.

Warning: Sweat- and testosterone-drenched alpha males ahead! More angst than an entire season of Downton Abbey! Wear a helmet—this could get messy!

Sometimes you only get one chance at a second chance.

No Place That Far
© 2015 L.A. Witt & Aleksandr Voinov

Still finding his footing after a long-overdue divorce, Marcus is looking forward to some mind-numbing drinking while ogling the grooms at Chris and Julien's wedding. He never expected his attention to be diverted by the gorgeous best man.

One of Julien's French Foreign Legion buddies, Timur doesn't speak much English, but language is no barrier to Marcus understanding exactly what the huge Tartar wants—a one-night stand.

Except that one night turns into two, three, then more, which puts Marcus on edge. After Timur is done house-sitting for the honeymooning couple, he's headed back to the Legion for another five years. Like it or not, once Timur gets on that plane, the fling is over.

Unfortunately, Marcus forgot to tell his heart not to fall in love. And this time, if history repeats and he makes another wrong decision, he may never see his tattooed Legionnaire lover again.

Warning: Contains a soldier who makes up for his lack of English by using his hands to read his lover's body; a chef-turned-bartender who no longer believes in love; a length of paracord that probably wasn't meant to be used this way; and a couple of newlyweds who are game for some four-way play.

A heart can live a lifetime in eight seconds.

Drawing the Devil
© 2015 Jon Keys

Ever since his father caught him with another boy and threw him out at the tender age of sixteen, Dustin Lewis has been fighting his way up the national bull-riding rankings. He's on the brink of qualifying for the National Finals when he draws Diablo, a notoriously rank bull—and the ride goes bad.

When bullfighter Shane Rees frees Dustin from the rigging of the same bull that nearly destroyed his face, he comes dangerously close to dropping his guard. Shane knows the potential consequences of being gay in a sport loaded with testosterone-overdosed cowboys, and the resulting scars of mind and body have left him with little self-worth.

Their near-death-by-bull first meeting sparks an attraction that awakens every last one of their personal demons. Yet as the National Finals draws closer, so do they. But they'll have to overcome emotional highs, near-tragic lows, and bone-crushing danger before love can bust out of the chute.

Warning: Contains man-on-man boot knocking, rawhide and raw emotions, badass cowboys and even badder-ass bulls. This ain't your old man's rodeo.

It's all about the story...

Romance

HORROR

www.samhainpublishing.com

CPSIA information can be obtained at www.ICGtesting.com
Printed in the USA
BVOW05s0827031115

425423BV00004B/38/P